P9-CMT-838

SORROW ON SUNDAY

The Lois Meade mysteries by Ann Purser from Severn House

MURDER ON MONDAY
TERROR ON TUESDAY
WEEPING ON WEDNESDAY
THEFT ON THURSDAY
FEAR ON FRIDAY
SECRETS ON SATURDAY
SORROW ON SUNDAY

SORROW ON SUNDAY

Ann Purser

This first world edition published in Great Britain 2007 by
SEVERN HOUSE PUBLISHERS LTD of
9–15 High Street, Sutton, Surrey SM1 1DF.
This first world edition published in the USA 2007 by
SEVERN HOUSE PUBLISHERS INC of
595 Madison Avenue, New York, N.Y. 10022.

British Library Cataloguing in Publication Data

Purser,   Ann
    Sorrow on Sunday. - (The Lois Meade mysteries)
    1.   Meade, Lois (Fictitious character) - Fiction
    2.   Cleaning personnel - England - Fiction
    3.   Country life - England - Fiction
    4.   Detective and mystery stories
    I.   Title
    823.9'14 [F]

    ISBN-13: 978-0-7278-6510-6

*The Author and Publishers are duly grateful to the Deputy Registrar
of the Royal Archive for permission to use the Quotation on p.vi.*

All Severn House titles are printed on acid-free paper.

Typeset by Palimpsest Book Production Ltd.,
Grangemouth, Stirlingshire, Scotland.
Printed and bound in Great Britain by
MPG Books Ltd., Bodmin, Cornwall.

Grateful thanks to Dave,
who has seen it all

How small and selfish is sorrow. But it bangs one about until one is senseless

HM Queen Elizabeth, the Queen Mother
in a letter to Edith Sitwell following the death of George VI
1952

One

Hazel Thornbull sat at her desk in the Tresham office of New Brooms – 'We Sweep Cleaner' – and looked out at Sebastopol Street, a street without character, consisting largely of terraced red-brick houses in varying states of decay. Shining out from the rest was the freshly painted corner office of Lois Meade's cleaning business, now well-established and popular in town and surrounding villages. Hazel managed the office, and Lois called in every now and then to make sure everything was running smoothly.

Lois also operated another business, a one-woman job, and unpaid. More of a hobby, she liked to think. She was a sleuth, a non-stipendiary private detective. A snout, a grass, an informer, some would say. She worked with only one man: Detective Chief Inspector Hunter Cowgill.

This Monday morning it was quiet, and Hazel disappeared into the small kitchen to make coffee. She heard the office door flung open and the warning bell rang loudly. 'Damn! Nothing happens all morning, and just when I—' She stopped, seeing her boss, Lois Meade, standing in the kitchen doorway, unsmiling.

'Mrs M! You made me jump! I'm just making a quick cup – d'you want one?'

'Might as well,' Lois said. 'It might cushion the blow.'

What blow? thought Hazel in alarm. There could be only one kind of blow. Mrs M was sacking her, or closing down the business. But why should she do either of these things? Hazel made the coffee rapidly, and they sat down in the office. 'Right then,' she said. 'Break it gently.'

After a couple of slurps of hot coffee, Lois began to speak. 'Now,' she said, 'guess what?'

'Josie's pregnant,' Hazel guessed. She couldn't bear even to consider the end of New Brooms. Josie was Lois's daughter, and ran the village shop back in Long Farnden. She had a partner, Rob, and it was common knowledge that Lois was hoping for a grandchild. But surely Lois would be joyful about that!

'No, not that unfortunately. No, it's something else,' Lois said, and Hazel's heart sank. *Hey, but wait a minute. Mrs M's smiling broadly now!* 'Are you having me on?' Hazel asked.

Lois took a deep breath and said, 'Just thought I'd keep you in suspense. Rotten trick. Sorry, Hazel. Now, hold tight . . . Derek's won the Lottery!'

Hazel had worked for Lois for a long time. She was one of New Brooms' original cleaners, until she'd married and baby Elizabeth had arrived. Then Lois had arranged for her to manage the office, and a friend next door looked after the baby. It had all worked out very well, and Lois had been pleased not to lose one of her best workers. Hazel trusted Lois, but now looked at her in amazement. 'You're joking?' she said.

Lois shook her head. 'I knew you wouldn't believe me, but it's true. Six of the men at the pub were in a sort of syndicate. They've won the jackpot. So even when it's divided up we'll still get a decent packet.'

Hazel was now in shock. She opened her mouth to say something, but nothing emerged.

'Mind you,' Lois said, 'it's not one of them five-million wins. Should be about a quarter of a million each, though. I had to come into town, and couldn't resist telling you. The others can have a nice surprise at our meeting.' She looked hard at Hazel. 'You all right, gel?' she asked anxiously.

Hazel came suddenly to life. She pulled Lois out of her chair, gave her a big hug, and began to caper around the office desk. 'It's *you-hoo* who's won the jackpot!' she sang at the top of her voice, brandishing the pointing finger. Then they both roared with laughter and did not notice the door opening until the visitor stood watching them.

'Oh!' gasped Lois. 'It's you! Well, have I got news for you!'

The man smiled slightly and Hazel said, 'Good morning, Inspector Cowgill. Can we help you?'

Two

The news spread like measles around the village. When Josie opened the shop on Monday morning, there had been a queue outside. This had never been known in all the years since the shop had been established in 1868. Josie, of course, knew why, and had yelled for her partner, Rob, to come down from the flat above the shop. 'Stand by,' she said. 'I'm going to need help for half an hour or so.'

'I have to go to work, Josie, you know that,' Rob said. But he was a gentle, thoughtful soul, and called his office in Tresham to say he'd been delayed. In the first hour, they sold more sweets, cigarettes, boxes of matches and newspapers than ever before. And each customer said a variation of the same thing. 'Glad to hear about your mum's good luck. Wish it was me!' Josie was almost relieved when that miserable old skinflint from the Baptist Church bought his usual half cabbage and said, 'The Lottery is the work of Satan, Josie Meade. No good will come of it. Retribution is mine, saith the Lord.'

'Thanks, Mr Goody,' she said. 'I'll tell Mum. She'll be delighted, I know. Now – next please?'

Finally it quietened down, Rob went off to work, and Josie was able to perch on her high stool behind the counter and consider what had happened.

Most people had been genuinely pleased for the Meades, and for the other winners, but a few had clearly resented this bonus from the blue. 'Why not me?' the pugnacious Colonel Battersby had said. He clearly thought that if the Lottery pointing finger was aimed at this area, then he was the most deserving recipient. 'Your turn next, maybe, Colonel,' Josie had said as pleasantly as she could. She had heard Rob snorting behind her as he fetched more supplies from the stockroom.

The telephone rang, and Josie picked up the receiver. 'Who's

that? Oh, it's you, Miss Beasley. Shall I take your order now?'
Josie packed up a number of boxes of groceries to deliver to
nearby villages where the village shop had not survived. Miss
Beasley lived in Round Ringford. She was a stroppy old lady,
a client of New Brooms, and a tough customer.

'No, no. Not yet, Josie Meade,' she said. 'First I want to
know what your father has been doing, gambling with that
no-good set at the pub.'

The 'no-good set' consisted of Lois's electrician husband
Derek; his plumber pal; the vicar's brother, who had retired
and come to live at the vicarage; a local farmer and Geoff the
publican. Josie giggled, and said that her father could not be
a more respectable citizen and it was all a bit of fun. They'd
never really dreamt they'd win the jackpot.

'Huh!' grunted Ivy Beasley. 'Anyway, I suppose your mother
will be giving up the cleaning? And the village shop won't
be good enough for you? It'll ruin your lives, you know.
Happens all the time. I've seen it on the telly. And what about
all of us in the villages? I'm too old and frail now to keep
my house clean, and you will certainly not catch me going
into one of them supermarkets. I've known our Doris to go
in for a loaf of bread and come out with a full trolley. No,
I'll just starve, surrounded by dust.'

Josie considered trying to cheer her up. She hadn't had time
to think about their future, so she said only that the money
was her parents', and that as for herself, she loved the shop
and would stay in it until she was carried out in a wooden
box. 'I suggest you ask Mum about the cleaning,' she added.
'But whatever happens, Mum would never leave you in the
lurch, Miss Beasley. You must know that. Now, I'm busy, so
shall I take your order?'

After a small celebration consisting of strong coffee and
squashed-fly biscuits, Inspector Cowgill asked if he could
have a moment with Lois confidentially. Hazel, drunk with
the news, grinned. 'Shall I make myself scarce? Would you
like the blinds drawn?'

Lois glared at her. 'Just go and wash these coffee mugs,
young lady,' she said. 'I'll talk to you later.'

'Don't be too hard on her, Lois,' Cowgill said, uncharac-
teristically mellow. 'It is the most amazing news. I'd come

here to discuss a minor crime with a colleague, and find a rich lady dancing the polka! Enough to make anyone tactless.'

'Well, what was this minor crime, then?'

'I'm sure you're not interested now, Lois. Maybe it's time to shake hands and say farewell.'

Was that a tear in his eye? Surely not. Lois looked at him closely. 'You don't get rid of me that easily,' she said. 'And anyway, I've never taken money from you, so winning the Lottery don't make no difference. Derek and me had a long discussion last night, and have decided not to make any big changes in our lives. Maybe we'll stay in hotels instead of bed-and-breakfasts, get a newer car, that kind of thing. But I've worked hard to establish New Brooms, and Derek loves his job. Why change it?'

'And your work with me?'

'Same applies,' Lois said shortly. 'Now, let's get on to this minor crime.'

'It's happened in Waltonby, that's why I came to you. Next village, and lots of people there either are, or have been, your clients. It's the horsy lot. Stable thefts. Saddles and bridles and harness in general. No horses as yet. And, thank God, no injuries to the animals. But this stuff is expensive, and can be sold easily in the right place. Have you heard anything?'

Lois shook her head. 'It happens every so often, but one at a time usually. Derek says it serves 'em right for not locking it away properly. More horses than people in these villages. The old village folk don't like them, incomers throwing their money about.'

Cowgill looked at her with a smile, and said, 'You're rich now, Lois. You could even buy a horse. Get to know these people with barmy ideas about country life.'

Lois's voice was icy as she replied that not for him nor for the Queen herself would she be seen on a bloody great horse. She added that she would, however, keep her ears and eyes open, and make a few enquiries. Derek sometimes heard useful stuff in the pub.

'Very useful!' laughed Cowgill. 'Perhaps I should start drinking in your pub – might be able to take early retirement!'

It was the first time she had heard Cowgill laugh, really laugh, with his eyes as well as his mouth, since his wife was killed in a road accident. So there, Mr Goody, Lois said to herself, if we're all doomed to hell, it will have been worth it.

Three

Colonel Battersby was in his late fifties, and married to a wife he had licked into shape over the last twenty-five years. He had inherited considerable wealth, and had conducted his life accordingly. He had the required two children – a son and a daughter – who had been a great satisfaction to him, the son following him into the armed forces, and the daughter having married well.

'I've had a bloody good life,' he would say to anyone with the ill luck to sit next to him at regimental reunion dinners. 'No complaints at all. That's what I shall say to my Maker when the day comes. No complaints. A bloody good life.'

His wife, Blanche, had been known to say quietly to him that it was tempting fate to talk like that. But he scoffed at her and took no notice. Then this morning, he had gone to the stables to inspect his fine, well-bred hunters, and found the tack room virtually empty. 'They've cleared the bloody lot!' he yelled at his wife when he'd run back to the house to ring the police.

She paled. 'The horses?' she said anxiously. She loved them, the sleek, elegant creatures. She respected their nobility, and never asked more from them than she thought appropriate. In return, the horses loved her and did their best for her.

The Colonel, on the contrary, made sure they knew who was master, and demanded complete obedience, exemplary behaviour and dumb bravery. They obeyed out of fear, and did not love him.

Reassured that the horses were not harmed, Blanche said, 'You've tempted fate once too often, Horace.' She had always thought it a ridiculous name, but he would have no other. 'Now look what's happened.'

'My fault, then?' But before a row could develop, he was through to the police station in Tresham, blustering and shouting. 'I shall expect the culprits found by sunset,' he said, 'and all my property returned forthwith. Yes, of course I expect you to come at once! And you will regret your insolence!' He slammed down the telephone and turned to continue to berate his wife, but she had slipped out of the room.

He sat down at the kitchen table and put his head in his hands. He would be the laughing stock of the village. Had Blanche locked up when she'd finished her ridiculous conversations with the horses last evening? Maybe he could blame her. He stormed into his study, found his silver flask and drank deeply, then picked up the telephone. 'Put me through to the Commissioner,' he said. 'I have a complaint.'

Blanche Battersby had escaped to her sewing room in the attic of the big house. It had been a farmhouse in the centre of Waltonby one hundred years ago, and had belonged to the Lord of the Manor. In the 1930s he had converted it into a comfortable home for his widowed mother, but she had had other ideas. She remained at the Hall, and suggested he and his ambitious little wife could move into the Dower House, as it was now known, until she joined her husband in the family vault. Eventually the Hall was destroyed by fire, and the family died out. Colonel Battersby had purchased the Dower House on the internet. He had regarded computer technology as a battle to be won, and set about it with characteristic thoroughness. Bidding for the house had been exciting, and he had practised his usual cunning, clinching the deal at just under a million pounds. 'Beat the other chap to it!' he'd crowed to Blanche. 'Worth every penny.'

Blanche was not so sure, but she found the house friendly enough. It was lovely to look at, built in dark gold stone that gleamed in the sun, and had a large garden where she could indulge her hobby. The borders and sloping lawns, the rose garden and walled kitchen garden were all too much for her alone, and so Horace had agreed to a lad from the village coming in once a week to do the heavy work. He was what the village children called a dimmie, and was certainly odd. He loved Mrs Battersby with respect and awe. As far as the Colonel was concerned, the lad kept out of his way as much as possible. His name was Darren, and on the whole he was happy.

In her sewing room, Blanche stared out of the window and wished herself back in the solid, four-square Victorian villa in the best part of Tresham, where she could manage the garden on her own, and, with Mrs Meade's help once a week, could keep the house clean and neat. There had been no tack room to burgle there.

Derek Meade was working over near Fletching, fitting a bathroom heater into an isolated farmhouse. The farmer, Joe Horsley and his wife Margaret, had gone into Tresham, so he could work steadily without interruption. As the lottery news spread, he was beginning to dread meeting people in the street, and the thought of being stuck in a bathroom at the housewife's mercy filled him with gloom. Still, he couldn't go into hiding, and would have to find a way of changing the subject away from lottery wins. It was amazing how many people were anxious to tell him stories of winners they knew who had been ruined by unaccustomed wealth, and how some had squandered the lot in the first three months.

He was comforted by the thought that Lois handled the family's finances. Since she had become a businesswoman, she was very sharp about where to put their savings, and how much they could spend. He was happy to leave her to it, and had been relieved when, on hearing of their win, she had immediately started making plans.

The bathroom overlooked a big farmyard, which was enclosed by barns and stables on three sides. A wide stone arch allowed access for vehicles and horses. Everything was tidy and well cared for, and Derek knew from the luxurious interior of the house that there was money here. Well, now he and Lois had money, lots of money, and it was a wonderful feeling. Security, that's what it was. He heard a car pulling up in the yard, and looked out of the window. He'd parked his own vehicle round the back of the buildings, out of the way. Now he peered out, but the glass was frosted and wobbly, and he could see only vague shapes. If it was Joe and Margaret returning, he would finish quickly and depart. But it wasn't the Horsleys. He could see the outline of a van. Delivering something, perhaps? A figure appeared, distorted by the glass, and he decided he'd better take a look. But he didn't hurry, and by the time he opened the yard door the van had moved off at speed, and all he could see was a trail of exhaust smoke down the track.

He returned to the house and resumed work, thinking about what he had just seen. Probably not important. Something to do with the farm. Still, he'd mention it when Joe and Margaret came back.

They drove into the yard as Derek was packing up to leave. As they unloaded shopping, he told them what he had seen, and was surprised at Joe's reaction. He rushed off to the tack room and emerged red-faced and shouting. 'The buggers have taken a saddle!' he roared accusingly at Derek.

'Don't blame me,' Derek said calmly. 'By the time I got downstairs, the van was moving off. I hardly saw it, let alone had a chance of stopping it. Any road, I didn't know they were up to no good, did I? You'd better tell the police.'

Joe deflated like a punctured tyre. 'A lot o' good that would do,' he muttered. 'No, we don't want them coming here asking a lot of damn stupid questions. I can handle this myself.'

'They might be able to help,' said Margaret mildly, and Joe rounded on her. 'Just mind your own business and get that shopping in the house!' he said roughly.

Derek judged it was time for him to go.

Lois was at home when Derek returned, and Gran greeted them with tales of what had gone on in the shop. 'Josie was unindated,' she said. 'Looks like it'll be good for shop business, if nothing else.' Gran had been feeling disorientated, as if walking on shifting sands. Everything would be changed. People talked of nothing else, and sometimes she wished the syndicate hadn't had the winning ticket. The family had been jogging along on Derek's job and what came in from New Brooms, though that wasn't a fortune. Mind you, she said to herself, with Derek's being a one-man business, if he was seriously ill or had an accident, they'd have been in trouble. There was still a mortgage to be paid off, and all the expenses of living in an old house. The lottery win had cushioned them against that, at least.

The three sat in silence for a while. There was so much to think about. Then Derek said, 'I had a bit of excitement today,' and told them about the Horsley drama. 'I didn't see a lot – just the back of some old van disappearing down the track. Joe discovered a saddle had been took, and he was furious. Looked as if he'd like to blame me. Nasty to his wife, too.'

Lois said swiftly, 'Did you say an old van? Have you seen it before? Did you get the number?'

'Oh, God,' groaned Derek. 'No, I didn't see anything much at all. Why are you so keen to find out? As if I didn't know,' he added. 'Lois rides again, with Cowgill close behind.'

Four

The Monday midday meeting of New Brooms was more of a party than the usual serious discussion of the week ahead and allocation of jobs. The cleaning staff were all there, except for Floss Pickering, who had gone to the doctor with a painful earache. Hazel, having closed the Tresham shop for a couple of hours, had followed Lois and was pouring champagne, and Bill Stockbridge, nearly the longest-serving cleaner, had a glass or two, enough to forget the broken nights and daily anxieties of a new baby. The others chatted excitedly, each with a story of lottery winners they knew, but none had had even a share of the jackpot.

'Now,' Lois said, a little flushed, 'we'd better get down to business. We'll keep it short today. I expect you'll be wondering what we'll do next. Well, there's one thing that won't change: New Brooms. With your help, I've built up a good business here with plenty of scope for expansion. No reason to change it. And, in any case, as Derek says, the amount we won is not big enough to retire on, but just right to give us some extra income and a few treats.'

There was a spontaneous burst of applause, and Lois laughed. 'And there's something else,' she said. 'Derek and me, we're nowhere near retirement, so what on earth would we do with ourselves? We're working class, and like to work.

Work is what we know. So there we are. Now, I'm due at the Battersbys' in ten minutes in place of Floss. I expect it'll be clean and tidy as ordered by the Colonel, but Mrs B likes somebody to talk to. So if there's nothing else to bring up, I'll just say thanks, all of you, for standing by me.'

One or two sniffed and all wished Lois and her family good luck as they departed. Lois, left alone, sat down for a few minutes to compose herself, then collected her things and set off for Waltonby and the Battersbys.

The moment Lois entered the house, she knew something was wrong. The atmosphere was charged with tension, and when Mrs Battersby clattered down the stairs in undignified haste, Lois was sure there had been some major disaster.

'Thank goodness you've come!' Mrs B said, twisting her hands.

'Of course I've come,' said Lois. 'Floss has gone to the doctor, so I'm here instead. If there'd been a problem, I'd have let you know.'

'Oh, I know, I know.' Mrs Battersby walked towards the kitchen, and Lois followed. 'Would you like a coffee before you start?'

This was new, and Lois almost declined. Then she looked at the poor woman's worried face, and accepted. 'I'll take it with me upstairs,' she said. 'Mustn't waste time, else the Colonel will have me on a charge!'

At this, Blanche Battersby burst into tears. Lois stared at her, and said, 'Goodness, Mrs Battersby, I'm sorry if I've upset you. It was just a silly joke.' She reached out and patted Blanche's hand. Slowly the tears dried up, and Lois stood up. 'Better get on,' she said, 'but thanks for the coffee.'

'Sit down again for a minute,' Blanche said. 'We've had a nasty shock this morning, and I apologize for losing control. It's just that when the Colonel went to check the horses this morning, the tack room was empty. All our stuff had been stolen. Nothing left. He was so angry, and I was frightened he'd have a stroke or something. He's gone out now, and I don't know where. Almost hit the gatepost when he drove out of the drive. I'll be so glad to see him back.'

I bet she hasn't always thought that, Lois said to herself, remembering how many times Mrs B had reportedly escaped to her sewing room when the Colonel had been in a shouting mood. Then she was struck by the full import of what Mrs B had said. The stable thieves had fallen straight into her lap! How lucky that Floss had earache. Lois knew she must ask more questions, and on the pretext of claiming Mrs B was in shock and mustn't be left for a while, she made her a cup of tea with plenty of sugar. It seemed that the Battersbys had heard nothing in the night. But then, the walls were thick, the curtains were heavy drapes which would shut out sound, and the stables stood a way off from the house. The Colonel was a little deaf, though he denied it hotly, and Blanche always slept with the bedcovers pulled up over her ears.

'What time did the Colonel go to the stables?' Lois asked gently.

'After breakfast. About eight o'clock. Never a lie-in for us!' Blanche seemed to be recovering, and even managed a small smile.

'No damage to the horses?'

'No, thank God. I immediately thought of those wicked people who cut horses, but ours were just frightened. And they *were* frightened, Mrs Meade. Very jumpy and nervous.'

'Do you think it had been in the early morning, then? Not long before you got up?' Lois knew very little about horses.

Blanche shook her head. 'Difficult to say. If something upsets them, they take a long while to settle down.'

The sound of the Colonel's car returning sent Blanche scuttling upstairs, and Lois quickly rinsed out the cups and put them away. She was on her way to start on the bedrooms when he came storming into the hall. 'Ah!' he said. 'Mrs Meade. Just the person. You go to lots of houses in the village, don't you? Can you throw any light on this tragic business?' He seemed confident that she knew all about it.

Lois shook her head. 'I am sorry for you, and for the horses,' she said. 'But I only know there's been rumours about stable thefts, and my husband actually saw a stranger making off with a saddle on one of the farms where he was working. He chased, but didn't catch him. The farmer was out, but when he came back, he didn't seem too bothered. Didn't want the police told. So Derek hasn't done nothing about it.'

'Send your husband to see me,' the Colonel said. Lois frowned.

'I'll ask him,' she said, 'but he's very busy just now. I must get on,' she added, and went upstairs, aware of a boiling Colonel behind her. But he said no more, and so she started work.

'Where have you been, dear?' Blanche said tentatively at lunch.

'When? Been here for hours.' The Colonel's appetite had not been affected by the disaster, and he lined up peas and carrots as if they were on parade, in order to dismiss them with relish.

'But earlier,' persisted Blanche. 'You went out in the car.'

'Ah, that. Just went into the village to find Darren. Thought he might know something.'

'You didn't frighten him, I hope, dear,' Blanche said.

'Frighten him? Of course not! In any case, he wasn't there. The neighbour said he'd gone shopping with his mother on the bus to Tresham. I'll talk to him later. He comes here tomorrow, doesn't he? I'll leave it until then. See what the police say first.'

Blanche stood up suddenly. 'Horace! It's them. The police have just driven in. Shall I go to the door?'

'Certainly not. I'll go at once. Trust them to come at lunchtime.' He strode out of the room, and Blanche heard the front door open and then loud voices. Well, one loud voice and two reasonable ones. She heard them go into the drawing room, and the door shut behind them. So that's that. I might as well creep to the kitchen and wash up, she thought.

But she misjudged the police. After a while, Horace came steaming back in, and said, 'Come along, Blanche. They want to talk to you, though I can't think why. It was I who discovered the burglary, after all. Still, they insist, so come now. And take that apron off! They'll think you're the scullery maid! What was that?' he added sharply.

'Nothing,' said Blanche, 'nothing at all.'

Five

'The Battersbys have been done,' Lois said at lunchtime. Derek was having a quick snack before returning to work.

'What d'you mean, done? You mean you've cleaned for them? So what's new about that?'

'Done over! Burgled, y'fool,' Lois said impatiently. 'The Colonel was purple. Went to check his precious horses first thing, and found the tack room empty. Poor Mrs B, she was the one I felt sorry for. He took it out on her, needless to say. She escaped to her workroom upstairs. He'd gone off in the car, but he was back quickly, huffin' and puffin'.'

'He's told the police, I suppose?'

'Practically accused them of negligence,' Lois replied. 'Then he asked me what I'd heard around the village. He more or less said that New Brooms eavesdropped wherever we went. That got me mad. I told him I didn't know much more than rumour, and then I mentioned you seeing the back of that van at a place you were working. Sorry about that, Derek. He asked – no, ordered – me to send you to him. I said you were busy, but I'd mention it.' Lois had regretted it the minute she'd told the Colonel, and decided to tell Derek in case the Colonel talked to him. 'Sorry about that,' she repeated.

Derek was unexpectedly calm. 'Don't worry, me duck,' he said. 'I reckon I'd have reported it anyway. I don't like keeping things like that to myself. Joe was furious, but he was determined not to tell the police.'

Lois blew him a kiss as he left in a hurry to get back to work, and sighed with relief. 'Right, Mum,' she said. 'I'll be in my office most of the afternoon. What are you up to?'

Gran said, 'Washing up, cleaning the sink where Derek left greasy marks, clearing out the grate in the sitting room and laying a fire.' Lois put her hands over her ears, and Gran shouted at the top of her voice, 'After that I might have time to take Jeems for a walk before tea!' Jeems was Lois's little white terrier, and this last snipe was too much for Lois.

'I'll take her after tea, so don't bother!' she said. Then she relented. 'Sorry, Mum,' she said. 'You know we couldn't manage without you. But you won't let me send one of the girls to help. I'd be quite happy to—'

'Get on with you,' Gran said. 'I was only teasing. I don't need one of your girls – and I'd not call Sheila Stratford a girl, by the way. What would I do with myself? Now, get out of my way while I clear the table.'

Lois sat at her desk in the office and smiled. She and her mother were very alike, and understood each other well. Still, it didn't do to take Gran for granted.

Derek finished his job down the road in Farnden, and came out of the client's gate to put his tools back in his van. He noticed a large car standing a few yards away, and as he shut the gate a tall, distinguished-looking figure got out and approached. 'Meade?' he said peremptorily. Derek guessed at once that this was Colonel Battersby. 'Yes?' he said.

'I want a word with you,' the Colonel replied. 'Come and sit in my car.'

Derek stared at him. 'What did you say?' he replied.

'I said, I want to talk to you,' snapped the Colonel. 'Are you deaf, man?'

'Look,' said Derek, with exaggerated reasonableness, 'I'm not one of your raw recruits. I have a business to run, and my time is precious. If you want to talk to me about the stable thefts, I'll see when I can spare ten minutes and let you know. Now, if you'll excuse me, I'm due at the next job. Good afternoon.'

He drove away, seeing in the rear-view mirror that the Colonel was left standing motionless, as if he couldn't believe what he had heard. Too bad, thought Derek, accelerating. I'll get in touch with the old sod, but when I decide to. God knows how Lois and the girls cope with all these people she cleans for, especially him! He drove on towards Fletching thinking about Lois and her decision to carry on with New Brooms and not let their windfall make any major difference to their lives. Was it possible? He looked back at his encounter with the Colonel, and wondered if he'd have been as confident in standing up to him before the lottery win? There was no doubt that having a large nest egg in the bank *did* make a lot of difference. How else would it affect them? It worried him sometimes. Still, he trusted Lois. She was strong and level-headed and would see that nothing disastrous happened.

There was one thing he wished she would give up, but there was no hope of her doing that. Snooping was in her bones, he reckoned, and now there was a new mystery for her to get her teeth into.

He slowed down as he approached the roundabout on the edge of Fletching village, and saw a dirty white van speeding along from another road. As it came towards the roundabout, he saw to his horror a shaggy-looking horse crash through the hedge and charge into the road in front of the van. The van swerved off and hit a road sign with force. A dreadful sound of crumpling metal and breaking glass was followed by a terrible silence. Derek was frozen for a few seconds, then shot out and ran to the scene.

The horse had miraculously escaped, and was galloping at full pelt back up the road. *Let it go*, thought Derek, and rushed over to the van. The front seemed to be completely destroyed. He looked anxiously for the driver. Trapped in twisted metal and broken glass, the man at the wheel was slumped forward, his face covered in blood, and was almost certainly dead. Derek dialled the police from his mobile, and gave them the details. He was told to stay exactly where he was. The ambulance would be there immediately.

Derek had another look at the man. He was young. If there was any sign of life, he would do everything he could to help him, regardless of police instructions. He peered closely through the shattered window, and realized it was hopeless. The man had been crushed horribly. He'd had no chance. Derek could see no sign of a safety belt. He straightened up and waited. He did a re-run in his mind from the moment he saw the horse crash through. It was a thick hedge, well-trimmed, and impossible to see in to the field beyond. Where, then, did the animal get out? He peered closer, and saw a narrow gap, and a broken fence, more or less overgrown. That was it. Perhaps there had been a stile there once. Some care-less farmer had failed to mend it. Ah, well, he'd have trouble finding his horse now.

Six

When Derek finally returned home, Gran was looking worried. 'Where've you been? I thought you said you'd be early today.'

Derek shook his head. 'It's a long story,' he said. 'I'd be glad of a good strong cup of tea. Where's Lois?'

'Taken Jeems out. She's gone over the meadows to the river walk. Should be back soon.' Gran made the tea and sat down opposite Derek. 'So what happened?' she said. Derek gave her an edited version of the crash itself, leaving out the gory bits. He told her about having to hang about for hours, telling the police what he had witnessed, and going with them to the woods to look for the horse. There had been no sign of it though the police were still busy up there when he left.

'Did you know the man in the van?' Gran had immediately thought of at least three people she knew who might have been driving white vans that way.

Derek shook his head. 'He was quite smashed up, though he was vaguely familiar. Still, the police'll find out who he is – was – and it'll all be in the local.'

It was getting dark, and Gran looked out of the window. 'Where's Lois got to?' she said. 'It'll be time for our tea soon. Steak and kidney pie today, and bread puddin' for afters.'

Ten minutes later, Lois arrived, out of breath and red in the face. 'She's in disgrace!' she said, tying Jeems to the table leg without taking off her lead.

Gran and Derek looked at each other. 'You're too soft with that dog,' Gran said. 'What's she done now?'

'Wouldn't come when she was called,' Lois said.

'So what's new?' said Derek. 'She never does.'

'Well, this time she'd found a rotting rabbit carcass and every time I approached her she retreated, with the disgusting green shiny object dangling from her mouth. In the end, I walked away and left her, then waited out of sight. It was hours before she came, and I'm frozen.' She started towards the door. 'Oh, and by the way, Derek, I met the Colonel. He said he'd seen you and you'd been helpful, and he was looking forward to hearing from you. I suppose you know what he's talking about, but anyway, I'm going to have a hot shower.' She slammed the door behind her and they heard her going up the stairs, tripping halfway up and cursing, and then all was silent.

'The Colonel?' said Gran. 'Old Battersby? What did he want?'

'To shoot somebody, I think,' said Derek gloomily, and opened the sports pages.

Halfway up Sebastopol Street, a police car cruised to a halt outside one of the small terraced houses. Hazel Thornbull, looking out of the window of the New Brooms office, watched it idly. Police cars were not uncommon in Sebastopol Street. She saw an officer approach one of the neglected, peeling front doors and ring a bell. At the same time he knocked on the heavy iron knocker, and waited. Then he peered through the grimy window facing the pavement, and looked up to see the same yellowing net curtains drawn across both upstairs windows. Back to the front door. This time, it opened a fraction, and Hazel could just see a pale face. Then the door opened wider, and the policeman disappeared inside. She shrugged. Another break-in, car theft, mugging. This area of Tresham was known for it.

'Now, Mrs Nimmo,' the policeman said. 'I need to have a few words. Shall we go . . .?' He looked around, and could see no room that he would willingly enter. The smell in the house was appalling, a cocktail of cigarette smoke, damp walls and stale cooking.

Mrs Nimmo led the way into a tiny kitchen, where she indicated a rickety chair drawn up to a small table covered in grubby oilcloth. So far, she had said nothing. She sat down on a rickety stool, and stared at him. He smiled at her, only too aware of the nature of his errand. She did not smile back.

'Have you got good neighbours here?' he said gently, not expecting her to say yes. Mrs Nimmo was small and thin, with dyed blonde hair falling over her face in strands. Her fingers were a deep brown at the tips, and a chipped saucer in the middle of the table overflowed with ash and stubs. At odds with all this was her mouth, carefully painted bright scarlet, and each of the cigarette stubs bore her scarlet signature.

'Rotten lot. Nosy parkers, all of 'em,' she growled. Her voice was husky with smoke.

'Family?'

'Only my Haydn,' she said. She pronounced it as in haystack. 'And you know him. He's working now, o' course,' she added with the trace of a smile.

The policeman took a deep breath. 'Indeed we do,' he said. 'Or should I say "did" . . . I'm afraid I've got bad news for you. Haydn has met with an accident.' He stretched out his arm and reluctantly took her hand. It shook violently, and he rescued her cigarette and stubbed it out.

'What . . . where . . . is he hurt?'

'I'm afraid so. He didn't stand a chance. An escaped horse ran out right in front of the van. Haydn must have stood on the brakes and the van skidded into a metal post. He wasn't wearing his safety-belt.'

Mrs Nimmo shook off his hand and stood up, tipping the stool over behind her. 'A sodding horse?' she screamed. 'I hope it was killed!'

The policeman was shocked. He shook his head. 'Bolted,' he said. 'Not touched. We haven't found it yet, but its owner will.'

After that, Mrs Nimmo let rip a string of expletives, some of which even the experienced policeman hadn't heard. She calmed down slowly, and protested that she would be perfectly all right. 'I don't need no friend wi' me,' she said firmly. 'I ain't got any friends, anyway. Just tell me what you want me to do. We've always known 'ow to cope with bad news. Get on with it, then.' She was still shaking, but refused a cup of tea.

He stood up, and said that if she was sure she would be all right he'd better be getting back to the station. He'd be in touch very soon. Mrs Nimmo followed him, and out of earshot, she muttered to herself, 'I know who's behind this, no mistake. He's bin asking for it, and now he'll get it, good and proper.'

Haydn Nimmo had been trouble since he was born. Arriving late, he was a ten-pounder and nearly split his mother in half.

He was a fractious baby, and an unwilling schoolboy, drifting through a series of schools, playing truant and learning as little as possible. Finally, when all the well-meaning helpers had washed their hands of him, he left school and as soon as he could – in fact, before he legally could – he drove any vehicle available to him and his dodgy friends. Whenever there was a job that needed a quick getaway, Haydn was the man. He loved driving, and had passed his driving test first time with flying colours, which was not surprising considering his several years of experience.

'It was the one thing 'e was good at,' Mrs Nimmo croaked to her sister Evelyn, who had several hours later heard the news through the grapevine and had come hurrying round to Sebastopol Street.

'He was a good boy,' she replied, 'on the whole. Fancy him dying in a road smash. None of us can believe it. He was so good with cars.'

'Us' applied to the family Mrs Nimmo had omitted to mention to the policeman. Generations of Nimmos had lived by their wits, mostly just the wrong side of the law. They were well known to the police, but each maintained an unwritten family rule that they never talked about each other. When Haydn's father had drowned in a gravel pit the other side of Long Farnden, though in broad daylight and with – for once – no trace of alcohol in his blood, the family had shaken their heads and remained mute. 'Must've missed his footin',' was the most they would say.

The two sisters were silent for a few minutes. Then Mrs Nimmo began to fill the kettle. 'Cup o' tea, Evie?'

Evelyn shook her head quickly. 'I must be going, Dot,' she said, glancing at the pile of dirty dishes in the sink. 'You know where we are if you need any help.' She paused. 'O' course,' she added, 'we all know it couldn't have been an accident, don't we?'

After she had left, Dot Nimmo sat down heavily on the wobbling stool. Apart from a whine from next door's dog, the house was heavy with a silence that would not be broken by Haydn bouncing through the door, full of news of his day to tell his mother. 'Never again,' she whispered to herself. She put her head down on her grubby hands and wept for a long time.

Seven

Lois had expected to see an account of the accident in the local paper the next morning, but there was nothing. Maybe it had happened too late for the early edition.

'Did you hear about the smash Dad saw yesterday?' she said to Josie, who was up on steps stacking the high shelves in the shop.

'I'm too busy for gossip this morning,' Josie said. She had had a row with Rob, and was not feeling sociable.

'Oops!' said Lois. 'Well, in that case, do you think I could have a loaf and a pot of raspberry jam? If you've got time, that is.'

Josie laughed in spite of herself, and put the food into her mother's basket. 'Here you are, and a pot of apricot that's just beyond its sell-by date. Gran'll eat it. The older the better, as far as she's concerned.'

Lois's mobile phone rang. She picked up her shopping and went outside, where the signal was stronger. 'Hello? I thought it might be you. What d'you want?'

'A word with you, Lois, if you can spare a minute.' Lois did not reply, and Cowgill smiled at the other end of the line. His Lois. 'Just checking in,' he continued, 'to find out how you are.'

'You don't fool me,' she said. 'That's *not* want you want to know, is it? You want to know what Derek has said about that road smash involving a white van.'

Cowgill sighed. 'Right as usual,' he said. 'I know Derek has made a statement, and a very good, detailed one, too. But people often remember things later.'

'Then why don't you speak to him? I'm getting cold standing here, so if that's all—'

'No, no, wait a minute, Lois. The young man killed in the crash was Haydn Nimmo. Straightforward accident with a

loose horse, it seems. Still, anything that happens to the
Nimmos has to be checked. A few years ago, his father, Handel
Nimmo, drowned in those gravel pits down the road from you.
Do you remember?'

'We'd only just moved here,' Lois said. 'I only remember
it because of the ridiculous name.'

'Nimmo Senior fancied himself as a joker,' Cowgill said.
'Practical jokes as well as funny names. Played one once too
often. We couldn't pin his death on anybody, but we reckon
it was in the family. Now there's Haydn. It is almost certainly
a genuine accident, but just could be something to do with
the old feud. Keep it to yourself, Lois.'

'Don't I always?' Lois said angrily. 'Anyway, what can I
do? They're not exactly among our circle of friends,' she added.

'Talk to Derek. Listen to Derek. Ask Josie to keep her ears
open in the shop. I don't have to spell it out to you, Lois.
Now go and get warm. Talk soon. And don't forget, officially
the police are satisfied there were no suspicious circumstances.'

Lois walked home fuming. *If he thinks I'm grilling my own
husband, he can think again. And if Josie hears anything interesting, well and good. But I'm not recruiting her into Cowgill's
private army.* She reached home to find Gran making leek
and potato soup, and propped herself up against the Rayburn.
'You're a wonder, Mum,' she said, and Gran nearly dropped
her wooden spoon in surprise.

'Feeling all right, Lois?' she said.

Eight

Hazel sat at her desk in New Brooms in Sebastopol Street
and looked at her watch. Soon it would be time for
Maureen to bring Lizzie for a hug and kiss before her morning
rest. Maureen was an old school friend, and by great good
fortune lived next to New Brooms. When Lois offered Hazel
the job of managing the office, the baby girl had been a

problem. The two grandmothers could help out, but not all the time. Then Hazel met Maureen, who had her own child, and the perfect arrangement was made. Baby-minding suited single mum Maureen, and she and Hazel devised a rota so that Lizzie could see her mother several times during the day.

'Here she comes!' said Hazel, opening the door and taking her daughter from Maureen's arms. 'Been a good girl?'

'As always,' Maureen said. 'She's an angel most of the time. Hey, Hazel,' she continued, 'you know them Nimmos up the street? Chronic lot, all of 'em. I've had trouble with smashed windows and graffiti on the door. The cowards know I've got no man in the house. It was a while ago, but I ain't forgiven them. Well, look at this,' she said, handing over the morning newspaper.

'I saw a bit in yesterday's late edition. About whatsisname Nimmo being killed in a crash. A horse ran in front of his van. Police were not regarding it as suspicious. Is that what you mean?' Hazel asked.

'This is a follow-up story,' Maureen said, and pointed to a picture with a few paragraphs. It was an interview with Mrs Nimmo, and the photograph must have been taken years ago. An attractive blonde looked out, with a confident smile. 'You'd not recognize the old bag from that,' Maureen said. 'But read what she says.'

It was a long complaint, full of resentment and blame. 'My Haydn was a good boy. And a real good driver. He'd never have crashed unless some bugger had scared that horse and sent it runnin'. He'd been doin' a building job, and was on his way 'ome with an empty van. Poor Haydn, he was bullied all his life, just one of life's victims. It was hell at school for 'im. Used to come home crying his eyes out. Too scared to tell who the bullies were. Then he got in with the wrong gang. They bullied 'im too. Scared stiff of 'em, he was . . . Yes, o' course I hope the police'll get that sod what set up that loose horse. Don't 'old yer breath, though. The likes of us don't matter much. You learn that, in Sebastopol.'

Hazel lifted her eyebrows and hugged Lizzie tight. 'Doesn't seem to occur to her that with a name like that he was an easy target?'

'None so blind as those that won't see, as Dad used to say,' said Maureen.

'Oh well, you'll see, some other poor sod'll pay for it, whether he's guilty or not. Tit for tat. That's the way they work. Now, Miss,' Hazel said, handing Lizzie a mug of orange, 'drink this nicely for Mum.'

When Maureen had taken the toddler away for her sleep, Hazel swept away biscuit crumbs and thought about Mrs Nimmo. Wasn't she a mother, just the same as herself and Maureen? She must have loved – what was his name? – Haydn, just as much. Maybe more, since he was bullied at school. But some kids, even with loving parents, went off the rails. It seemed to be there from birth.

The telephone rang, and Lois spoke briefly. 'I'm coming into Tresham this afternoon,' she said, 'and I'll drop in. Not sure what time, but earlyish.' Hazel smiled. She suspected that Lois liked to check up on her. Well, fair enough. She was the boss.

Before she went to Tresham, Lois had to call on the Battersbys. Floss was back at work, and she needed to make sure everything was going smoothly. She hoped the Colonel had calmed down, though doubted it. Derek had not yet been in touch with him, and did not intend to be, she knew. With any luck, the old martinet would be out, attending one of the many committees he chaired.

Floss had seen her coming and opened the door. 'He's out,' she whispered with a smile. 'But she's in, upstairs in her room. I'll tell her you're here.'

'It's you I've come to see, Floss,' Lois said. 'Just want to make sure you're feeling better. How's the ear? Still painful?'

Floss shook her head. 'Not really. I'm still taking the tablets, but it'll be fine by tomorrow. Nice of you to come, though.'

'Better tell Mrs Battersby I'm here now, else she'll have her feathers ruffled. Her sort do.'

Lois heard Floss's voice, and then Blanche Battersby came downstairs. The Colonel's lady was smiling, and greeted Lois in a friendly fashion. 'Floss assures me she is feeling fine,' she said. 'I wouldn't want her to be in pain.'

'Nor would I,' said Lois. 'For one thing, she wouldn't do the job properly.' Floss, standing behind Blanche, made a face. 'Is there any news of the theft?' Lois continued casually. 'Last time I was here, poor Colonel Battersby was so upset.'

'Yes, well,' said Blanche, 'he had good cause . . . for once,' she added quietly, looking away. 'No, there's no news,' she continued, 'at least, the police haven't told us anything. I believe your husband, Mrs Meade, had some experience of this nasty business? I know the Colonel is hoping to speak to him.'

'Mm,' said Lois. 'Well, I must be off. I'm going into Tresham, Floss. Anything you need?'

As she walked into the yard, she saw a young lad in the distance, carrying an armful of dead twigs. That must be Darren Smith, the garden boy. She quickened her step and caught up with him. 'Morning, Darren,' she said. She had heard of the Smiths in Waltonby. They were a mother and young son, and lived in a council house on the Wycherley Estate. The father was still alive, but never came near them.

Darren looked round with a startled look. He did not recognize Lois, and was scared of strangers. He found it impossible to relate to people in the usual way. Words meant little to him, and he often repeated what had been said to him with no apparent comprehension, but he understood simple commands. He was like a person from another planet, where time, space, language and human behaviour were totally at odds with the one he had landed in. But his mother looked after him and loved him. She was in tune with him, made sure he got where he was supposed to go, and came back safely. His job with the Battersbys was ideal, and he worked hard. He loved the garden, but he loved the birds even more. He seemed to understand them, and looked anxious when a blackbird squawked its alarm as dusk fell.

'I'm Mrs Meade, from Long Farnden,' Lois said quickly. 'It is a nice morning, isn't it?'

Darren nodded. 'Nice morning,' he echoed politely. 'Goodbye,' he said, and began to walk away.

'Oh, don't go,' Lois said, reluctant to be dismissed so quickly. She tried again. 'Mrs Battersby has a lovely garden, hasn't she? Thanks to you! And lovely horses, too. Do you like them?'

'Nice morning, goodbye,' he repeated.

Sad that she had failed, Lois turned around and went back to her car.

*   *   *

Hazel had a sandwich and coffee ready when Lois walked in. 'Bet you've had nothing to eat yet,' she said. 'Here, sit at the desk and I'll keep an eye out for customers.' She perched on a chair, and they discussed New Brooms matters until Hazel stood up suddenly and retreated from the window. 'Blimey!' she said. 'There's Mrs Nimmo coming this way, and she's got up like a dog's dinner! Where's she off to?'

They soon discovered the answer when Dot Nimmo paused by New Brooms' door, gave a push, and came into the office.

'Good afternoon,' Lois said, 'can we help you?' She shoved her half-eaten sandwich into a drawer, and Hazel disappeared into the kitchen behind the office.

'Yer needn't do that,' said Dot Nimmo, observing the half-open drawer. 'Everybody's got to eat.' She walked forward and stood within inches of the desk. 'Now, it's not what you can do fer me,' she said. 'It's what I can do fer you. I want a job. I'm a good cleaner, and reliable. You can ask anybody. I'll take whatever wages the rest get, and I can start on Monday.'

Nine

Long Farnden post was delivered by Josie, who was postmistress as well as shopkeeper. Post office business was a lifeline for village shops, and the thought that one day it might be taken away sometimes kept her awake at night. She had sorted and delivered the post this morning, including a handful for her parents. A mail-order catalogue for Gran would keep her happy for hours, and Josie had smiled as she pushed it through the letterbox.

It was an exciting time for the family, and she wondered if she'd be able to go along to the presentation ceremony. She hoped so, and maybe Gran as well. She must remember to ask Mum. By the time she was back in the shop, she was immediately plunged into an argument about a loaf of bread that Miss Beasley had refused to accept, and had sent back with her friend, Doris Ashbourne. 'Not cooked properly,' Doris said apologetically. 'Ivy says it's soggy in the middle.'

It was mid-afternoon when Lois arrived home and picked up her letters. Gran had sorted them and was already immersed in her catalogue. 'There's some lovely things here,' she said as Lois came into the kitchen. 'I'll let you have a look later.'

Lois's letters were dull. Four charity appeals, and notice of a Well Woman Clinic at the local surgery. She put the appeals in the bin, feeling guilty, and decided the clinic could wait another year. She felt fine, except somewhat bruised by her encounter with Dot Nimmo. She glanced at Derek's letters, and saw an official-looking envelope with a London postmark. 'Oh no,' she said. 'Don't say it's all been a big mistake, and we haven't won the Lottery after all!'

'Don't be ridiculous,' Gran said. 'Anyway,' she added doubt-fully, 'if you're really worried, we could open it. I could say *I* opened it by mistake?' She picked up the envelope as if it contained a bomb.

'Mother!' Lois said sharply. 'Put it down at once. Derek'll be home soon, and then we shall know all. I'm going up to change. Perhaps you'd better give the letter to me.'

Gran exploded. 'So you don't trust your own mother!' she said, and threw the letter across the table to Lois. 'For two pins I'd move to where I was appreciated. See how you get on without me!' Then she burst into tears, and Lois was morti-fied. It took a good fifteen minutes to put things right, and by that time Derek's van was drawing into the drive.

'Come on, Mum,' Lois said. 'Buck up. I've a good story to tell you and Derek. Something that happened in the office this afternoon. I'll just whiz up and change first.'

They were on to their steamed jam roll and custard before Lois felt relaxed enough to describe the visit of Dot Nimmo to New Brooms. Derek had looked at his London post-marked letter and it had been an insurance company touting for busi-ness. So that was all right. Now she could make a good story of Dot's strange appearance in the office.

'We saw her coming down the street,' she said. 'Make-up, tight jeans, scrawny neck and dangling earrings. The lot. Hazel had just been showing me a crash follow-up story in the paper, with a picture of our Dot taken about thirty years ago. She was a good-looker then, poor woman. Anyway, to our surprise, she came into the office, and launched into a long speech about how she needed a job, and said we really needed her. She could start on Monday, she said!'

'I know all about them Nimmos,' Gran said darkly. 'You don't want to touch them with a barge pole. Not unless you want to lose all your customers.'

Derek laughed. 'Time to listen to Gran, Lois, from the sound of it.'

'You don't think I took her on, for God's sake!' Lois stared at them. 'No, it was quite difficult for Hazel and me to get rid of her. What beats me is why she wanted a job with us, anyway.'

'Information, that's what she'd want. She's not stupid, that Dot Nimmo. Her folks lived on the estate, just up the road from me.' Gran's eyes were misty as she recalled the days when her husband was alive and they were regulars at the whist afternoons. 'I remember they told me once that she'd been bright at school and had a good future. Then she met that Handy Nimmo, as they called him, and fell for him, hook, line and sinker. She went from bad to worse, and is now just like the rest of 'em. But she's not stupid, Lois. She'll be wanting to nose around to get some way of paying back for the death of her beloved son.'

'Ha!' said Derek. 'So you're not the only one, Lois, to spot how goin' cleanin' can be useful. You could hire Dot Nimmo as your side-kick.'

'Thanks very much for the suggestion,' said Lois, not liking the way this conversation was going. 'Anyway, how was your day? Seen the Colonel yet?'

Derek shook his head. 'But I have had a call from your friend Cowgill. Seems the Colonel told him about what I saw at Joe Horsley's. He wants me to call in at the cop shop tomorrow.' He watched for Lois's reaction, and got it.

'Just wait till I speak to him! He knows I won't talk about you, so he's trying the direct line!'

Derek sighed. 'Don't worry, me duck,' he said. 'I told you I was goin' to tell them, anyway. Won't take more than five minutes to tell what I saw. Shan't mention Joe, though. I shan't say he didn't want the police told. They can find out for themselves why he didn't.'

'Fine,' said Lois. 'And he's good at his job, is Cowgill, so don't let him worm anything out of you what you don't want told.'

Later that evening, while they were watching boring football on the television, Lois was thinking about stable thefts, and remembered what Derek had said. Why didn't Joe Horsley want to report it to the police? Didn't want the hassle, he'd said. But that thief could have had another go at the farm. Why had Joe taken it so casually?

'Derek,' she said.

'Sshh! He's gonna score! Hey!! Yes!' After several moments of triumph, he turned to her and said, 'Did you say somethin', me duck?'

'Oh, forget it,' Lois said. 'No, on second thoughts, don't forget it. I was thinking about Joe Horsley. How well do you know him?'

'Only what I picked up while working there. He seemed a good enough bloke. His wife was very nice.' He grinned at her, and Gran laughed.

'I'm serious, Derek. Is it a big farm? What's the house like? Did he pay up promptly?'

Derek groaned. 'Why don't you just leave it to your policeman to ask the questions?'

Lois didn't answer, but fixed him with an icy look. He sighed. 'Oh, all right. It's a middlin'-size farm. The house is just an old farmhouse, but they've made it posh. Tennis court, billiard room, all that. And yes, he paid me in cash before I left. Will that do? Can we concentrate on the football now?'

'One more question,' she said. 'Who are his friends?'

'God knows. I've heard them talking to people on the phone, but I've got no idea who they were. That's more in your line than mine, Lois.' He stared at the screen for five minutes, and then added, 'I heard the two of them talking about the Domino Club in Tresham a couple of times. Seems he goes there quite a lot. Don't think *she* does, though. Now, if you don't mind, I'd like to see the rest of this exciting match.'

Lois yawned exaggeratedly, and said, 'I think I'll go on up now. Night, Mum. See you in a bit, Derek.'

He blew her a kiss without taking his eyes off the screen.

Ten

Tresham's night life centred around a multi-screen cinema, a small theatre where skilled amateurs put on popular plays for an audience of mostly pensioners; and a couple of clubs: the Domino and the Ace of Diamonds. Lois knew the cinema well, and had been occasionally to the theatre with Gran, but had never been clubbing. She had never even considered it, rightly supposing that Derek would hate it – and anyway, such clubs were for the young. But now she was intrigued. Joe Horsley wasn't young. Josie would be the one to ask about clubs. She had gone mildly off the rails as a teenager. Then there was Hazel, who'd had direct experience of the drug scene and still had many contacts. But there was no reason to suppose Joe Horsley's taste for clubbing had anything to do with drugs. No, she would try Josie first.

Lois had also been toying with the idea of organizing an accidental meeting with one of the Horsleys. Joe's wife Maggie must have her hair done somewhere, or she might catch Joe at the market in Tresham. Most farmers congregated in the pub in the Market Square. That was probably the best bet. Then she could settle the niggling thought that she should try a bit harder on the stable thefts, find out at least some pointers for Cowgill. She smiled to herself. They'd been close for years, in a manner of speaking.

She closed down her computer and went through to the kitchen, where Gran was ironing fiercely. Her technique was a battle between her and Derek's shirts, rumpled pillowcases, and tea towels, which, in Lois's view, did not need ironing. Gran thumped the iron down on obstinate creases and rolled-up edges. Clouds of steam hissed, and she folded and pressed as if inflicting a necessary punishment.

'Shall I do the rest?' Lois asked.

'Why?'

'To give you a rest.' This was a recurring conversation, and Lois knew the conclusion, but it made her feel better to ask.

'If you do them, my dear,' Gran said on cue, 'I shall just have to go over them again. So I might as well finish now. Derek loves the way I do his shirts.'

'Right,' said Lois. 'Have it your way. Don't forget I offered.' She looked at the clock. 'I think I'll just slip down to the shop,' she added. 'Something I need to ask Josie, and I think we're out of eggs. Shan't be long.'

Gran did not reply. They were not out of eggs, but it was no good arguing with Lois.

Josie was preparing to hand over the shop to Rob, who had come home early. 'I've got work to do in the stockroom,' she'd said, 'and it's so much easier without interruptions.'

Now Lois came in and lifted her eyebrows in surprise. 'Hi Rob, where's Josie?' she asked.

'Out the back,' he said. 'I'm in charge, so what can I sell you? Josie thinks I'm no good at selling, so you could do me a favour and spend a tenner or two.'

'Not a chance,' said Lois, laughing. 'Just a dozen eggs please. And then I'll go and have a word out the back. She can carry on working. Just something I need to know.'

'And I can't help?'

'Well . . .' Lois considered for a couple of seconds. 'Well, actually, Rob, you might be able to. I need to know about the club scene in Tresham. Needless to say, I don't know much. But Josie used to go with friends at one time, and I expect you did too. What are the clubs like? Are they both much the same?'

Rob shook his head. 'The Ace of Diamonds is a rough place, with a bad reputation. Kids go there to show how big they are. They buy stuff and get high, and then have to be picked up off pavements and sometimes end up in hospital – and occasionally the morgue.'

'Why don't the police close it down?' Lois could not imagine Joe Horsley in this scene. She had a mental picture of him in tweeds and brogues, bluff and pipe-smoking. No, no, not that one. Anyway, she was sure Derek had said the Domino.

'The Ace is clever. Always got a get-out clause when anything bad comes up.'

'And the other one?' she asked.

'The Domino? Ah, now that's a different kettle of fish. Smart, with excellent music for dancing, no drugs – not on the surface, anyway – and a good class of customer. They have visiting show-biz stars, often ones who make it to the top later. I used to go there a lot at one time, when I could afford it.' He smiled, gesturing towards the stockroom. 'Too many expenses now,' he added.

'Well, you've been a help,' Lois said. 'I don't need to bother your expensive partner now. Far be it from me to interrupt a vital part of this money-making business.' She was irritated by his insinuations. She had brought up her daughter to keep an eye on spending, and run an economic household. And what was Rob bringing in? Not a fortune, that was for sure.

'A joke, Lois,' Rob said, seeing her face. 'Your Josie is a wonder. I'm sure she'll be sorry to have missed you. Shall I call her?'

Lois shook her head. 'No, not now, thanks. I'll be getting back. Sorry I can't be a better customer,' she added, picking up the eggs. 'Bye.'

Oops, said Rob to himself, put my foot in it there. Just when I was thinking of popping the question to Josie. I'm not sure I could manage a mother-in-law like Lois. He wondered why she wanted to know about Tresham clubs. Deciding that she was sleuthing again and was not likely to tell him, he sat on the stool and picked up a paper to read until the next customer came in.

'Put those eggs behind the other ones in the larder', said Gran when Lois returned. 'How was Josie?'

'Didn't see her,' Lois said casually. 'Rob was in the shop, and she was busy in the stockroom. I had a chat with him, bought the eggs and came straight home. Happy?'

'I don't know why you are so difficult,' Gran said. 'You had loving parents, were a spoilt only one, and have a very patient, wonderful husband.'

'Not to mention my long-suffering, hard-working mother!' Lois gave her mother a big hug, said some people reckoned she, Lois, was exactly like her mum, and so there was nothing to be done. 'I'll be in my office for an hour or so,' Lois continued. 'Paperwork to catch up on.'

Sitting at her desk, Lois looked at her diary. Tomorrow

would be market day in Tresham, and usually she and Gran went together. It was a routine outing, and Gran loved it, trawling the market stalls for bargains and meeting old friends. Lois chewed the end of her pen. Could she take Gran into the pub? And then what would she do with her if Joe Horsley was there? Come to that, how could she introduce herself to a perfect stranger without sounding like a middle-aged whore?

She doodled on her pad, then realized she had drawn the face of a heavily made-up, raddled old woman. *Exactly*, she said to herself, screwing up the paper and throwing it in the bin. But wait a minute. If she and Gran decided on a snack lunch at the pub, a special treat, she could keep her ears open for mention of Joe Horsley – maybe at a game of darts, or standing his round. Lunch was more respectable than just a drink, and then she could do some serious eavesdropping, somehow concealing it from Gran. Yep, that was worth a try. If he wasn't there, nothing would be lost.

The telephone rang. She picked it up, and heard the familiar voice of Cowgill. 'Hello, Lois. How are you?'

'If you've nothing better to do than enquire after my health, then don't waste my time,' she answered sharply.

'Only keeping up standards of politeness in the Force,' he said. 'You sound fierce. Any reason why I've irritated you more than usual?'

'Yes. You have gone too far, Cowgill. You had already asked me to talk to Derek, see if he'd remembered anything extra. Then you go and approach him direct! If you don't trust me, then we'd better end all this malarkey right now.'

'Slow down, Lois!' he said firmly. 'I asked you to talk to Derek about the van crash. My suggestion that he might come in and tell us what he knows about stable thefts is another matter entirely. Fair's fair, Lois. You must admit that.'

Lois said nothing for a few seconds, and then conceded that he was right. 'But I'm working on the thefts, and at the moment it'd be best if you left Derek to me. By the way, have you got any useful info?'

'Nothing beyond speculation at the moment, Lois. But you'll be first to know if we get something concrete.'

'Like a block of it through the police station window?' she answered. 'I should know better than to ask.'

Cowgill chuckled. 'I love you, Lois,' he said, but his voice was carefully light. 'And have you anything to tell me?'

'Nothing beyond speculation at the moment,' she said, and ignored his declaration of love.

Eleven

Dot Nimmo, neat and clean and smelling of cheap scent, left her house by the front door, carefully locking up behind her. She walked past New Brooms with her head down, and turned into the next street. There she waited for a bus to take her into one of the wealthier areas of Tresham, where there were big old houses and tasteful new housing developments. Dot had been there before, but not for a long time.

The bus was full. It was market day, and many people went into town early to catch the bargains and fresh food, and were now on their way home. Women with bulky plastic shopping bags, and young mothers with pre-school children clogged up the aisle when Dot wanted to alight. 'Make way!' she said sharply. 'Some of us 'ave a livin' to earn.'

A woman of her own age turned round, and said equally sharply, 'Wait yer turn, missus. We're all gettin' off here.'

Dot glared at her, but noticed she had an old tapestry bag and work-worn hands. When they were both off the bus, Dot said, 'D'you live round 'ere, then?'

'What if I do?'

'Just wondered. I'm lookin' for work. Cleanin' work.'

'That's what I do,' the woman said, warming up slightly. 'There's plenty of work round here. More money than sense, some of these housewives. Still, it's good fer the likes of us. Now,' she said, looking thoughtful, 'I 'eard of somebody needing help. Yes, I got it. That road over there, there's a new estate of luxury dwellings, as they call 'em. Number three, I think it was. Try there. Can't remember the name. I'd do it meself, except my week is full up. Good luck, missus.'

Dot reflected that luck seemed to be with her already. The woman wasn't such a bad old cow, after all. It had begun to rain, and she hurried down the road until she saw what must be the 'luxury dwellings'. Number three was off the road, in a large crescent, with a series of big gardens leading to mock-everything houses. Tudor, Georgian, Queen Anne, all cheek by jowl, with coach lamps and statues of nymphs and expensive-looking cars in the driveways.

Dot pressed the bell. It was a while before the door opened slowly. 'Yes?' said an elderly woman, leaning on a stick.

Dot stood firmly on the doorstep, and said, 'I bin told you're lookin' for a cleaner. I've come about the job.'

The woman nervously half-closed the door. Dot said, without having planned to do so, 'I work for that cleanin' business in the town. They sent me. A friend of yours got in touch. I'm very respectable and 'ave lots of experience. Would you like me to come in for a minute?' She was quite pleased with this, and wondered if she should have mentioned New Brooms by name. But no, that was too easy to check up on.

With a doubtful look, the woman moved back painfully, and motioned Dot in. 'Just for a minute, then,' she said.

Dot moved swiftly, and went ahead into the sitting room. 'You just come and sit down, dear,' she said. 'Then we can talk comfortably.' Her late husband had once told her she had the tongue of a serpent, and she had taken it as a compliment. 'Not many say no to Dot,' he had been fond of saying. Except for that stuck-up Mrs Meade, of course. Well, she would show her.

After ten minutes or so, Dot and the infirm woman were like old friends. Dot said she could start tomorrow.

'What's yer name, dear?' Dot asked.

'Mrs Parker-Knowle,' the smiling woman said. 'Just like the chairs.'

Dot laughed heartily. 'I do like a lady with a good sense of humour,' she said. They arranged days and times and rates of pay, and then Dot left. 'Don't get up, dear,' she called from the front door. 'And don't forget, 'ave a key ready for me when I come tomorrow. Oh, and I forgot to say, we get paid direct by the client. So if you need any help gettin' money from the Post Office 'n that, just let me know.'

Then she was gone. As she walked back to the bus stop,

she considered calling at other houses on the way. But perhaps it was best to start with one nice old lady, who would recommend Dot to her friends. And one of her friends might be the one Dot was looking for.

The market in Tresham was a pretty sight when the sun was out, with blue and white striped awnings over the stalls flapping gently in the breeze. Lois and Gran went across to the flower stall, to buy chrysanthemums for Josie. 'Yellow ones, don't forget,' said Gran. Lois said nothing. They had been buying yellow chrysanths for Josie for years. 'I need some new tea towels,' Gran added. 'We'll go to old Bill's stall by the hamburgers. Are we going to have ours yet?'

'No, I thought we'd treat ourselves today,' Lois said. 'I fancied a steak and kidney pie at the pub. How about you?'

Gran's eyes brightened. 'Good idea!' she said. 'I might even have a half of Guinness.'

'Well, let's get the towels first, then it's pie and chips for two.'

They settled themselves at a table by the window and looked out on to the market square. 'We should do this every week,' Gran said, beaming. 'Now, are you having a Guinness with me?'

'Better not. I'm driving,' Lois said. 'But you have one. Here, let's look at the menu board, and I'll order at the bar.'

They were happily shaking brown sauce on to their pies when a knot of farmers drinking at the bar turned round to look at the door. A big man with a ruddy face and thick grey hair came in and approached them. 'Morning, Joe,' said two or three of the farmers, and Lois pricked up her ears. Joe was a common enough name, but still . . .

'How's Margaret?' another said, and Joe replied that she was very well, and just as talkative as ever. 'That's why I come in here,' he said, 'to get a bit o' peace!' They laughed, and the circle closed up, all talking at once.

So it was him, thought Lois. Derek had said his wife's name was Margaret. She wished she could hear their conversation, but Gran was saying something about puddings. Were they having ice cream or tiramisu? Lois took the opportunity to go back to the bar to order ice creams, and positioned herself next to the men.

One of them turned and looked at her. 'Morning, gel,' he said, winking at the others. 'Excuse me asking, but ain't you the one who's won the lottery? Saw your picture in the paper.' He smiled invitingly.

'If you saw my bank account, you wouldn't ask me that.' It wasn't a lie. They hadn't had a penny of their winnings yet.

'Oh, sorry, me duck. Mistook you for somebody else. Can I buy you a drink?'

Lois shook her head. 'I'm driving,' she repeated. 'But no offence taken. Are you lot regulars here?' she asked. 'That's my mum over there. She likes to come and shop the old way. Some of the stallholders know her well.'

'Yeah,' said the one called Joe, looking her up and down. 'We're a fixture in this pub on market days. You won't know Derek Meade, then? He's the one who won the lottery, and he came and did some electrics for me. I suppose he'll not be doing that kind of work now?'

Lois shook her head, and began to walk back to her table. She could see Gran staring at her. She must have heard, but she said nothing. Lois had answers ready, but there were no questions.

When they had finished and paid for their meal, they headed for the door. Lois let Gran go first, and hung back for a second or two. 'See you next week?' called Joe Horsley. 'Is it a date?' Lois smiled faintly, and followed Gran into the market square.

Half an hour passed before they were in the car and heading back to Farnden. Then Gran said, 'What are you up to, Lois?'

'What d'you mean?'

'In the pub. Flirting, at your age! I was ashamed of you. I hope it don't get back to Derek. I shan't say anything, but you know how bad news travels.'

'What on earth are you talking about?' Lois tried hard to sound annoyed. 'Of course I wasn't flirting. Just being polite. No harm in a friendly word, you know. And anyway, there were five of 'em. Safety in numbers.'

Gran snorted. 'Well, don't ask me to go there again if you intend to behave like that. We Weedons still have a good name in Tresham. We had enough trouble keeping it when you were young, and I don't expect to go through all that again.'

Lois was firm. She told her mother she was being ridiculous. She would tell Derek herself. And, even if it was a white lie she had told about the lottery, Derek would agree with what she'd done. They didn't want to talk about it with every nosey Tom, Dick and Harry. So that was an end to it.

Gran said no more. She bided her time.

Twelve

'Just a moment, sir,' said the young policeman behind the desk. 'I'll tell the chief you're here.' He smiled. Blimey, thought Derek, there must be a new policy of being kind to visitors to the station. He sat down and glanced around at the two others looking anxiously at the reception desk. An elderly woman, respectable and neat, twisted her purse over and over in her veined hands. A young man – how young it was difficult to say – slumped in his chair, his face defiantly hidden by his grey hood.

If it hadn't been for Lois, I wouldn't be here, Derek thought. I could be getting on with my job, enjoying it and dreaming of what we could do with our windfall. Instead, I'm sitting here feeling like a criminal, even though I've done nowt wrong. Why couldn't she be like other blokes' wives? Housework, children, keeping herself lovely for me . . .? In spite of himself and where he was, Derek laughed out loud. His Lois was special, and though he sometimes wished for a quiet life, he loved her just as she was. When they'd first met, she was trouble. Shoplifting, truanting, in with the worst gang in Tresham – and more fanciable than all the other girls put together.

'Mr Meade? Will you come this way, please?'

'Morning, Derek,' said Cowgill pleasantly. 'Have a seat. This shouldn't take long.'

Their conversation was indeed brief and to the point. Derek described in detail all he could remember of the episode in Horsley's yard. Cowgill wrote steadily on his pad.

'And so you told the farmer – Mr Horsley – what you saw?'

'Yep, when he and his wife came home. I told him all what I've told you.'

'And what did he say?'

'Not a lot, really. I expect he was a bit shocked. I finished the job, and I left after that. Told Lois about it. The rest you know.'

'And what about Mrs Horsley? How did she react?'

'Didn't really notice.' Derek shrugged. 'She was busy unloading shopping, I think.' He stood up. 'That's all then. I've told you all I can remember. I suppose I should have been quicker off the mark, but didn't think much of it at the time.'

Cowgill got to his feet. 'Just a minute, Derek,' he said. 'Thank you very much for coming in and giving us your help. Invaluable. And please reassure Lois that you have been treated with courtesy and consideration. Good morning.'

Derek left the station and walked across the car park. So that was all right, then. Credit where credit's due, old Cowgill had stuck to the point, except for his message to Lois. Derek grinned. His Lois could put the fear of God into most people.

He was just about to get into the van when a loud 'Good morning, Derek!' stopped him. He looked around and saw to his dismay the upright figure of Colonel Battersby. The last person he wanted to see right now. And what gave him the right to call him Derek? Maybe he should try calling him Horace.

'Morning, Horace,' Derek said.

The Colonel swallowed hard. 'What luck meeting you,' he said bravely. 'Is there a chance we could go and have a coffee and a short chat? I've just been to the police station, and as far as I can gather from a senior officer, they've got nowhere with the wretched stable thefts.'

Derek hesitated. He could do with a coffee, and he supposed the stiff-necked idiot wouldn't rest until he'd heard Derek's story. 'All right,' he said. 'I can't be too long. Let's go to that coffee shop in the market square. The service is quick there.' He looked at his watch, and was surprised to see it was nearly lunchtime. A beer would be more acceptable, but he supposed the Colonel wouldn't stoop to drinking with an electrician.

'Yes, dear,' said the waitress when they went in, 'what can I get you?'

'Two coffees,' said the Colonel, and before she could reply, he added, 'and none of those frothy things. Just two cups – and I mean cups with saucers – of good coffee. And hot milk.'

'I'd like a latte, please, me duck,' Derek said. 'And a biscotti, please.' He smiled sweetly at her.

'So that's two cups of coffee and one latte?' she said tentatively.

'Of course not!' said the irritated Colonel. 'One proper cup for me, and whatever it was that, um, Derek ordered. And we haven't much time.'

'Mistake there, Horace,' said Derek. 'Never say you're in a hurry. They put you to the bottom of the list.'

'Not in my club,' said Colonel Battersby pompously. 'Respect is the byword there. Bit of a shock to come to places like this.'

Derek laughed. 'You'll get over it,' he said. 'Now, what do you want to know?'

'Exactly what happened when you witnessed a stable theft at Horsley's farm? Your wife did not – or would not – give me any details, but the more I know about all these stable thefts, the better chance I stand of catching the culprits.'

'I can tell you very little,' Derek said firmly. 'First sight I got was through the frosted bathroom window. The sort with wobbly glass. Just vague shapes, so I didn't take much notice. Then I thought maybe I should take a look, but the vehicle was halfway down the track, trailing exhaust fumes, by the time I got down into the yard.'

'Did you tell the police all this?' the Colonel said in a court-martial voice.

'O' course. What d'you think I was doin' at the station? I'm not a regular there, y'know.'

The Colonel said nothing, and Derek considered what his inquisitor had said. Something not quite right there, he thought, trying to remember the Colonel's exact words. Oh, yes, that was it. He'd referred to *Horsley's* farm. Lois wouldn't have told him which farm it was, and he certainly hadn't mentioned the name. So how did the Colonel know?

A young girl with nothing much covering her midriff appeared with their coffee, and Derek forgot all about farms and saddles. 'Thanks a lot, ducky,' he said with a fatherly smile, and the Colonel looked suspiciously at Derek's foaming mug.

'Is that any good?' he said.

'Want a try?' Derek held out a spoonful of creamy coffee, and to his surprise Horace took it. 'Mmm, not bad at all,' he grunted, and licked the spoon.

*   *   *

In a quieter, more dignified part of Tresham, Dot Nimmo was changing from slippers into shoes, and taking off her wrap-around overall. 'There we are then, dear,' she said to Mrs Parker-Knowle. 'All tickety-boo. I must say your last char was taking you for a bit of a ride. Lots of dirty corners! My old mum used to say if you take care of the corners, the middles'll take care of themselves. And she was right. Still, I think you'll find I take care of all of it.'

Alice Parker-Knowle smiled. Even if it wasn't true, she was cheered up already by this perky woman from Sebastopol Street. She reached for an envelope tucked behind her radio. 'This is for you,' she said. 'You'll find it is correct.'

Dot hesitated. Every brain cell told her to check it, but she was about to take a risk. For the sake of establishing trust, she put the unopened envelope in her pocket. 'Well, I must get the bus. See you soon, dear.'

'Um, what's the time?' Alice asked.

'Five minutes past my three hours,' Dot said sharply. Trust should work both ways.

'Oh, I'm not checking up on you,' Alice said hastily. 'I was just thinking it is lunchtime and you have a bus ride before you get home. I'd be happy for you to have another coffee and something to keep the wolf from the door. You'll have to get it yourself, of course.'

Now we're talking, thought Dot, and slipped off her coat. 'Why don't I get *you* something nice for lunch, dear,' she said, 'and have a bite myself? Save you the trouble of bending and stretching in that lovely kitchen of yours?'

They sat companionably with trays on their laps in the sitting room. Dot had made an appetizing salad for Alice, and a rough sandwich for herself. Alice had a fresh table napkin from the drawer, and Dot had a square of kitchen paper to catch the crumbs.

'How long have you lived in Tresham?' Dot asked conversationally.

'All my life,' Alice said. 'But not in this house, of course. My family farmed over towards Waltonby. A large acreage, and father was what I suppose you would call a gentleman farmer. Lovely old house, and we kept horses. Hunting, pony club – all that. My nephew is there now. Unfortunately, my husband and I had no children.'

'Shame,' said Dot. 'They can be a comfort. And, then again, they can be a sorrow.'

It was all going to plan, and Alice dutifully asked what experience Dot had suffered. She was told a heart-rending story, including the strange death of Handel in the gravel pit and Haydn's fatal crash at the roundabout. 'He was my only,' Dot said. 'The light of me life, and a comfort, as you can imagine, after I lost my husband.'

'How frightful! You poor thing,' said Alice, reaching for a box of chocolates by her chair. 'Here, have one of these. They are my comforters, and I eat far too many of them.'

They had two each, and then Alice said, 'Whose was the horse that ran in front of your son's van?'

Dot shook her head mournfully. 'Dunno,' she said. 'Leastways, I don't know for sure, but I have my suspicions. All to do with a stupid feud that should've been stopped years ago. My Handy – we called him that – was a good husband, but he didn't forgive nobody who done him a bad turn. Man called Battersby. Nasty piece of work. He refused to pay a bill for work Handy done for 'im. Said it was skimped, and threatened to report him to the police. Handy wrote it off, but he never forgave 'im. What he did was, he made sure nobody else would work for Battersby. It was in Handy's power, see. Sort of union, his friends. The Tresham Mafia! Made life very difficult for Battersby. Years ago now, but the feud went on.'

Dot looked mistily out of the window, and Alice shook her head in amazement. 'Fancy that,' she said. 'I had no idea these things were so close to home. How awful for you. D'you know, funnily enough, I knew some people called Battersby.'

Dot's head jerked round to her. 'Did you?' she said.

'Oh, ages ago. Met them through the Conservative Association. You know the sort of thing. Cocktails and bits of sawdust to eat!' She laughed, but Dot did not. She could not believe her luck. Should she ask more questions, tickle the old girl's memory? No, better to leave it till next time. She might remember more then. Could it be the same Battersbys? It was a common name around Tresham, but you never knew. A morning well spent, she thought as she put on her coat.

'I'll be off, then,' she said.

'Right, and thank you so much,' said Alice.

'Don't you get up, dear,' Dot said. 'I'll see meself out. Take care, and don't do nothing I wouldn't do!'

Alice heard her cackling down the drive, and smiled. What a treasure she was, and how splendid to find someone so obliging.

Thirteen

Seven nervously excited people settled into two cars outside the shop, and Josie leaned into the driver's window of the first one. 'Have a nice day!' she said to Derek, who had hired a smart Toyota for the purpose. It was the syndicate's big day, and Josie was not going, in spite of dropping heavy hints.

'I shall be there, of course,' Lois had said. 'Your Dad will need me there. But that'll be it, I'm afraid. We'll tell you all about it when we get back. Don't forget to take Jeems for a walk after closing.'

'Don't worry, me and Gran will take care of everything,' Josie said, and wiped away a tear as she waved to the retreating cars. Please God, she said to herself, don't let them be disappointed. It was an odd prayer for people about to collect a couple of million, but they looked so apprehensive and somehow vulnerable . . . Still, her mum was usually neither of those things, so they'd be all right.

'Nice of Josie to wave us off,' Lois said. She was sitting in the passenger seat next to Derek, and turned to smile at Matt the plumber and Geoff the publican sitting in the back. 'Did you get any sleep last night?' she said.

'Not a lot,' Matt said. 'I set the alarm, but didn't need it. And the wife was making tea at half past five. I feel as if I've done a day's work already.'

'I have,' said Geoff smugly. 'Got everything ready for opening time. I'm always an early riser. Must admit, though, I hardly got a wink last night.'

Derek said, 'Lois snored all night, as usual.'

'Liar,' Lois said amiably. She was not about to spoil the day by arguing, and they drove steadily on towards Staines, where the unbelievable was about to happen.

'Geoff, have you got the ticket?' Matt asked suddenly as they were approaching their destination.

'Don't be ruddy daft,' Geoff replied. 'O' course I've got the ticket! Would I come all this way without it?'

He felt in his pocket for his wallet. Then he felt in another pocket. A deadly quiet fell on the car's passengers. 'Um, just a minute,' he said, 'it's here somewhere.'

Derek pulled into a layby. 'Better make sure,' he said calmly. 'Might have to turn back.'

Now Geoff searched frantically, and finally pulled his leather wallet out of a hidden pocket in his jacket. 'Phew!' he said. 'I remember putting it there now. Somewhere really safe, I thought.'

'Stupid bugger,' said Matt. 'Then you forgot.'

'We all do it,' said Lois soothingly. 'Especially when we're in a bit of a state. Drive on then, love. We're almost there.'

Derek drove into a development of modern office buildings. The Camelot block blended in with the rest, and from the outside there was nothing to indicate that inside awaited a piece of paper that was going to change their lives. Large, expensive cars were parked all around, and Derek said he was glad they'd not come in a van.

'Oh, I dunno,' Lois said. 'Might pick up some business for New Brooms here. Must be thousands of offices need cleaning.'

'Lois!' chorused the others. 'Not today of all days!'

A parking space had been reserved for them, and when they pulled up and Derek switched off the engine, all gave a rousing cheer for driver and navigator. They announced themselves into the entry phone, and a security man admitted them. As they walked in, a little uncertainly, he directed them to seats in the reception area, and said that in a few minutes he would take them to see the Camelot representative. They watched in silence as impeccably groomed girls and dynamic young men came and went. Nobody took much notice of them, and they were glad when they were ushered into the lift and escorted upwards.

As the doors opened, Lois saw a smiling, pleasant-faced

woman waiting for them, who introduced herself as Debbie. It was the first sign that there was something special about this visit. Debbie was dressed as if for a party, and Lois's spirits began to rise. But not for long. She was shattered to see that once they had been shown into the windowless room, the door was firmly locked behind them. The group filled the room, and Lois felt a claustrophobic stab. She looked at the framed photographs of happy, smiling faces of past winners, and told herself not to be an idiot.

'Why've you locked the door?' she asked bluntly. 'We're not likely to run away, are we?' It was explained that security was vital, and Camelot would have to carry out a number of checks to make sure the ticket was authentic, and that they were who they said they were.

'Please do help yourselves to coffee and sandwiches,' Debbie said. 'You've had a long journey, and must be starving.'

Geoff the publican bit into a sandwich and frowned. 'We could do better than this,' he whispered to Lois. 'Tastes like fish paste.'

Questions were asked, and the group found it difficult to answer with a mouthful of fish paste. Publicity was mentioned. Did they want national publicity or not? It was entirely their choice, and if any of them did not want it, their privacy would be completely protected. They had talked about this in the car, and decided that none of them would mind. 'It'd just be a nine-day wonder,' Matt had said. 'People know, anyway, so it won't come as any great surprise.'

The moment came. Debbie presented the cheque to Geoff, the nominee, together with a single bottle of champagne to enliven the photographs. They were given souvenir mugs and pens, and Lois's eyes widened. 'Wow!' she said with heavy irony, as she examined them. They reminded her of a day at the seaside. 'Terrific!' she added. 'We shall treasure these.'

'Shush!' said Derek.

After that, they got down to business. They were told their money was safely banked, and were advised that the safest option was to leave it where it was until they had decided what they were going to do with it.

'Not for long,' muttered Lois. 'We want it where we can get at it.'

'Shush,' whispered Derek.

More advice followed, and they were offered the services of a solicitor or a financial adviser. By this time, the winners' heads were spinning.

'We can't take all this in at once,' said Lois. 'Don't forget it's a first for us!' They were reassured that they could take time to consider all of it, and they would find the help they needed in their winners' pack. 'Out of the blue – it's you!' the booklet told them, and Lois held it tight for reassurance. She was feeling breathless and wanted desperately to open the door.

At this point, all the lights went out.

'Derek!' Lois's panic escalated. No windows and a locked door were bad enough, but now they were in pitch darkness.

Debbie's voice was loud and authoritative. 'Sorry about this!' she said. 'If this was a crime novel, there'd be a body on the floor when the lights came up!' She laughed, but none of the others did. This was nearly the final straw for Lois.

Finally the lights returned and, shaken and pale-faced, Lois was first out when the door was unlocked. She took a deep breath, and looked down at her hands. She would not have been at all surprised if they had been surreptitiously mana-cled in the darkness. They went down in the lift in silence, and were then escorted from the building. Lois turned to Debbie and said, 'Are you sure it's safe to let us go now?'

The woman frowned. 'Most people say thank you,' she said curtly, and turned to walk away.

It was not until they were in the car and driving off towards home that the silence was broken by Matt suddenly bursting into raucous laughter. 'My God, Lois!' he said. 'You were great! Told her straight!'

Derek looked at Lois. 'Very embarrassed, I was,' he said. 'Sounded like you'd been falsely arrested instead of given a cheque for a couple of million.'

Lois muttered that it had felt a bit like that. Then she turned to the others with a smile and said, 'Still, it's our great day, isn't it? Why don't we stop at that pub comin' up and have a real celebration? We can just about afford it now.'

'Why are we waiting?' chorused the lads, and they pulled into the pub car park in a heady atmosphere of relief and excitement.

Fourteen

A fine sunset greeted them as they drove into Long Farnden, and Derek was temporarily blinded as they approached their house.

'Stop! Derek, stop!' Lois grabbed the handbrake, and they juddered to a halt.

'What the bloody hell . . .? I *was* stopping, Lois! For goodness sake!' His voice tailed off as he looked out of the window into the road in front of him. A barrier of people holding high a banner greeted them. 'WELCOME HOME, LUCKY WINNERS!' it declared in huge red letters on what was clearly a white sheet torn into suitable strips. Josie stepped forward.

'Hi, you lot,' she said. 'Had a nice day?' They all smiled and nodded, speechless – even Lois, at least for the moment. 'Right, well it's not ended yet,' Josie said. 'Dad, will you drive on round to the village hall, and you'll find everyone there.' She turned to the cheering barrier, and shouted, 'Let them through, now! Everyone to the village hall!'

Late that night, Lois and Derek could not sleep. But this time it was happy thoughts that kept them awake. 'That banner was very well done,' Lois said softly, in case Derek had drifted off at last. He hadn't.

'Did you hear who done it?' he said. 'It was Josie's Rob. He's good at graphic art, she said. Whatever that might be.'

'I wonder whose sheet it was,' Lois giggled. 'Hope it wasn't Gran's.'

'Nope. She said they got it from jumble sale stuff, and it had already been sides-to-middled. Apparently everything was done by the village. Ben's mother did the catering; Floss's dad gave the drinks. Her at the Hall gave flowers, and guess who donated the chocs? You'll never guess.'

'Miss Ivy Beasley,' Lois said.

'How did you know, you old fraud?' Derek turned towards her with a dig in the ribs. In due course, they were celebrating as was entirely appropriate at that moment.

Gran, also lying awake, heard laughter and shouts, and smiled. 'What a day! I just wish you were still here to see it,' she whispered to the photograph by her bed. 'You'd have been proud of our little gel.' She picked up the photo and put it on the pillow beside her, and then drifted quietly off to sleep.

Next morning, Gran was up bright and early, but with the tea made and breakfast sizzling in the pan, there was no sound from upstairs. 'Mmm, thick heads all round, I reckon,' she muttered to herself, putting the teapot on the Rayburn to keep warm. She sat down to eat a bowl of cornflakes, and picked up the local paper, which had been delivered at its usual early time by a man in a cherry-red van.

'Well I never!' she said, staring at the smiling face of Derek, looking gleefully up at her. She read the accompanying news story, and laughed out loud. 'Cheeky devil!' she said, and thought she was justified in calling up from the foot of the stairs that they'd better get up, as they were famous.

Lois appeared in her dressing gown, rubbing her eyes. 'What d'you mean, Mum?' she said as she came slowly downstairs.

'Look at this!' said Gran. 'And read what Derek says here . . .'

She came to the bit where Derek was reported as saying that he wasn't all that surprised, as he'd expected it to happen sometime. 'We've been doing the lottery since God knows when, so I knew we'd come up sooner or later. It'll come in handy,' he added, with masterly understatement.

Lois gasped. 'Can you believe it, Mum?' she said. 'He's so laid back, he'll fall on his bum sooner or later.' She went upstairs two steps at a time, then Gran heard yells and shrieks, and she sighed.

'Better put the bacon in the oven,' she said, and returned to the kitchen.

Collapsed on the bed a bit later, Derek and Lois agreed that it was time to get up. Lois folded the crumpled newspaper, and her eye was caught by a familiar name. 'Tresham man involved in tragic accident' the headline announced, and the story described how two teenagers out for a walk in the Municipal Gardens had seen a foot sticking out from under a bush. Investigating, they had seen the body of an old man. At first they thought he must be a homeless vagrant, sheltering from the rain. But when the police arrived, he was pronounced dead. The man was later identified as Albert Nimmo, from Gordon Street. He was ninety-eight, and had wandered away from the old folks' home when nobody was looking. A fatal heart attack had carried him off. 'His favourite relative,' Lois read, 'Mrs Dot Nimmo, of Sebastopol Street, who has lately lost her son Haydn in a car smash at the Harrington roundabout, said, "We are an ill-starred family."'

'Derek! Read this,' Lois said, and hastily went to have a shower. 'I'll have to miss breakfast,' she called through the cascading water. 'Can you square it with Mum?'

Before Derek had dressed, Lois was shouting goodbye and slamming the door behind her. He heard her van starting up, and then grating gears as she backed out of the drive and was away.

'What do *you* want!' Dot Nimmo was far from the scrubbed-up creature last seen tackling Lois in New Brooms' office. Her hair was wild and her eyes sunken, with heavy shadows accentuating the narrowness of her face. No lipstick this morning, and the varnish on her nails was chipped and dirty. The smell wafting under Lois's nose was overpoweringly awful. Much as she was reluctant to go in, Lois said could she have a word. She was sorry to hear about old Albert. 'He was fond of you, wasn't he?' She couldn't think of anything else to say.

'Yes. And me of him.' Dot said, swallowing hard. She continued, 'Anyway what do you want? I can't waste time with you this morning. I expect you've just come to poke your nose in where it's not wanted. So say what you've got to say, and bugger off.'

Lois took the plunge, hoping against hope that this was not a step that she would live to regret. 'I've reconsidered your application,' she said formally, 'and under the circumstances would like to give you a job. Usual probationary period of four weeks.'

Dot Nimmo stood with narrowed eyes staring at her.

'What're you up to?' she asked suspiciously. 'Changing yer mind s'sudden? Still, I'll take it,' she added hastily. 'I know I look a mess right now, but I clean up all right, as you've seen. When shall I start? Oh, and by the way, I've got another little job a couple of mornings a week. Quality job over in one of them new estates of luxury dwellings. I don't want to give her up. She's a nice old gel. I suppose you'll want to take it over, like, and be responsible an' that. Well, I don't mind that. I expect you're covered for breakages and such like?'

As Dot Nimmo drew breath, Lois was able to interrupt. 'Of course,' she said. 'But first I'd like to see you in my office over the road, cleaned up. And one more thing: I'm not doing this for charity. I shall expect high standards from you, like the rest of my team. And don't dress for a night in the Butcher's Arms, please. Quiet, efficient and able to merge into the background. That's how I like it. Good morning.'

Lois walked swiftly down the road, and surprised Hazel in the middle of a telephone call. 'Who was that?' she said.

'The Colonel's lady,' Hazel replied. 'Trying to track you down. I didn't know you were coming in this morning. How are you, after yesterday – especially the evening?'

'Fresh as a daisy, thanks.' Lois picked up the phone. 'What's Battersby's number?' she said, and prepared herself for a tale of woe. She hoped Floss hadn't overstepped the mark and offended the Colonel. 'Mind you,' she muttered, 'easily done.'

'What is?' Hazel eyebrows were raised. Mrs M was in a funny mood today – and what was she doing in Tresham anyway?

'Yes, it's Mrs Meade,' Lois said into the telephone, her fingers crossed. 'Gone missing? What do you mean? Yesterday? And he didn't come home? Is it his day to come to you? And he didn't turn up? He might be ill . . . Oh, you've done that. What else did his mother say? Right. It's not really anything to do with New Brooms, but I'll see what I can do.'

'Who's missing?' Hazel said.

'Darren. The Battersbys' garden lad. He's a bit slow on the uptake, and his mum is frantic. Apparently the Battersbys were taking him to a point-to-point yesterday to watch the races. He was going to stay with them for the night, to give his mum time off to visit a friend. He's fond of Blanche, and she's very kind to him. But he slipped away from them at the races, and they thought he'd gone home with somebody from the family after all. Didn't do nothing about it, which was pretty stupid, I reckon. Anyway, Blanche rang his mum when he didn't turn up to garden this morning, and the poor woman is hysterical. She thought he was safe with the Battersbys. She called the police straightaway, and they've searched the village, but no trace. Called me, in case I'd seen him on my rounds. Poor lad, I hope he's OK. He's frightened of everything.'

'Anyway,' she continued, 'I just came in to tell you we've got a new recruit. She'll be coming in for a talk.'

'Who is it?' Hazel said curiously. She didn't know Mrs M was looking for another cleaner.

'Dot Nimmo,' said Lois, and waited for the earth to quake. It did.

Fifteen

'You've done *what*?' Next morning Gran stood, duster in hand, by the piano in the sitting room. It was scarcely ever played, now that Jamie had gone off to study music. Lois remembered the night when Derek and his mates had smuggled it into the house after Jamie had gone to bed, ready for Christmas morning.

'I felt sorry for her,' Lois lied.

'Yes, yes, and now tell me the truth,' Gran said.

She speaks to me as if I'd just bunked off school and was covering up, Lois thought. 'It's really my business, Mum,' she said. 'But I'll remember what you said about the Nimmos.'

'It'll be too late then,' Gran said darkly. 'You must be out of your mind. Well, don't come complaining to me when things go wrong.'

'Wouldn't dream of it,' Lois said. 'Now let's change the subject. I need to go over to Waltonby to see the Battersbys this morning. Their garden boy, young Darren, has gone missing, so they say.'

Gran nodded. 'It's all round the village this morning,' she said. 'People are being asked to look out for him. Goodness knows what's happened to him. He'll never cope on his own, poor lad. His mum's frantic, they say. Josie had the police in the shop this morning, asking her to put up a notice.'

'Mum,' said Lois, looking at her watch, 'how do you know all this by ten o'clock in the morning when, as far as I know, you haven't been out of the house?'

'It don't take long for that kind of thing to get round. And before you get all high and mighty, it's just as well. People in villages know everything about everybody, and sometimes it comes in useful.' Gran sniffed, and turned to get on with her dusting.

Lois collected her jacket from the hall, and went out. She was not at all sure she'd done the right thing with Dot Nimmo. Gran could well be right. But Lois justified her decision to herself by saying she'd rather have Dot under supervision than getting up to God knows what on her own. She'd obviously made a start with the nice woman in Tresham. And one thing was sure: the Nimmos would not need to go out scrubbing. Money was their business, and they were certain to have plenty of it. No, Dot was driven by revenge, and if, as Lois increasingly suspected, the Nimmo deaths had something to do with the stable thefts – which in themselves could be the tip of a much worse iceberg – Dot's connections could be very useful.

She drove through the twisting, narrow lanes towards Waltonby, and had to slow down dramatically when a couple of large horses with beefy women aboard came trotting along. They arranged themselves into single file, and raised hands in thanks as they passed. What enormous creatures they were! All those rippling muscles and powerful legs. Lois chuckled to herself. 'And the horses too,' Derek would say. She accelerated, and thought about Darren.

Horses. He was very good with horses, and had been at a point-to-point. If someone had wanted to frighten Darren out of his wits, a horse would not be the thing to do it. The Battersbys had horses, and Blanche was known to be very fond of Darren. He was a gentle, silent lad, who walked around with his head down, and worked solidly when he was in their garden.

Perhaps some of the roughs at the races had thought it would be a joke to have a go at Darren. He would be an easy target. But he was more likely to just run home than retreat into hiding.

Lois turned into the Battersbys' drive and pulled up alongside the Colonel's Range Rover. Everything about the Colonel was threatening, thought Lois. His huge great horses, his dominating vehicle looming over her, his puce face when in a rage, and his leader-of-men stuff.

Blanche answered the door. 'Come in, Mrs Meade, please. Nice of you to come round,' she said pleasantly.

'Best thing *you* could do,' said the Colonel, appearing out of his study and addressing Lois, 'is mind your own business. The police have it in hand, and will soon turn up the silly idiot. Frightened of his own shadow, that one. Now, Blanche, if you're ready, we have an appointment.'

'Do we?' Blanche turned to him in surprise. 'I'd like to have a chat with Mrs Meade just now.'

'Dentist,' said the Colonel. 'He can fit us in straight away.'

'But I don't need—'

'Don't stand there wasting time, Blanche. We must be off now. I'll see you out, Mrs Meade,' he said, walking to the door and holding it open.

Lois had no alternative but to leave. As she brushed by Blanche to cross the wide hallway, a whisper reached her ear. 'Come this afternoon. He's out.'

'Leave it to me, Mrs Meade,' the Colonel said, as she stepped out into the courtyard. 'I shall make sure the police find the lad. They'll try a bit harder than they have with my tack, I expect. Don't forget, now, it's nothing to do with you.'

'Bollocks to you,' said Lois under her breath. She revved up the van and screeched out of the yard. She was very angry, and decided to take the long way home to give herself time to cool down. She'd get no sympathy from Derek or Gran, who would probably think the same as the Colonel.

As she left the outskirts of Waltonby village, she drove slowly, mindful of women on horseback. The way she felt, she would really have liked to drive fast with headlights flashing. But she didn't, and as she came to a straight stretch of road, she kept a curb on her speed. Besides, she could see a figure in the distance, walking towards her in the middle of the road.

Sixteen

D arren saw her coming. At least, he saw a car coming, and stood stock still in the middle of the road. Car, not horse. Might be a horse behind it. Might be that man in the car. Better go away. Better run. Another place to hide.

He darted to the side of the road, then sped back a few yards to where he'd noticed a field gate. He was over it in seconds and running clumsily, but with the speed of panic, across the field and into a spinney where the trees were planted far apart and light came through to the ground below. Over brambles and fallen saplings he dashed, until he came to the other side of the spinney. He was out of breath now, and had a pain in his side. Then he saw a figure pulling a trolley. Darren froze, and stared. The man took a stick out of the trolley, and hit a small white ball into the air.

Darren did not wait to see where it landed. He was off again, and disappeared into a thicket where the fairway met the spinney. He crouched down, hidden now from sight, and shut his eyes. He would count, to make the time go by. One two three, one two three, one two three, one two three . . . The repetition calmed him down, and he began to hiss, a breathy whistle, as if soothing a crying baby. Shh, shh, shh, shh . . .

It was this sound that Lois heard as she went quickly through the spinney. She stopped and listened. That was no animal or bird. She moved as quietly as she could towards the sound. Then there was a loud cry from the golf course. 'Fore!' A man's voice, which carried through the trees. The hissing stopped, and Lois saw a movement in the thicket. It was Darren Smith, and he could not find his way out through the thorns.

By the time she reached him, his hands and arms were bleeding, and his jeans were torn in a couple of places. Tears were streaming down his cheeks, and Lois took him by the hand and led him out into a clearing. Then she put her arms around him and hugged him tight. 'It's all right, Darren,' she crooned. 'You're safe now, safe with Lois. We'll go back home, shall we? Take you back to Mum? She'll make you a nice cup of tea, and you can tell her about your adventure . . .'

In this way, she propelled him forward gently and eventually they reached her van, which was parked by the field gate. Darren backed away when she opened the door, but she persuaded him quietly to get inside, and then shut the door. In the driving seat, she pressed the button to lock all the doors. It would be a disaster if Darren tried to jump out whilst they were moving.

On the way back to Waltonby, she kept up a monologue. She sensed that it didn't much matter what she said, as long as she kept talking. She was tempted to tell him about the horse riders she had met, just to see his reaction, but decided that it would be cruel, and her first duty was to take the poor lad home to his mother.

Wycherley Estate, just off Waltonby's main street, had been built as council houses, but many were now privately owned. Lois wondered how she would tell which was Darren's house, until she saw a familiar car parked. It was Cowgill's, and he was standing at the gate, his hand on Mrs Smith's shoulder. Lois pulled up slowly, and stopped. Both of them turned to look at her, and then Mrs Smith's hand went to her mouth, and she swayed. Lois got out of the car fast.

'He's fine, Mrs Smith!' she called. 'Just hungry and thirsty. Looking forward to a nice cup of tea!'

Cowgill pushed open the gate and put his arm around Darren's mum. He led her forward, and Lois opened the passenger door and waited.

'Mum,' Darren said, and struggled out. Mrs Smith moved towards him, and he was safe at last.

After they were settled inside the house, and Cowgill had arranged to call the next day to talk to them, he and Lois walked down the narrow garden path. A small crowd had gathered outside, and Lois was about to send them packing, when

Cowgill put his hand on her arm. 'My job, Lois,' he said, and in a steady, authoritative voice advised them to go home. 'The Smiths will need your support,' he said, 'but not until tomorrow.' The neighbours dispersed, shepherding the staring children across the square of grass and into their own homes.

'Will the Smiths be all right? Shouldn't Darren see a doctor?' said Lois anxiously.

'All taken care of,' Cowgill said. 'I'd been preparing Mrs Smith for what she should do when he turned up,' he added.

'And if he didn't turn up?'

'That too,' said Cowgill. 'Now, Lois, I'm afraid I have to ask you to give me an account of how you found him. And also, I fear, I have to ask you why you didn't tell me you were on his trail?'

'I wasn't. I just saw him, in the middle of the road, on my way home from Waltonby.'

'I'd like you to follow me to the station, please. Then we can get down what you remember, while it is fresh in your mind.' He saw her expression, and added hastily, 'That is, if you can manage it right now? Can you ring Derek . . . or Gran?' Before she could reply, he hopped into his car and started the engine.

'How kind of you, Inspector Cowgill,' Lois muttered to herself, 'to congratulate me on restoring the missing boy to his family.' She reached for her mobile phone, and dialled her home number.

Inside the Smiths' warm sitting room, Darren sat curled up in his big armchair. His mum brought him a mug of hot chocolate, his favourite. She smiled at him, and leaned forward to kiss his scratched cheek. The terrified look in his eyes was slowly fading, and as he sipped the hot drink he seemed to relax a little.

'Better now?' asked his mum.

He nodded, and managed a small smile. 'Horses,' he said, and drained the mug.

Seventeen

Lois went in through a back entrance at the police station. Was this a good idea? It was certainly official, but if something nasty was going on, it might be stupid to be seen anywhere near the cop shop. After several years of sleuthing for Cowgill, her name was known amongst the criminal fraternity.

'Right,' said Cowgill in his best policeman voice. 'Sit there. Would you like a coffee? Feeling a bit upset?'

Lois couldn't be bothered to reply. 'Let's get on with it, shall we,' she said. 'I've got an appointment this afternoon.'

Cowgill sighed. His dream of a nice cozy chat with Lois was clearly not going to happen. But then, he should have known that. 'Fire away, then,' he said. 'Just begin at the beginning and tell me what happened.'

He was right in saying it would still be clear and fresh in her mind, and she gave him a lucid, chronological account. 'Darren doesn't talk at all, really. Just has a few words, and when scared to death he can't get anything out,' she said finally. 'Mostly he just parrots what people say to him, and I reckon even them words don't mean anything to him. "Mum" *is* real to him, and so, apparently, is "horses".'

'*Horses*?' said Cowgill. 'Why horses?'

Lois shrugged. 'Don't know,' she said. 'All I know is that he is very good with them. He was at a point-to-point with the Battersbys. Something must have happened to make him run, but God knows what. It'll make your job difficult, won't it?'

Cowgill explained that they had long experience of people who couldn't, or wouldn't talk. In Darren's case, a lot would depend on how much his mother could get out of him.

'Pressure will obviously be a bad idea, so we shall take it gently. Meanwhile, Lois,' he added, 'I'd be most grateful if you—'

'Yes, yes,' Lois interrupted, 'I'll see what I can find out.

And, by the way, I might as well tell you, seeing as you're bound to find out.'

'Tell me what?' said Cowgill, smiling lovingly at her. Oh, dear, would he ever be able to tell her how he felt? Of course not, you silly old fool, he said to himself. Get on with your job, else you'll be relieved of it before your time.

'I've taken on Dot Nimmo as a cleaner. Member of the team.' She stood up. 'I'll be off now, before I get a lecture. Cheers.'

'Just a minute!' said Cowgill. 'I know better than to lecture you. If you have taken on a devious, dirty and unreliable widow, I am sure you have a good reason for doing so. Keep in touch, Lois. And thanks for this morning. Darren Smith was lucky that it was you who found him. Take care.'

Gran was standing arms akimbo when Lois came into the kitchen. 'And what time is this to come home for your dinner?' she said.

'You knew I'd be late, so don't go on, Mum,' Lois said. 'Couldn't tell you before, but I found Darren. Just came across him in the road a mile or two outside Waltonby. He ran, but I caught up with him and got him home. Then I had to go to the police station to make a statement. Is there anything left to eat?'

Gran opened the oven door and drew out a plate. 'Fish and chips,' she said. 'I hope they're not dried out. Sorry, love,' she added. 'Me and Derek, we worry about you, y'know. I'm not asking any questions about Darren until you're ready to tell, so sit down and get this inside you. A nice walk across the meadows this afternoon with Jeems, that's what I suggest. I might come with you, now the sun's out.'

Lois shook her head. 'Got an appointment,' she said, and began to eat. 'Can't change it, but after I come back we could maybe get a walk before tea.'

Gran bit back a sharp retort, and put on the kettle. 'You'll have time for a coffee, won't you?' she asked, then changed the subject. 'Women's Institute this evening,' she said. 'Should be good. We've got an old bloke coming in to tell us all about the Tresham Studio Brass Band. How it started an' that. Doris Ashbourne from Ringford suggested it. She said she'd heard him speak once before, and he was brilliant. Memory like an elephant, she said. You can come as my guest, if you like?'

Lois smiled. Her mother never gave up trying to enlist Lois into the WI. Lois knew they were a nice bunch, and had interesting speakers, but held out against it. She could never tell Gran the reason, but she felt quite strongly that she did not want to be a mother-and-daughter pair, always out together, seen as one. She was not proud of this.

'Not tonight,' she said. 'I'm looking forward to a bit of peace in front of the telly. Been quite a day so far.' And it hadn't ended yet, she realized. Blanche had something to tell her, and it could be important.

'Better be going,' she said. 'Can't be late. Fussy client.'

'Where?' asked Gran suspiciously.

'Other side of Waltonby,' Lois replied. 'Sooner I go, sooner I'll be back for a walk. Bye, Mum.'

In the old inn in Tresham market place, the knot of farmers was breaking up. They'd had a fair bit to drink, and were placing bets on who'd get breathalysed on the way home. 'I'm meeting Margaret shortly,' said Joe Horsley. 'She's been spending m'money all morning', so she'll drive us back home.' He was the last to leave, and lingered, saying he'd arranged for Margaret to come and find him. It was quiet after the others had gone. There were not many left in the bar, and Joe turned to talk to the landlord.

At that moment, the door swung open, and a tall, commanding figure strode in.

'Morning, landlord,' Horace Battersby said firmly. 'Whisky, please, same as usual. Morning, Joe. Shall we sit over there in the corner, where we'll not be disturbed?'

When Lois rang the bell at the Battersbys' house, it was opened immediately. 'I was looking out for you,' Blanche said with a smile. 'He's in Tresham this afternoon, so you can come in without fear of being turned out again!'

She's as perky as a dog with two tails, thought Lois. Obviously not something dire she has to tell me. She followed Blanche into the drawing room and sat down as instructed. She refused refreshment, saying she had another call to make. This was a lie, but Lois had an uncomfortable feeling that the Colonel might appear, steam coming from his ears, before she could get away.

'Fine,' said Blanche, 'then I'll come straight to the point. We have decided to sell the horses. Now that our saddles and bridles and stuff have all gone, Horace is reluctant to buy more. We were insured, of course, but it has made us realize we're getting a bit too old to handle those big creatures, and perhaps now is the time to give up.'

Lois looked puzzled. 'Um, but how does this affect me?' she said. Surely Blanche hadn't set up this meeting just to tell her that?

'Well, I'll tell you,' Blanche said, settling herself comfortably in her chair. 'We've both got quite fond of Floss, and once or twice she has said how much she loves horses. Used to ride quite a lot, apparently.'

Lois nodded. She knew Floss had admired the old mare up at the Hall, and had softened Mrs Tollervey-Jones's gorgon heart as a result.

'You probably won't believe it, but it was Horace's idea. He wants to give the young mare we bought last year to Floss. Her name is Maisie, and she has a really gentle nature. We would offer to keep her here, as we shall have empty stables, and there's the paddock doing nothing, too. A plus for us is that we would still have a lovely horse to look at.'

'I still don't understand why you're telling *me*,' Lois said. 'It's really between the Colonel and Floss. I must say I think it's a very generous offer.'

'Ah, well, you see we thought you might object to a gift to one of your employees from one of your clients. Bad business practice. All that. So I promised to sound you out first. Of course, if you object, then we shall do no more about it.'

'So you haven't mentioned it to Floss? Or her parents? I presume they would have to buy new tack, and pay for upkeep?'

Blanche nodded. 'Yes, there would be that,' she said.

Lois thought for a moment, and then said, 'I'd like to think about it for a couple of days, if that's all right. Meanwhile, we'd better not mention it to Floss.' She got up to leave, and Blanche put her hand on Lois's arm.

'Horace is not one for generous gestures, Mrs Meade. It would be so nice if we could encourage him this once.'

As she drove home, Lois felt so weary that she had to make a conscious effort to concentrate. One overriding thought was still with her when she entered her house. What was the Colonel up to? She did not believe for one moment Blanche's generous gesture theory. He would have a good reason, and it would not be affection for his cleaner, however blonde and attractive. Good mares cost money, lots of money. Well, she had a couple of days to find out.

Eighteen

Gran didn't mention the walk. She took one look at Lois's weary face, and went off to light the fire in the sitting room. When she came back, she said, 'I've put the telly on and it's *The Clangers*. Why don't you sit down and watch for a bit. You know how you loved them.'

Lois looked at her sharply and frowned. 'Kids' television? I haven't sunk that low, Mum. Anyway, I've got a few notes to make.' She hesitated at the kitchen door. 'Still, I suppose I could do those later . . . Are you sure it's *The Clangers* now?'

The twilit other-world of the tiny knitted creatures, with piping sounds their only form of communication, the soup dragon and the trumpeting hoots, were oddly soothing. Maybe Darren would be more at home on the Clangers' planet. The pleasant voice of the story-teller lulled her into a calm that soon turned to a doze.

Gran later came in with the tea tray, with a pot-bellied teapot under a quilted tea-cosy, and set it down. Lois opened her eyes. 'Oh, has it finished?' she said, and sat up straight. 'Mum,' she said, 'I've been thinking. Do you know anything about the Battersbys? Where they came from, who their friends are, anything at all?'

'Why do you ask me that out of the blue? Battersbys? Them over at Waltonby, where Floss cleans?'

'Are there more somewhere else?' Lois asked.

'How should I know? I'm a Tresham girl, don't forget. I only know about the Waltonby family from what you've told me. He's an army man, isn't he?'

'He certainly was,' Lois replied. 'Retired now. I'm not sure what he does with his time. Keeps horses, and loses his temper quite a bit. Was mad about having his tack stolen. Floss says he treats his wife like a servant. That's about it.'

'Horses, yes. I remember your father used to talk about him at the point-to-point racing. I've heard his wife is very nice, but under his thumb. Military men are like that, Lois. Good thing Derek was never in the services. Mind you, you'd never've been under his thumb!'

Lois ignored that. 'To get back to the Battersbys,' she said, 'I wonder if they've always lived in Waltonby?'

'I've told you all I know,' Gran said, 'but if you're that keen, why don't you come to WI with me, and you could ask around. You can bet Ivy Beasley knows all about them. She's a bottomless pit as far as local knowledge goes.'

Lois said she was really too tired, but was sure her mother could bring up the subject with Ivy. 'I think she likes you,' she said. 'Met her match, for once.'

Gran denied this hotly. 'She beats me hands down,' she said. 'Not often I'm lost for words, but Ivy can do it every time. Still, if she's there, I'll have a go.'

It was a chilly evening, and the WI secretary had put fifty pence in the meter to have an hour or so's heating in the hall. The system was not very efficient, as Ivy Beasley had been quick to point out. 'Either you roast under one of them electric things, or you freeze to death from the draughts coming under the door,' she had said to the long-suffering President. A project to raise funds for a new community hall had been set up years ago, but as fast as small sums of money were raised from local events, the cost of the project went up. The present hall had been the original old school in the village, and some said it was just right for the number of people likely to use it. But the main users were the daily playgroup, who without so much as a by-your-leave had taken up all the storage space in the shed behind the hall. The whist group couldn't reach their card tables, and the carpet bowlers had to step over mounds of toys to reach their carpet runs. It was a continuing battle, without much chance of a solution.

This evening, the plates of cakes were set out in the kitchen, with cups and saucers and a simmering urn, all ready to take into the hall when the speaker had finished. In the semi-circle of chairs, Gran settled herself next to Floss's mother, Mrs Pickering, and glanced round for Miss Ivy Beasley. So far there was no sign of her, but a kerfuffle in the porch signalled her approach.

'No need to push me along, Doris!' The harsh voice was unmistakeable. Ivy made her entrance as usual, glaring at anyone already sitting under one of the heaters. Gran jumped up nervously. 'Here, Miss Beasley, have this seat, it's a chilly night, and it's really warm here . . .' Talking too much, she said to herself. The old bat will do exactly as she likes, even if it means asking some poor soul to move.

'That's very kind of you, Mrs Weedon,' Doris Ashbourne said, guiding Ivy towards the seat. Ivy grunted, and sat down. Gran was now next to her, and, recalling her promise to Lois, felt this was all to the good.

'So how are you, Miss Beasley?' Gran said.

'As well as can be expected,' Ivy said. 'I begin to feel my age, though. Can't do what I used to do.'

'That probably goes for all of us,' Gran answered, remembering too late that Ivy always considered herself unique in all fields. 'Still,' she added hastily, 'I know my daughter thinks you're wonderful for your age.'

'Is that meant to be a compliment?' Ivy laughed suddenly. 'You don't do so badly yourself, Mrs Weedon,' she added, visibly softening. 'I'm looking forward to visiting you for a cup of tea. Soon,' she said firmly. Gran's heart sank. It was a date she hoped Ivy had forgotten, but she might have known there was no chance of that. Ivy Beasley had an uncomfortably encyclopedic memory. Gran was not the only one waiting in trepidation for Ivy to correct the speaker on a number of points.

Now, how to bring up the subject of the Battersbys? At least Ivy's memory could be useful there. But not time now. The President had finished the business of the meeting and was getting to her feet.

'Now, members,' she said, smiling benevolently around, 'it is my great pleasure to introduce our speaker for this evening. I know we are in for a real treat. Mr Blenkinsop has been involved in the Studio Band since it began, and is going to tell us all about it. Over to you, Mr Blenkinsop,' she concluded, and sat down.

A bespectacled, smartly dressed man in his seventies walked round to the front of the President's table and beamed at the assembled women. He knew some of them, had known them for years. He'd been at school with one or two. He felt completely at ease. 'Just listen to this, ladies, before we begin,' he said as he twiddled a couple of switches and a cheerful burst of brass instruments playing the *Dambusters* theme filled the hall.

Ivy immediately put her hands over her ears. 'Does he think we're all deaf?' she said in a loud voice. Mr Blenkinsop grinned. He'd been at school with Ivy, too. 'Goes down well on the parade ground, Miss Beasley,' he said, and turned down the volume. After a few minutes, he began to speak, and for an hour his audience listened, spellbound.

'Just one of those naturals,' Doris said to Gran, when they were seated around a rickety card table, covered with a pink plastic cloth. Nothing rickety about the cakes, though. They were light and creamy, very bad for the figure, but consumed with gusto.

'A born story-teller,' agreed Gran. 'I loved hearing about how it all began, with the two Miss Battersbys setting it all up to keep the local boys off the streets.'

'Nothing changes,' said Ivy. 'Some folk daren't walk in the streets at night now.'

Gran couldn't believe her luck when Mr Blenkinsop had named the benefactors of the band. She turned to Ivy, and said lightly, 'I expect you're too young to remember the Battersby ladies?'

'Flattery will get you nowhere,' Ivy replied. 'Of course I remember them. Thought a lot of themselves, they did. Lived together in a big house by the Town Park in Tresham. Pillars of the church. Always doing good, buying their places in Heaven. Hope they didn't get a nasty surprise when they got to the pearly gates,' she added comfortably.

'What *do* you mean, Ivy?' Doris asked.

'You know as well as I do. A couple of dark horses, they were. One or two of the so-called bad boys on the streets were rumoured to be adopted, mothers unknown. At least, known only to a few. Rumour had it that them prim women were no better than they should be. Plenty of money, of course, to cover it up. Long holidays abroad, coming back a lot thinner than when they went. Still, a lot of water under the bridge since then.'

'New Brooms cleans for the Battersbys in Waltonby,' Gran said nonchalantly. 'Any relation, are they?'

'Course they are,' Ivy said, helping herself to another wedge of chocolate sponge. 'The Colonel's one of them. Big family, they were. Too many, maybe. Gentleman farmers the other side of Tresham. Somewhere along the line the money ran out. People say the Colonel's as mean as muck, but I reckon he's not got that much to throw around. Married money, luckily for him, but some of that's gone too, from what I hear. Now, Doris, get me another cup of tea, will you. And ask for it hot this time.'

Subject closed, thought Gran, and took up a stack of dirty plates to offer help in the kitchen.

Nineteen

Monday morning, and Lois had asked Dot Nimmo to come in half an hour before the team meeting. As promised, Handy's BMW had been serviced and cleaned, and as Lois looked out of the window to where the car had drawn up by the kerb, she reflected that it was not exactly what clients would expect to see when their cleaner arrived for work.

'Morning, Mrs Meade,' Dot said briskly. She was neatly dressed and carried a bag the size of a suitcase. 'Just in case you wanted me to start straight away after the meeting,' she said.

'What's in *there*? Lois asked, with a sudden mental picture of Dot scooping valuable antiques from the Hall into the bag.

'Cleaning things, o' course,' Dot said. Lois replied that these were supplied by New Brooms, but that it was very thoughtful of Dot to bring them.

'Now, let's get a few things sorted out before the others arrive,' Lois said, and in spite of frequent interruptions from

Dot, who said she was sure she knew all there was to know about scrubbing floors, by the time there was a knock at the door Dot had been told all the rules and practices of the cleaning team. 'And we do work as a team, Dot,' Lois said, 'helping each other out when necessary.'

'Well, one thing,' said Dot, 'I'm always available. Got nothing else to do now. Nothing else at all.'

Except to have a blitz on your own house, thought Lois, and went to let in Bridie and Floss, the first to arrive. Introductions were made, and when all were sitting comfortably, Lois began with the schedules for the coming week.

'And where shall I be going?' Dot asked when jobs had been allocated.

'With Bridie,' Lois said. 'You can go with Bridie for a start. She'll show you the ropes at Bridge House. It's in at the deep end, but I'm sure you'll be up to that. Get together after the meeting, and Bridie can explain.'

Lois had a moment's panic. Was she wise in sending Dot, an unknown quantity, to her richest and most particular client? The Bucklands were a young couple with small children, a nanny and a housekeeper, and lived a life that seemed based elsewhere. They were never seen in the village, but loud voices calling 'Shot! Good shot, Camilla!' floated from the tennis court over the barrier of their laurel hedge in summer. In the autumn, their children stood behind a stretch of stone wall and threw conkers from the towering chestnut tree on to the villagers passing below. The Bucklands were not disliked in the village, but once people saw how they wished to live, they were ignored.

'Blimey,' said Dot. 'You're right there. Them Bucklands are rich as Croesus. They say she inherited from her dad, who was, so they say, a rag-and-bone man who made his pile in Birmingham.'

'And that reminds me,' Lois said sternly. 'I don't want no gossip. None at all. The good name of my business is at stake, and if I hear a whisper of gossip coming from any member of the team, they'll be for the high jump.'

All the others looked affronted. 'I don't think you need tell the rest of us that,' Bill Stockbridge said. 'And I'm sure Dot will be very careful,' he added, but he looked doubtful. Lois had expected some animosity towards Dot. The Nimmos had a local reputation, and all of the team had read the news-papers. It was with some relief that Lois closed the meeting and sent them on their way.

Bill hesitated at the door, the last to leave. 'Could I have a word?' he said, and Lois sighed. Bill was her most level-headed, responsible cleaner, and she had relied on him for a long time now, discussing problems and sometimes accepting help with gathering information. When Derek accused her of using the team to collect gossip, she denied it hotly. 'Not gossip,' she had said. 'It's valuable information.'

'Can't see the difference,' he had shrugged, and changed the subject.

'I expect you know what I'm going to say.' Bill looked uncomfortable, and fiddled with the door handle.

'Dot Nimmo?' Lois suggested. 'You don't approve. Well then, tell me why.'

'Just one thing,' Bill said. 'I know for a fact that the Nimmos are probably some of the wealthiest crooks in Tresham. So why should Handy's widow need to start cleaning? It can't be the money, so what is it? You must have asked yourself, Mrs M. In case you hadn't, I thought I'd mention it.'

'You're right, Bill. And why does Dot live in a small terrace house in Sebastopol Street? Rumour isn't always right. Anyway, trust me, and keep your ears open for any . . . er . . . anything you hear that might be useful.'

After Bill had gone, Lois sat at her desk thinking. She was certain that Dot would not be able to break the habit of a life-time and keep her mouth shut. Her outburst about the Bucklands showed that she was a mine of information. But tread softly, Lois said to herself. Dot was not stupid, and if she suspected Lois was ferreting down in the underworld, she would shut up like a trap.

Lois picked up a pen. Time to sort things out. She wrote a sentence in capitals and underlined it. 'WHERE IS THE CRIME?' A run of stable thefts that seemed to have come to a halt. Derek had seen a scruffy bloke escaping from the Horsleys' farm. Haydn Nimmo had been killed in a car smash, and there was so far no official suggestion of foul play. His father, Handy, had drowned in Farnden gravel pits, but that was years ago. Darren Smith had disappeared and reappeared shaking with terror within twenty-four hours, but he had very special difficulties, could hardly speak or understand much, and had possibly got lost in a wood. And then the Colonel. The Battersbys were victims of the thefts, of course, but Lois felt uneasy about the Colonel. Derek had dealt with him efficiently, but on every occasion that Lois saw him, he seemed anxious to get away from her. Sent me packing last time, she remembered. Why? And what was the real reason for giving Floss a valuable horse?

Cowgill was certain something serious was going on, that was plain. And not just the stable thefts. There was something niggling away in her mind about the thefts. She would ask Cowgill how many there had been in the area, and who were the victims. That wouldn't be confidential information, surely, though he would probably make it sound like it.

'Lois, hello. Nice to hear from you. Have you something for me?' Cowgill had answered his phone at once, and Lois hoped he was sitting in his office in front of a computer. 'No, I haven't,' she said, 'but I want information from you.'

'Ah,' he said. It was too much to hope that Lois had called for a chat. Never mind, he said to himself, the sound of her voice is enough. 'What exactly do you want to know?'

When she told him, he asked her to hold on for a couple of minutes. Then he began a search, and meanwhile attempted a pleasant conversation. 'How are Derek and Gran?' he asked.

'Why?' said Lois. 'Are they on your list of suspects?'

Cowgill laughed. 'For what?' he said.

'You tell me. Stealing saddles? Fixing white vans?'

'Lois,' he said patiently, 'you know perfectly well I was merely being polite. Now, I'm afraid the information about victims and perpetrators of the saddle thefts has to be confidential at the moment.'

'Thanks very much!' Lois exploded. 'Have you got the villain yet?'

'Getting close,' Cowgill said. 'Following up leads, and we'll soon be there.'

'And are you close to knowing who abducted Darren Smith?'

Cowgill sighed. 'We're not miracle-workers, Lois, but we do our best. Any help you can give us is greatly appreciated.'

'Yes, well,' Lois said. 'I'll be in touch. Thanks for nothing. Bye.'

Cowgill looked at the phone in his hand and smiled. She had no idea how she brightened his day.

Lois thought of the people she knew who had been burgled. Both within a fairly small area. And there were others, of course. Did that mean local knowledge? And was it one devious character doing them all, or a smart little syndicate organizing the thefts and moving the loot on quickly before it could be discovered? Battersbys and Horsleys were the latest, she reckoned. Their reactions she knew, and they couldn't have been more different. The Colonel had been apoplectic, but Joe Horsley had seemed not to care. Still, he'd not actually lost anything.

If there was a syndicate or gang, surely one of them would make a mistake sooner or later. Lois remembered the syndicate that Derek had been part of, and laughed. They'd been successful enough! She'd had an idea for investing their winnings, and intended to talk to Derek about it this evening. She looked forward to that.

'Dinner's ready!' It was Gran's voice from the kitchen. 'Or lunch, if you prefer!'

Twenty

Lois waited until Gran went upstairs to watch her favourite reality TV show. She was a great fan, but Derek couldn't abide them. So that left the two of them alone, and Derek was dozing with the newspaper over his face.

'Derek,' Lois said, and nudged him.

'Wha' . . . wha'? No, o' course I'm not asleep. Just thinking,' he mumbled, and slumped down.

'Derek! I want to tell you something.'

'I'm listening,' he said, and dragged himself awake. 'How about a nice cup of tea?' he added.

'Talk first,' Lois said. 'It could be important.'

Derek groaned. 'Stable thefts? Abducted lads?'

Lois was quiet. Derek's words jumped around in her mind. Stable . . . lads . . .

'Come on, speak out,' he said. 'I won't eat you. Leastways, I might,' he laughed and made a lunge towards her.

'No, really, Derek. Be sensible for a minute. I just thought of this idea. Nothing to do with Cowgill, if that's what you're worrying about. It's about our money, and what we should be doing with it.'

'I thought we'd agreed to leave it in the bank?'

'Yeah, well, that's a bit boring. I was thinking we could buy a little house somewhere, probably in Tresham, and rent it out. It'd be income, and we'd always have the property. Couldn't lose on it.'

'And what about repairs and council tax and all that ruddy nonsense? Ownin' a house is an expensive business, as we know,' he said, serious now. 'And tenants can be lousy, causing damage and doin' moonlight flits. It could be a real worry.'

'We could get agents to manage it for us. They'd take about ten percent, but if we got a good rent it would be worth it.' Lois had thought a lot about it, and was anxious to convince a reluctant Derek.'

He stood up. 'If you're keen on this, Lois, you'd better get facts and figures and let's go through them together. I know what Gran would say: "What do you want another house for? You've got a nice one already. Ideas above your station, Lois, if you ask me."' His mimicry was so exact that Lois laughed.

'OK,' she said. 'I'll do what you say, and we won't even mention it to Mum. It's not her money, anyway.'

'Bedtime, me duck,' said Derek, and took her hand. 'Let's see if we can lighten up a bit, shall we?'

Gran switched off her television, and hopped into bed. It had been a good episode tonight, and she loved to think about those idiots, and what they got up to in front of millions of people. How did they persuade so-called celebrities to take part? They nearly always came out of it badly. Still, she was glad they did. Good for a laugh, and it put her in a good mood before sleep.

Lois hadn't seemed too happy this evening. Gran wished for the thousandth time that she'd been able to have another child. Lois had had far too much attention, especially from her father, and had always behaved as if the world revolved around her. Derek had gone along with this. Gran presumed that this was because she was a bobby dazzler, as her Dad used to say, and because he loved her so much. If there'd been a brother or sister, Gran could have shared the responsibility of Lois with them. Mind you, the last thing Lois would want was Gran feeling responsible. She'd probably turf her mother out on her ear! It *was* difficult, though, to watch Lois trying Derek's patience to breaking point, and not seeming to care.

Gran turned over in her cool sheets and shut her eyes. In minutes, after starting a re-run of the show behind her eyelids, she was asleep.

Twenty-One

Gran had faithfully relayed the information gleaned from Ivy Beasley at the WI meeting, and Lois had listened attentively. Now they sat in silence at the kitchen table, staring at each other.

'Doesn't help much, I'm afraid,' Lois said finally.

Gran was affronted. 'You didn't tell me what you were looking for! That's the last time I do your dirty work,' she said. 'Anyway, I found that story about the Miss Battersbys very interesting. I've worked out they'd be the same generation as the Colonel's father. Must've been big families down the years.'

'There was something,' Lois said in a belated attempt to placate Gran. 'That thing you said about money . . . money running out. And Blanche Battersby's money going too. Did Ivy say anything about where it had gone, or why?'

'Family too big, I expect. Too many people taking money out of the farm. It happens, even now.'

'That wouldn't explain why Blanche's money is draining away.' Lois frowned. Something elusive hovered at the back of her mind, and she couldn't recover it.

'It's them horses, I shouldn't wonder. Very expensive things to keep. Probably why he's selling them.'

'How d'you know that?' Lois hadn't mentioned it to her mother.

'People were talking about it last night. Mrs Battersby sometimes comes to WI, but not often. She wasn't there last night, but sent her apologies. She always sends apologies if she's not coming. Nice woman, I reckon.'

Lois didn't mention the Battersby offer to Floss. She had been thinking about it, and decided she would not object. But she would have to have a chat with Floss about it. Maybe the girl wouldn't accept. Her father might have something to say!

'Thanks, Mum,' Lois said.

'No need to thank me. I was just making conversation, and it was natural that the Battersbys were talked about, after hearing about them do-gooding spinsters, an' that.'

Floss was at the Hall that morning, and Lois rang her mobile. 'Floss? Everything all right? No problems, I hope.' There frequently *were* problems with Mrs Tollervey-Jones, but Floss assured her that everything was going smoothly so far.

'Could you call in on your way home, Floss? I need to have a word.' Then she wondered what she would say. She couldn't upstage the Colonel and mention his generosity before he made his offer to Floss. Perhaps she would sound her out about how she felt in the job. She'd made no complaints, and had never mentioned the Colonel being unpleasant to her. Maybe to his wife, but not to Floss. The girl was, of course, a young and attractive blonde, but she'd heard no rumours of a flirty, dirty old man!

'You still there, Mrs M?'

Lois said that she was, and would see Floss later.

'Was that the telephone?' Mrs T-J had appeared in the drawing room, where Floss was polishing the grand piano.

'It was for me. Message from Mrs Meade. Not a personal call, Mrs Tollervey-Jones. You know me better than that.'

Mrs T-J smiled. 'Of course, my dear,' she said. 'I am perfectly satisfied with your work. And so, I know, is my friend Blanche at Waltonby. She needs a friend,' she added quietly, and then shook herself. 'Must get back to work,' she said. 'Important meeting this afternoon. Carry on, my dear.'

Lois saw Floss arriving and went out to open the front door herself. Gran, annoyed, hovered in the background.

'Come on in, Floss,' Lois said, and ushered her into the office, firmly shutting the door behind her. It opened again immediately.

'I usually offer to make coffee,' Gran said in a martyred voice.

Floss smiled. She liked Gran, and thought privately that Lois was a bit hard on her. 'I'm dying for one, thanks,' she said. Lois muttered that she supposed she would have one too, and Gran disappeared.

'Is there a problem, Mrs M?' Floss had been with New Brooms long enough to recognize the signs.

'Not exactly a problem,' said Lois, 'but something I have to discuss with you. Has Colonel Battersby or Blanche said anything to you about their horses?'

Floss nodded. 'They've decided to sell them,' she said. 'Mrs Battersby said they're getting too old to ride properly, and the Colonel has finally agreed to sell. It took a bit of persuading, apparently! He fancies himself on the hunting field and gossiping with his friends at point-to-point races.'

'Nothing more? Nothing about keeping just one?'

Floss shook her head. 'No, I think they're all going. The Colonel said that if they couldn't manage a horse with guts and spirit, he'd rather not have them at all. I think Blanche would've liked to keep a gentle one, just to go for a ride on a nice sunny day.'

'Yes, well, that's what they are planning to do, so they have told me. They would keep a reliable mare in the stables and graze it on their meadow – but give it to you.' Lois waited, watching Floss's face carefully.

Floss stared at Lois, her eyes wide. 'What on earth do you mean?' Her colour had risen.

At that moment, Gran opened the door and brought in two mugs of coffee and a plate of biscuits. She took her time putting it down on Lois's desk, and fidgeted about, moving piles of papers to make way for the tray. Lois and Floss sat in total silence, and Gran looked from one to the other. 'Are you two having a row?' she asked sharply.

'Sorry, Mum. No, we're not,' Lois said. 'And thanks a lot for the coffee.'

Gran left, leaving the door ajar. Lois got up and shut it quietly.

'Now,' she said. 'I'll explain again what I mean. Colonel and Mrs Battersby say they are fond of you and are very satisfied with your work, and they would like to give you the mare as a present. They realize you've got nowhere to keep it, and so are offering to have it there, where they can keep an eye on it, but it will be yours. That's about as clear as I can make it.'

'I can't believe it,' Floss said slowly, and then, seeing Lois's expression, added hastily that of course it must be true, and it was very nice of the Battersbys. 'But it's such a surprise, Mrs M. And a bit of a shock, to tell the truth. I've always thought the Colonel had no time for me, except as a hired help who should know her place.'

'Give it some thought,' Lois said. 'I must admit I can't help thinking there's something more than meets the eye about this. But it's really between them and you. If you want to have it, I'm not objecting, provided it doesn't compromise New Brooms or me. I expect you'll want to talk it over with your parents, too?'

'Oh, yeah. I'll have to tell them. I can just imagine what Dad will say.'

'What will he say?'

'"How dare they patronize my daughter like this! If she wants a horse, I'll buy her one! Refuse at once, Floss!" That's what he'll say,' she answered sadly.

'Mmm, well, he could be right,' said Lois. 'Let me know what you decide, Floss. It's a tricky one.'

'I'll talk it over with Ben first,' Floss said defensively. 'Now we're engaged, we share everything. We're as one, Mrs M.'

Lois swallowed. 'How nice,' she said.

Twenty-Two

As fate would have it, Floss woke up with the symptoms of flu the next day, and her mother telephoned Lois to give her the news. 'She's got a high temperature, Mrs Meade, and not making much sense. Rambling on about horses! Anyway, I've phoned the doctor, and I'll let you know what he says. Sorry she's off work again so soon. Can't be helped, though. She probably caught it from Ben . . .'

'I know,' said Lois, 'they're as one.' Mrs Pickering laughed.

Lois rang off, and looked down the schedules. It was a busy week, and the only one who could spare extra hours was Dot Nimmo. 'Bugger it,' Lois said aloud. She was reluctant to send Dot on her own so soon, but it looked as if she had no alternative.

'Well,' said Derek at lunchtime, 'at least Dot will give the Colonel a piece of her mind if he don't behave.'

'That's what I'm afraid of,' Lois replied. 'For all his bluster, they are good clients, and I don't want to lose them.'

Gran raised her eyebrows. 'You should've thought of that before you took on that Nimmo woman in the first place,' she said.

Lois didn't answer. Her mind was working fast. Maybe it wouldn't be such a bad idea to send Dot Nimmo to the Battersbys. She was a nosy old bag, and might well glean something interesting from Blanche about the Colonel and the mare. The Nimmos had been around in the area as long as the Battersbys, and Dot was bound to know of a skeleton or two in their cupboards.

'Thanks for lunch, Mum,' she said, and disappeared into her office to use the telephone. 'Bridie?' Lois had dialed Bridie's mobile, remembering she was at the Bucklands in Fletching, and that Dot was with her. 'Bridie, it's me. Is Dot there? Oh, upstairs. Well, could you put her on the phone, please, and keep your voices down, both of you.'

She could hear Bridie's footsteps on the stairs, and then Dot's voice, whispering. 'Yeah? What y'want?'

Lois explained about Floss being ill, and gave Dot instructions on getting to the Battersbys and being very careful not to offend either the Colonel or Mrs Battersby when she arrived.

'You're joking!' said Dot in her normal harsh smoker's voice. 'Just bein' alive offends him!'

Lois heard Bridie shushing her, and then coming back on the phone. 'Mrs M? I'll make sure she knows where to go, and how to handle it. Leave it to me. Cheers.'

Thank God for Bridie, thought Lois. She refused to think about whether Dot was a good idea or not, and instead dialled the Battersbys.

'Lois Meade here, Mrs Battersby. Unfortunately Floss has flu, but I am sending Dot in her place. She'll be with you at the usual time, and I hope you'll find her satisfactory. Please don't hesitate to explain what you want, if need be.'

'I hope she's reliable.' Blanche sounded doubtful. 'You see, the Colonel is not here, and I'm always a little nervous on my own, with new people in the house. Did you say Dot? Is she new? What's her other name?'

But Lois pretended not to hear the last question, and said a cheery goodbye. Nimmo was not a name to boast about.

Horace Battersby drove into Joe Horsley's farm drive and parked his car in the stable yard. He got out and looked over at the house. Joe's vehicle was nowhere to be seen. 'Blast!' the Colonel muttered to himself. 'I told the stupid idiot I'd be coming.' He walked over to the door and pressed the bell. After a few seconds he heard footsteps, and the door was opened by Margaret.

Her face fell when she saw him, and she half-closed the door again. 'He's not here,' she said.

'No matter,' said the Colonel, and pushed his way through the door and into the kitchen. 'I'll wait. A cup of coffee would not go amiss.'

'I don't recall asking you to come in!' said Margaret with spirit. 'In fact, I'm very busy, so you can just go and wait in your car. Joe might be some time. He's gone into Tresham to the bank, and then he'll probably go for a drink with the boys, and God knows what time he'll be home.'

'He'll be here soon,' countered Horace. 'We arranged to meet. Now, how about that coffee?'

His voice was quiet, and Margaret shivered. It was worse than when he blustered. Oh well, she couldn't physically turf him out, so she put on the kettle and said he must excuse her because she was in the middle of doing the farm accounts.

'They can wait,' he replied. 'Sit down and talk to me, Margaret. It is a long time since we were alone together.'

Oh God, not that again, thought Margaret. Please, Joe, come home soon – like now. She made the coffee and set it in front of him.

'Sugar?'

'No thank you, Margaret. Surely you haven't forgotten that?'

Margaret perched on the edge of a chair, and asked after Blanche. 'Is she well? Still riding those lovely horses? She was so good with them. I think they really love her.' If I can keep the conversation on these lines, she thought, maybe it'll be all right.

'Too soft with them,' Horace said. 'Lets them get away with murder.'

Margaret looked up at him sharply. 'What did you say?' The colour had drained from her face.

'I said,' Horace replied in measured tones, 'that Blanche is too soft with the horses. Still, not for much longer. I'm selling them. After the tack theft, it is not worth replacing it.'

Margaret opened her mouth to say something, but at that moment she heard the sound of a car in the yard. 'There's Joe!' she said with obvious relief. 'I'll go and tell him you're here.'

Horace Battersby shrugged. 'He knows,' he said to Margaret's retreating back. Then he laughed.

Blanche, meanwhile, was surreptitiously following Dot around the house, checking on her every move. Dot was aware of this, but had the sense to pretend not to notice. She was practised in dissembling. She had merely said a polite hello, and got on quietly with the work. Bridie had prepared her well, and she was especially careful with the antique furniture and porcelain figures that were Blanche's prized collection.

'Do you usually have a cup of tea? Or would you like coffee?' Blanche asked finally.

'Tea, if that's awright with you, Mrs Battersby,' Dot said. Tea was offered first, and so she took that. She wanted to keep on the right side of this woman, at all costs.

'I'll call you when it's ready. Floss usually sits down for a minute or two. Just a little break.' Blanche made it quite clear that the break would be very little indeed.

When the call came, Dot appeared in the kitchen and proceeded to wash her hands at the sink. 'Dust and vittles don't go together,' she said smugly. Just as well she can't see my house, Dot thought, and suppressed a smile.

'Here, dry your hands on this,' Blanche said quickly. It looked like the dog towel to Dot, but she said, 'Ta,' and sat down.

'How long have you worked for Mrs Meade?' Blanche asked. 'I don't remember her mentioning a new cleaner.'

'Oh, on and off for quite a while. I've been a temp, as they say, but now I'm on the permanent staff. Had one or two clients myself, in a private capacity, in Tresham. I expect you'd know some of them,' she added speculatively.

'Like who?' Blanche asked suspiciously.

'Mrs Parker-Knowles. Up in that posh estate near the hospital.'

Blanche frowned. 'The name does sound familiar. We may have met her through the Conservative Association. The Colonel has been Chairman for ages, and given long service to the party. Is there a Mr Parker-Knowles?'

'Dead,' said Dot in a funereal voice. 'Poor lady is a widder-woman. We get on, though. Perhaps the Colonel will remember. Now,' she said as she got to her feet, 'I must get back to work. We like to give value for money at New Brooms.'

Blanche looked impressed. 'Right,' she said. 'I won't keep you.'

'Oh yeah,' said Dot, as she reached the door, 'I meant to ask you. Have you still got them horses? The Colonel used to be a racing man, didn't he?'

'At the moment, yes,' said Blanche, determined not to prolong the little break. 'Now, what did you say your name was?'

'Dot,' she answered, and vanished.

Twenty-Three

Horace and Joe strolled across the stable yard and Horace eased himself into his car. 'Right, then,' he said peremptorily, 'it should go well, as long as we all do what we've planned. Can you trust the other two? Is it safe to leave that job to you?'

Joe scowled. 'Of course it is. What d'you take me for? I've been in this business long enough – longer than you, if you think about it.'

'What business?' said Margaret, coming up behind Joe. He turned swiftly. 'Farming, of course. What else do I know?' He turned back to the Colonel. 'You know the way back. Take care in the narrow track through the copse. They say there's highwaymen in there.'

After the Colonel's car had disappeared, Margaret took Joe's arm. 'I wish you wouldn't have anything to do with him,' she said quietly.

'You did, once,' Joe said shortly, shaking her off, and strode back into the house.

Horace Battersby sped down the narrow track, his face dark with irritation. If only he did not have to deal with Horsley. The man was far too arrogant, considering he had little education and a dubious reputation to boot. Horace had seen him lording it over his companions in the Tresham pub, downing pint after pint. Still, they all did that. He sighed. He had to make the best of it. He turned out into the main road without looking to right or left, and heard a furious hooting behind him. Idiot! He accelerated and shook his fist.

As he turned into his drive in Waltonby, he saw a strange woman getting into a BMW parked by the front door. Who the hell was that? He drew up and got out. But the BMW was too quick for him, and had disappeared out of the drive before he could hail the woman.

'Who was that?' he said abruptly to Blanche, who stood by the door waiting for him.

'Hello, dear,' she said. 'Did you have a good morning?'

'Who was that?' he repeated impatiently.

'Dot.'

'Dot who?'

'Don't know. She's new with New Brooms. Oh, that's good,' laughed Blanche. 'A new broom with New Brooms!' She was well aware that she was provoking Horace, but felt quite perky after Dot's visit. She'd dealt with her well, she thought, and the woman had quite a sense of humour.

'Well, find out,' said Horace. 'We don't want unknowns going through our things. Could be dangerous.'

Blanche laughed. 'Oh, for goodness sake, Horace,' she replied, 'what have we got to hide?'

He didn't answer, but went swiftly through to his study and banged the door.

'Old fart!' muttered Blanche, and giggled at her new-found courage.

The Battersbys were in Floss's mind as she lay sweating and shivering by turns. Had she dreamed they'd offered her a horse to ride? No, it was Mrs M who had told her, and she trusted Mrs M to tell the truth. She hadn't yet mentioned it to her parents, and certainly did not feel up to telling them now. It was coming back to her now, and she remembered Mrs M's face as she told her. It was as if she was reluctant to give her the good news. As if she didn't think it *was* good news . . .

Floss drifted back to sleep, and was awoken after a while by her mother coming in with a glass of hot lemon. 'You have to drink lots,' she said. 'Try and get it down, to please me.' She had the motherly voice that Floss remembered from childhood. Propping herself on her elbow, she drank a few mouthfuls and then fell back on the pillow. 'Leave it there, Mum,' she said. 'I'll drink some more in a minute or two.' She closed her eyes, hoping her mother would go away. She wanted to concentrate on the gift of a horse.

Why hadn't the Battersbys spoken to her first? Oh, yes, she remembered Mrs M saying they were anxious not to break New Brooms rules. Cleaners accepting gifts, and all that. It made it more difficult for her to decide, though at heart she was thrilled at the idea of having her own mare to ride and care for. Expense, that would be another factor. Horses were expensive things, and her salary was not huge. She'd have to check that the Battersbys didn't want rent for the stable and field. And then there'd be new tack. There was none of that left in the stables. Vet's bills and feed supplements. Farrier to keep hooves in good nick. Her mind got stuck on farriers, and she wandered off into a hazy dream about a curly-haired young farrier who'd run off with a rich wife in Fletching, leaving behind young daughters and a sorrowing husband . . .

Dot had also been thinking about the Battersbys. She was pleased with herself, and as she drove into Tresham, deciding to go straight to Mrs Parker-Knowle, she reckoned she had made a good start. Then she passed the entrance to Sebastopol Street, and changed her mind. Just time to dash home and eat a sausage roll. It had been a cup of tea only with Blanche. No delicious shortbread biscuits or slice of date and walnut cake. She backed the car and turned into Sebastopol Street. As she went by the video shop, a couple of youths parked outside watched her until she stopped outside her house.

The kitchen clock, thick with dust, told Dot that she had ten minutes to spare, and she took a sausage roll from its packet. It was well past its sell-by date, but she habitually took no notice of these arbitrary limits. As she said to her sister Evie, 'Sausage rolls don't suddenly go rotten at midnight, do they?'

'Like Cinderella,' Evie had said, and they'd cackled at this shaft of wit.

Time's up, Dot said to herself, and left the house. She looked at the car. Something not right. 'Oh, sod it!' she said aloud. She walked round the car, and found a bright yellow triangular clamp attached to her offside wheel. There were no parking restrictions in Sebastopol Street. She looked up and down the street. Not a soul in sight. Still, there wouldn't be, would there? She sighed, and went back into the house. Dialling a number, she reflected that anyone else would have sent for the police. But not a Nimmo. She laughed wryly, and said, 'Stan? Is that you? Help needed.'

She told him about the clamp. 'It's the cheap one, with a padlock. I can't move it. Can you get up here? Yeah, cut it. Damage? Nope, can't see anything. Ta very much. See you.'

Next she phoned Alice Parker-Knowle, and said she'd be
a bit late. Reassured that Alice was not unhappy about this,
she went out to look once more at the car. There was something else – a scrap of paper tucked under the windscreen
wiper. '"Mind yer own business, Dot,"' she read. '"Or else".'

Dot looked closely, and then screwed it up and put it in her
pocket. She scowled. Fools! They don't scare me that easy,
she thought, and waved to the garage truck now speeding up
Sebastopol Street.

'You got enemies, Dot?' asked the mechanic, as he unloaded
tools.

'What do you think?' said Dot. 'Won't take you a minute
to cut through that,' she added confidently. 'I could've done
it meself, 'cept I'm due at my next client, an' I don't have
the tools.'

Stan had the clamp removed in seconds, and said, 'Better
check there ain't no scratches nor nothin'.' He examined the
bodywork carefully. 'No, you bin lucky,' he said. 'This time.
Who d'yer reckon done it, then?'

'You know as well as I do, Stan,' she said. 'But they don't
bother me. It's one of the other lot that done for my Haydn.
Police are sayin' it was a tragic accident, with that loose horse.
But I know different. Horses don't bolt into the road for no
reason.'

'You on the warpath, then, Dot?' Stan was grinning affec-
tionately. 'If I hear anythin' I'll let yer know. The others might
know somethin'. I'll spread it around.'

Dot delved into her purse, but Stan waved her away. 'Don't
be daft. Gotta stick together, us lot. Save yer pennies, Dot.
Never know when yer might need a penny.'

'More like ten pence nowadays,' Dot replied, and laughed
heartily. 'Thanks, anyway, Stan. Mind how y'go.'

She locked up her house and drove off, looking from side
to side along the street, but she could see nothing. She was
certain someone would have seen the culprits, but Sebastopol
kept itself to itself. Might be dangerous to do otherwise. Ah
well, the message would get round. She expected to be left
alone from now on.

Twenty-Four

L ois had not mentioned it, but she planned to drop in on Mrs Parker-Knowle while Dot was there, just to make sure that everything was going as would be expected from a New Brooms cleaner. The fact that Dot had worked there before joining the team made her slightly uneasy. Everything about Dot made Lois uneasy! Dot Nimmo was, as Gran would say, a law unto herself. Lois drove through the town and out towards Meadow Crescent.

A BMW was parked outside Alice Parker-Knowle's house, and Lois drew up behind it. She looked at her watch. Three o'clock. Dot should be nearly through by now. She walked up the driveway and rang the bell. 'Come in, Mrs M! Door's not locked . . .' It was Dot's voice, and Lois immediately objected to the familiarity in her tone. She should be at the door, opening it politely, and ushering her in to see Alice P-K. That sounded like a bottled sauce: P-K Tomato Sauce. She pushed open the door.

'In here!' called Dot, and Lois followed the voice. A dreadful sight met her eyes. Alice and Dot sat either side of a coffee table which bore a neat tea tray, with a plate of chocolate biscuits, clearly much depleted.

'Cup of tea?' Dot said cheerily. 'I'll get another cup. You sit there, Mrs M.' Dot disappeared off to the kitchen. Alice looked at Lois's face and whispered quickly, 'Don't be cross, Mrs Meade. We have had this arrangement since she began. I like her company. She cheers me up. If you like, I'll pay a little extra.'

Lois sighed. 'No need for that, Mrs Parker-Knowle,' she said.

'Do call me Alice, please, Mrs Meade – Lois . . . I do dislike formality among friends. I regard Dot as a friend, and I'm sure you will be one too.'

'Yes, well, we'll see. But thank you, Alice. Apart from the social side of the job, are you satisfied with Dot's work?'

'Oh, yes, she's an excellent cleaner. You are lucky to have found her, Lois.'

At this point, Dot, who had crept up close to the open door to listen, now appeared, smiling and carrying a cup and saucer. 'Here we are then. Now, what have you been telling Mrs M?' she said. 'No complaints, I hope!'

Lois couldn't believe her ears. She had never had an employee like Dot, and it was a going to be a challenge. 'Not so far,' she said with a frown.

The conversation ranged from cleaners Alice had known to Dot's tragedies with the men in her family. Lois purposely blocked questions about her own personal life, and was beginning to think it was time to go, when she heard Alice say, 'And wasn't it strange that Dot should have been cleaning at the Battersbys? *We* knew the family, years and years ago.'

Lois sat up straight. 'How interesting,' she said. 'Did you know them well? Where were they living then?'

Alice then recounted what she had already told Dot, about the farm and the family, and Horace's military career. This time she also mentioned the spinster sisters who had done good works in the town, and had become a legend. 'You'll have seen Battersby Road on the Eastern Development? Named after them.' Lois knew it, but said that most people kept away from that side of town unless they had a very pressing reason to go there. She also knew from Gran about the spinster sisters, but she kept quiet.

While Alice was talking, Lois noticed that Dot was also very quiet and seemed to be concentrating hard on what she was saying. This was unusual, as Dot could not resist interrupting whatever was being said with a contribution of her own.

'Of course,' Alice said, coming to the end, 'Dot could tell you some stories about the Battersbys.' Lois was still looking at Dot and saw her shake her head almost imperceptibly at Alice. She made a mental note to hear those stories later.

Driving away from Meadow Crescent, Lois looked in her rear-view mirror. Two youths were in conversation on the pavement opposite Alice's house. As she waited at the corner for the traffic to clear, she glanced again into the mirror. One of the youths was walking across the road towards Dot's car. He leaned across the windscreen as if to clean it, and Lois saw that he had a spray can in his hand. Ah well, maybe Dot had asked them to do it while she was working. But why, as she watched, did the pair of them scarper at top speed?

Lois reversed into the nearest driveway and went back to look at the BMW. Sure enough, the windscreen had been sprayed, but not with detergent. A message had been left for Dot in bright purple: SHUT YER TRAP DOT!

At this moment, Dot came rushing out. 'What's up, Mrs M?' she shouted. Then she saw her windscreen and her face hardened. 'I'll have 'em lynched,' she muttered under her breath.

'What did you say?'

'I said, did they pinch anything?' Dot replied, quick as a flash. She tried her car door, and shook her head. 'Locked, thank God. Don't worry, Mrs M,' she added. 'I can have that got off in no time. I know your time's money, so you get going.'

Lois reluctantly returned to her car. 'I'll see you tomorrow,' she called to a rapidly disappearing Dot. 'Come around ten o'clock when you've finished the early job on the surgery. I need to talk to you.'

She drove off, and this time there was no traffic. She was well on the way home before she remembered she had wanted to call into Sebastopol Street to see Hazel. Memory going, she silently cursed. Don't say the senior moments are starting already. Gran's memory is better than mine these days. She sighed, and turned around, heading back into Tresham.

'Message for you from our mutual friend,' Hazel said. 'Could you ring him as soon as poss?'

Lois frowned. 'Why didn't he try my mobile?' she said.

'He did, but you're switched off, apparently. Do you want to do it here?' she added, getting up from the desk. Lois nodded, and sat down in the chair.

'Ah, thanks for ringing,' Cowgill said. 'Got some good news for you. Young Darren has been talking to his mother, in fits and starts, and is now asking for the lady in the van. Mrs Smith is certain he means you. Can you go?'

'What's he been saying to his mother?'

'Mostly about horses. Big horses. And the big man, which is how he always refers to Colonel Battersby. She says he has clearly been very frightened.'

'Right,' said Lois, looking at her watch and feeling a sudden surge of energy, 'I'll call in on the way home.'

'Let me know what emerges, won't you?' Cowgill dared to say.

'I'll think about it,' said Lois, and ended the call.

Twenty-Five

After a quick sandwich at home, Lois drove to Waltonby and into Wycherley Close. She parked outside Darren's house, and glanced across to see Mrs Smith watching out for her.

'Hello, Mrs Meade,' she said, opening the door. 'It's very nice of you to come over. I'm sure Darren means *you* when he says "the lady with the van". He's out the back, in the garden. Please sit down and I'll go and get him.'

'No, hang on a minute,' Lois said. 'I'll come with you, and then we'll see if he recognizes me, and if I'm really the person he wants to see.'

They walked through the sitting room and spotless kitchen, and into the garden. A grassy pasture bordered the back fence, where Darren was leaning, looking at a group of horses grazing a few yards away.

'I thought he was frightened of horses now?' said Lois.

'Not those ones,' Mrs Smith replied. 'He knows those. They belong to the farmer – his house is over there.' She pointed to a big farmhouse a couple of fields away. 'It was him that taught Darren to ride. He loved it. Very good, he was, too. They say some children like him have one thing they're very good at, and with Darren it was riding horses. They were gentle with him . . . they seemed to know, like.'

As Lois watched, one of the horses looked up and came over to where Darren stood. The lad had not heard the women talking, or, if he had, he was ignoring them. But now he put out a hand and patted the mare on her head. She snickered, and Darren made a hissing noise close to her nose. Then he leaned over the fence and put his face next to the mare's cheek. They stood there for a few seconds, and Lois was embarrassed to find tears coming to her eyes. She sniffed. 'Oh dear,' she said.

Mrs Smith patted her hand. 'It's all right,' she said. 'You see, he does have friends.'

Darren suddenly looked round. He saw Lois, and his face lit up. 'Lady with the van!' he shouted, and came running awkwardly towards them.

'I was right, then,' Mrs Smith muttered. 'Come on, Darren,' she said in a louder voice, 'come and meet Mrs Meade. She brought you home, didn't she? Let's go in and give her a nice cup of tea.'

Darren tucked his hand under Lois's arm, and beamed at her. 'I go for a ride in your van?' he said.

'Maybe later,' Lois said. She hardly recognized this confident and smiling Darren as the terrified, dumbstruck boy she had chased across the fields and brought home.

He nodded. 'We have a nice cup of tea,' he said. 'Then I go for a ride in your van.'

They sat in the comfortable sitting room and drank their tea. Lois noticed that Darren gulped his quickly, as if anxious to get going.

'You've got nice horses in your field,' Lois said, trying to keep it simple. Darren nodded again. 'Very nice horses,' he said. 'I ride one. She's called Maisie, and she loves me and I love her. And I love my Mum.'

'And your Dad too, I expect?'

'Not Dad,' Darren said firmly. 'Dad gone away.'

Lois looked at Mrs Smith and said, 'Oh, sorry.' But Mrs Smith smiled, and said it didn't matter. He'd been gone a long time.

'Couldn't get used to his son not being normal, as he put it.'

'I saw you once before,' Lois said to Darren, changing the subject. 'You were working in Colonel Battersby's garden. Do you remember?'

The change in him was marked, and Lois wished she hadn't mentioned it.

'Don't love the big man,' he said. 'Love the horses out the back, and my Mum. Shall I love you too, lady with the van?'

'Yes, please,' Lois replied, dangerously wobbly again. 'And you love the big man's horses, too?'

Darren stood up suddenly, knocking back his chair. 'Not the big man's horses!' he said, and seemed near to tears. 'Darren not going back to the big man's garden?' he asked, turning to his mother.

She shook her head and kissed him. 'Ssh, Darren. No, you're not going back there until you want to. You stay with Mum.'

He gradually relaxed, and sat down again. Lois finished her tea, and turned to Mrs Smith. 'Would it be all right to take Darren for a quick spin in the van? I'll bring him back in half an hour or so . . .'

Mrs Smith frowned. 'I don't know,' she said slowly. 'He gets frightened easily, and then he might try to get out.'

Darren had wandered back into the garden, and his mother explained he found it difficult to sit still for long. Lois was glad, not being sure how much he understood of their conversation.

'I can lock the doors,' she said. 'We won't go far, and certainly nowhere near Colonel Battersby's house! What on earth happened to Darren there? I thought he mostly worked for Mrs Battersby, and she's a very nice person.'

'She is. Mrs Battersby always took him out, and told me he could have a future in the horsey world when he'd matured a bit more. I doubted it myself, but was pleased that it was going so well. Sometimes Darren would spend the whole day at the stables, and then stay the night, so's I could have a break. Once the Colonel and his wife took him to the local point-to-point. He was very excited when he came home, going on about the horses for hours. They'd taken him to another one, and that was when he ran away.'

'So what happened?'

'Don't know. I couldn't make it out. I was frantic, but you found him, thank God. He wouldn't tell me where he'd been, or why he'd gone, and he wouldn't go back to the Battersbys' after that. I still haven't found out what happened, and the police seem to have forgotten about it. Written him off, I dare say. Most people do.'

'Well, I don't,' said Lois. 'I'll give him a shout, and we'll be off. I promise to take care of him.'

Darren came in again straight away, and Lois took his hand. 'Come on, Darren, let's go for that ride in the van,' she said in a comfortable voice. He took her outstretched hand.

'Mrs Meade,' he said, and managed a tentative smile.

'Take care of Mrs Meade,' said Mrs Smith. 'Be a good boy. See you soon.' She waved them off with an anxious face, and watched until they disappeared out of sight.

'Where shall we go, Darren?' Lois asked, once they were safely locked inside the van. He didn't answer, but smiled at her. 'Would you like to see my little dog?' she said, with a sudden flash of inspiration. They would have time on the way to Farnden to talk, and then Gran and Jeems might help him to relax and talk some more. She knew that Darren held the key to whatever had happened at the Battersbys to make him run away. The only other people were the Colonel and his lady, but they were not saying. It was possible that not even Blanche knew, but she probably suspected.

On the way out of Waltonby village, they passed by the Battersbys' house, and Darren went rigid. 'Not going there,' he said in alarm.

Lois shook her head, 'Of course not, Darren. We're going to see my little dog, and my mother. You'll like them. The dog's name is Jeems, and she loves games. She loves to chase after a ball. We can throw a ball for her.'

Darren relaxed, and nodded. 'I love dogs,' he said. 'And I love my Mum . . . and Mrs Meade,' he added, and smiled.

Lois felt absurdly glad that Darren loved her.

Twenty-Six

Derek had finished the job he was doing over at Fletching, and decided he was near enough to home to go back for one of Gran's fry-ups. He had some jobs to do in the house and garden, and would take the afternoon off to do them.

He hardly ever did this, and Lois had to bully him to take a holiday. Although he preferred working for himself, he did occasionally reflect that it must be nice to do a nine-to-five job, with weekends free and paid holidays. Still, the fact that all the money he earned came direct to him was worth a lot.

As he turned into his driveway, he saw Lois on the lawn with a skinny lad, who was laughing and jumping up and down with obvious delight. They were throwing a ball for Jeems, who was catching it mid-air. When the little dog saw Derek, she lost interest in the ball and ran towards him. Just before she reached him, she saw the open gates and changed direction. Like lightning, she streaked down the drive and out into the road. Derek could hear the sound of a heavy vehicle approaching, and shouted at the top of his voice in a furious tone, which was the only one Jeems obeyed. 'Come here! Get back here, you bad dog!'

Lois joined him quickly, and neither noticed that at the sound of Derek shouting, Darren froze, then ran down the path to the bottom of the garden and out of sight.

Jeems turned back in time, and was told off in no uncertain terms by Lois. 'Still,' she pleaded with a still angry Derek, 'she's only young. And she was so excited to see you.'

'Hmm!' said Derek. 'Anyway, who's that you've got with . . .' Both looked at once to the empty lawn, and Lois began to run.

'It's Darren,' she shouted back to Derek. 'Come and help, and get Gran.'

This time thankfully he had not gone far. He was cowering behind the garden shed, and refused to come out. 'You and Gran go back into the house,' said Lois. 'He'll come to me in a minute.'

'I expect I frightened him,' Derek said glumly. 'But . . .'

'Not your fault,' Lois said quickly. 'Jeems would be flattened by now if you hadn't shouted. We'll be with you in two shakes of a lamb's tail. Now, Darren,' she continued gently, when the other two were out of sight, 'shall we go in and have a nice cup of tea?'

Darren shook his head violently. 'Big man in there,' he said. 'Not nice to Darren. Want to go home to Mum.'

'Yes,' Lois said, realizing that the big man was Derek, and it was indeed the shouting that had frightened the lad. 'We will go back to Mum soon. But Gran has made a cake for you, and will be sad if we don't go in and eat it.' This was a safe enough lie. Gran always had a cake in the tin.

'Is the big man there?' said Darren.

'Maybe,' Lois replied quietly. 'But this man's name is Derek, and he is never unkind. He just has a loud voice. He saved Jeems from being killed by the big lorry. So that was kind of him, wasn't it?'

Darren looked doubtful. 'Big man . . . Derek . . . got horses?' he said.

'No, no horses,' Lois said. 'He is my husband, and very nice. You will like him.'

'Not love him,' said Darren.

Lois laughed. 'Maybe not,' she said. 'But you will like him. I promise you. And you love me, don't you, so I won't let anything bad happen to you.'

Darren got slowly to his feet, and came forward. 'Hold my hand,' he said, and Lois led him gently down the garden path, back towards the house. It all depends on Derek now, she thought as they went into the kitchen. The table was laid with a chocolate cake in pride of place in the centre. Gran stood with her back to the Rayburn, smiling, and Derek had disappeared. When he came back into the kitchen, Darren began to back away.

'Have you seen this, Darren?' Derek said, and held out his hand. He was holding a small glazed pottery model of a dog – a white Westie, just like Jeems. 'For you, Darren,' he said, 'to keep in your room at home.'

Lois held her breath. Darren stood still, then took a tentative step towards Derek. 'Jeems,' he said, and Derek carefully placed the figure into Darren's outstretched hand. Darren held it to his cheek, just as he had with Maisie, the horse in the field. 'I love Jeems,' he said, and looked at the table. 'And chocolate cake,' he added, and sat down.

As she drove Darren back to Waltonby, Lois reflected that he had said nothing useful about the Battersbys, but this didn't matter. His reaction to Derek's shouting, and the fact that a 'big man' had terrified him, and then the question about Derek having horses, all told her a great deal. He had without doubt been frightened out of his wits by Colonel Battersby, and perhaps by the big hunters that lived in the Colonel's stables.

Mrs Smith was waiting at the gate. 'Ah, there you are,' she said, with obvious relief. She looked at Darren's beaming face and the knot of anxiety in her stomach gradually gave way to a tearful welcome. 'So he enjoyed himself, Mrs Meade,' she said, taking his hand.

'Look, Mum, look what kind Derek gave me,' he said. 'I love Jeems. She's for my room. Upstairs, in my room. I put her on my shelf.' He turned to go up the path, and then looked back. 'Thank you, Mrs Meade,' he said, like a well-drilled child. 'I come again in your van? See Jeems, and Gran . . . and Derek?'

'Yes, soon,' said Lois, and waved her hand.

'A success, then?' Mrs Meade said. 'I can't thank you enough. He'll be happy for days now. Don't worry about taking him again. He'll not remember for very long.'

'I shall come again,' Lois said firmly. 'For one thing, this afternoon gave me several things to think about. Maybe when he really trusts me, we'll get to the bottom of what happened to him to make him run away. Bye now, Mrs Smith. Take care.'

Mrs Smith watched Lois drive away, and turned to go into the house. For some reason, she felt optimistic for the first time since Darren's disappearance.

Derek was waiting for Lois, and gave her a hug as she got out of the car. 'I messed that up, didn't I, me duck?' he said. 'Sorry. Was he all right when he got home?'

Lois kissed his cheek, and said, 'Fine. He was fine. But I've got a bone to pick with you. Who said you could give away my little pottery Westie? You gave me that at Christmas, and it was special.'

'Emergency,' he said. 'I'll get you another.'

She kissed him again. 'Only teasing,' she said. 'Couldn't have done better meself.'

Twenty-Seven

'Hello? Is that New Brooms? Ah, good. This is Mrs Margaret Horsley here – Willow Farm.'

Lois's eyes widened. 'Good morning, Mrs Horsley,' she said, gathering herself together. 'How can I help you?'

Lois was sitting at the office desk in Sebastopol Street, holding the fort for Hazel, who had gone to the dentist. She couldn't believe her luck. This was definitely the wife of Joe Horsley, farmer, and colleague of Colonel Battersby – though just what 'colleague' meant, Lois was not yet sure.

'Do you remember your husband doing a job for us? Yes? Well, I know you won the lottery, and I was thinking maybe you'd packed in the cleaning business?'

'No, no,' Lois said. 'New Brooms is still here, and I'm still running it. And Derek is still doing electrical work. No problems, I hope?'

'Goodness, no! No, the reason I'm ringing is that I was talking to my friend Blanche Battersby, and she says you'd sent her a wonderful cleaner called Dot. Strongly recommended, she said. Now, I need a couple of hours' help in the house every week, and wondered whether you could fit me in. But I would like Dot, if that's possible. What is her other name, by the way?'

Antennae waving about madly, Lois felt sure there was something odd about this call, something that told her this was not just a lucky chance.

'We always try to fit in with clients' wishes,' she replied firmly. 'But because of illness, or need to change schedules, we reserve the right to send whoever is available. All our staff are thoroughly trained and completely reliable. Now,' she added, deliberately ignoring the question about Dot's surname, 'I would like to come and see you at a convenient time to discuss the work and answer any questions.'

There was a pause before Margaret replied, 'Yes, of course. I'm free on Wednesday morning, around ten thirty. Would that suit?'

'Fine. I'll see you then. Goodbye, Mrs Horsley.'

'Just a minute! You haven't told me Dot's—'

Lois heard Margaret's question, but she put down the phone and entered the appointment in her diary.

Margaret Horsley swore. Was the Meade woman deliberately withholding Dot's name? In which case, there was something funny going on, as Horace had said. She had lied about being a friend of Blanche, but thought it would sound more convincing. On the rare occasions they had met, Blanche had either patronized her or ignored her all together. Well, she supposed that was fair enough. Her fling with Horace had been a secret at first, but had become general knowledge after a while. Once Joe found out, and seemed reluctant to do anything about it, news of the affair got round all the drinking and gambling circles. Margaret still couldn't forgive Joe for not putting a stop to it, but had become more and more convinced that Horace had some hold over him.

Horace had asked her to ring New Brooms, suspecting that Dot was a plant. He hadn't seen her, but from Blanche's description, he guessed she was one of the Nimmo lot from Tresham, and he was certain he knew who had planted her. It would be Mrs Meade, the cleaning boss and part-time sleuth in cahoots with the police, according to information he had received.

Now Margaret had to ring Horace to tell him she had failed, and to ask what she should do next. She dialled his mobile number and waited. His reply was like staccato gunfire. 'Damn! Hire the woman! Report back!' Margaret sighed. She wished she was married to one of those nice, jolly farmers they met at the Hunt Ball. Comfortable wives in cushy situations, matriarchs of farming dynasties, indispensable and contented. Or were they? At the farm bordering Willow Farm, Margaret knew that the farmer's wife had not been able to have children, had had a nervous collapse, and was now virtually a recluse, while her husband played the field at the club in Tresham.

She shook herself. These were useless thoughts, and she

might as well forget about it until Wednesday, when she might be able to find out more.

Hazel came into the office holding her cheek. 'These dentists!' she said. 'I reckon they find something to do, even if it's not necessary. It was only a check-up, and now I've been tortured for half an hour under the drill. Ouch!'

Lois stood up and put her arm around Hazel's shoulder. 'Now listen,' she said, 'it's home for you. Painkillers and some nice sloppy food. Bridie's not working today, is she? She asked for time off, in case you weren't able to cope with Lizzie.'

Hazel nodded, and said in a voice that sounded as if she had a hot potato in her mouth, 'Yeah, Mum's got her. Are you sure, Mrs M? Will you be able to stay?'

'Yes, I can work from here. The wonders of laptop computers! Get off now, and then you'll be fine tomorrow. Take care, Hazel. Oh, and a little whisky and water helps, so Derek says. But then, he doesn't need toothache to try that remedy! Go on, gel. Off you go.'

Hazel tried to smile, but yelped again, and left, waving a pathetic hand.

Lois picked up the phone. 'Mum?' she said. 'Shan't be back for lunch. Hazel's gone home with a painful tooth. Yes, Bridie's looking after Lizzie, so they'll be fine. Love to Derek, if he turns up. See you later. Yes, I'll get a sandwich. Promise. Bye.'

Bringing up the week's schedule on her computer, Lois looked to see where Dot Nimmo was working today. She was pretty sure she was at Alice Parker-Knowle's. Yes, Dot was there from two o'clock. Right. She got through to her, and asked her to call in at the office when she had finished at Alice's. 'And don't stay longer than your three hours,' she said. Dot exploded. She protested that she never got paid for any extra time, and she wouldn't dream of asking for it. It was a good turn she was doing for a nice old lady.

'Yes, all right,' said Lois. 'But it's important that I see you as soon as possible before I go home. Yes, I'm here all after-noon. Thanks, Dot.'

The day went quickly, with phone calls from potential new clients, and one or two existing ones. There were seldom complaints, and when Mrs Pickering telephoned in to talk to Lois about Floss, she wondered what was up. Floss was not allowed to work for her mother. This was one of Lois's rules, and so it couldn't be a cleaning problem.

'It's about this horse, Mrs Meade,' Mrs Pickering said. 'Floss is feeling a bit better now, and has said she really would like to have it on the Battersbys' terms. She's had a bit of a rough time with illness lately, and her father and I would like to help her out with paying for upkeep and so on. As you know, she's saving up to get married, and says she couldn't possibly afford it herself.'

'Are you getting round to telling me Floss wants to get a better-paid job? If so, Mrs Pickering, I would quite under-stand, though I'd be very sorry to lose her.'

'Gracious, no! Floss loves working for New Brooms. She's never been so happy. Says she's found her métier!'

Lois laughed. 'Good. Then what's the problem? I'd be quite happy about that, as long as you make sure she's under no obligation to the Battersbys. I wouldn't want her to feel indebted to them. No need to oblige them in any way that she didn't want to.'

'What do you mean by oblige?' Mrs Pickering said.

'Oh, well, extra jobs without telling me, that sort of thing.'

Mrs Pickering sounded relieved. 'Yes, of course,' she said. 'For a minute I thought you meant oblige the Colonel in . . . er . . . well, you know, in some unpleasant way . . .' She tailed off lamely, and Lois laughed again.

'Don't know him that well, Mrs Pickering,' she answered, 'but I'm sure he's not a dirty old man. If you can ever be sure,' she added honestly. 'But she only has to leave at once and tell me. New Brooms has ways of dealing with that sort of thing.'

What *had* she meant? Lois asked herself later. She was beginning to distrust anything connected with the Battersbys. All roads seemed to lead back to the Colonel. She knew what Derek would say. How could she expect to trust anybody named Horace?

Twenty-Eight

Dot arrived at the office exactly ten minutes after the time she had finished at Alice's. Lois glanced at her watch, and wished she hadn't.

'No need for you to check the time,' said Dot crossly. 'If I say I'll do a thing, I do it. And I'll be glad if you could show the same trust in me as you do with the others. You've had no cause to doubt me so far, and you won't have. So if it's all right with you, as I'm out of paid time, I'll go home and get me tea.'

'Sorry, sorry!' said Lois. 'I apologize! I wasn't checking up on you, though I can see it looked bad. Now come and sit down, Dot. I want to talk to you about something important. D'you want a cup of tea?'

A little mollified, Dot nodded and said she'd make it for both of them. Once they were settled, she looked at Lois and said, 'It's about the Battersbys, isn't it?'

'Sort of,' Lois said. 'I need to know for my business purposes what previous connection you've had with the Battersbys. I've had roundabout requests for your surname from them and their friends. I've stalled them so far. It wasn't an unreasonable request, but I got this feeling. I have it sometimes, and it never lets me down.'

Dot was silent for a minute or so. Then she squared her shoulders and began to talk. 'I've not told you everything,' she said, 'and you could say I hadn't been straight. Well, you give me a chance, when I bet everybody tried to turn you against me. The Nimmo name is not a good'un in Tresham. My Handy sailed close to the wind in more ways than one, and he had friends and relations to back him up. People were scared of him, not to put too fine a point on it. There's other mobs in town, o' course. But Nimmos was known to be the most powerful. Can't tell you a name for the others. Honour among thieves, my dad would say. Dad didn't approve of my marryin' Handy, but the old devil always treated me well. Not stingy, not with me.'

'And the Battersbys?' prompted Lois.

Dot told her what she had already told Alice. It had been a case of non-payment of a bill, with the Colonel accusing Handy of screwing him over, and refusing to pay. 'Handy got his revenge, though. Nobody would work for Battersby after that. Not Tresham builders. It was only a poxy kitchen extension he wanted, and Handy did a good job. It was a fair price, too.'

'So if they knew your name, you'd be out on your ear at once? Well, that is even more important than I thought.'

'Yeah, well, I'm sorry about that. But there's more. Y'know my Haydn was killed in a so-called accident? Well, I think old Battersby had somethin' to do with it, and I reckoned that if I could go to work there, I could find out more.' There was a pause, and then Dot added, 'So I s'pose you'd like to give me m' cards straight away. Fair enough. I wouldn't blame you.'

Lois sighed. 'Oh, Dot,' she said. 'Now what am I to do? I know you're good at the job, and another client has asked for you specially.'

'Can I ask yer something, Mrs M?'

'Go on,' Lois replied, wondering how honest she should be herself.

'Why did you hire me? I'm not a fool, and I know I got a disgusting house. I look a sight when I'm not scrubbed up, and the Nimmo reputation goes before me. So why?'

Lois made a decision. 'Because I thought I could use you,' she said. 'My Derek witnessed the accident, you know. When he told me all the details, I reckoned there was something not quite right. Your son was a young man, and I don't like young blokes being killed for some trumped-up accident story. I've got sons, too. I don't know what Haydn was involved in, but whatever it was, it needed the truth told. So when you came in here, applying for a job, I thought I could use you.' She did not mention Cowgill.

'And now it looks like you can?' Dot said hopefully.

'Maybe,' Lois said. 'So I'll give you another chance. What I get to know I'll share with you. And you can tell me everything you know about them. And you can start by explaining why the Horsleys at Willow Farm should also be interested in who you are. And what do you know about the stable thefts?'

'Easy,' said Dot. 'Close as a couple o' toads, Horace and Joe are. Gambling, women, money. Been goin' on for years. Mind you, they're close in other ways, too. Nothing much leaks out. Got away with it for years, too. If you want to know more about them, I got contacts. As for the stable thefts, I'll see what I can do.' She stood up and held out her hand. 'Partners?' she asked.

'For now,' answered Lois, shaking her hand. 'But with a get-out clause at any time.'

'Goes for me, too,' said Dot cheerfully, and made for the door.

Lois began to tidy up the desk, and as she took the dirty mugs into the kitchen, she heard a loud squeal of brakes, and then an engine revving.

'Oh no!' she yelled, and rushed out into the road. Not far from Dot Nimmo's house near the top end of the road she could see a dark shape lying in the road. People were beginning to run towards it, and Lois joined them.

'Let me through!' she shouted, and pushed her way to the front of the gathering spectators. 'Oh, God,' she said in a shocked voice. 'Not Dot! Please God, not Dot!'

But of course it was Dot, and in due course police and ambulance arrived, and Lois was making another call to Gran, saying she would be home later than expected.

Twenty-Nine

'And guess who was quickly on the scene?' Derek asked grimly.

Gran, Derek and Lois were in the sitting room, and for once the television was not on. It was quite late, and Lois had forced down a meal, with Derek and Gran sternly standing over her. Now, after a long pause, Derek had made his sour remark.

'Yes, you're right. Cowgill was there,' Lois said flatly. Gran reckoned she was in shock, and had said so. Lois had denied it hotly, but was like a zombie going through the motions of the day.

'You haven't told us much, lovey,' Gran said gently. She remembered when Lois was a young girl, reluctant to confide in her parents. She needed coaxing. 'Was Dot all right when she left you in the office?'

Lois gave herself a little shake and made an effort. 'She was fine. We'd had a good talk, and sorted things out. It was going to be easier in the future for both of us. I admire her, you know. Dogged and brave, in her way.'

'What did the ambulance man say?' Derek said. 'Was she . . . well, you know, had she snuffed it?'

'Nearly,' said Lois. 'They reckoned she couldn't live much longer. Extensive injuries, they said . . .'

Suddenly Lois collapsed and hid her face in her hands. Derek moved to sit next to her on the sofa, and put his arm around her shoulders. She pulled herself together in seconds. Lois Meade did not blub. But the lapse in self-control had relaxed her, and she began to tell them the whole story, from beginning to end, but leaving out the partnership pact. 'I keep thinking that if I'd let her go earlier, it wouldn't have happened.'

'Had you thought, me duck,' said Derek, 'that whoever ran her down might have been waiting for her? It wouldn't have mattered what time she came out of the office, she'd still have been in trouble. Didn't anybody see the sodding hit-and-run merchant?'

'Don't know,' Lois said, 'but you know what Sebastopol is like.'

'I expect you'll be hearing from Cowgill, anyway,' Derek said. 'You can bet on it.'

'I have to make a statement,' Lois said. 'So I expect I'll know more after that.' She was quiet for a minute, and then said angrily, 'Who the hell would do a thing like that to a woman like Dot?'

Derek raised his eyebrows. 'You're not telling me Dot was

a poor defenceless widder woman, mindin' her own business and no threat to nobody?'

Lois shrugged. 'No, I'm not,' she said, 'but I shall still do my best to find out who killed one of my team and then buggered off.'

'She's not dead yet,' Gran reminded them.

Later in the evening, the telephone rang. 'It's for you, Lois. It's him,' called Derek.

'I'll take it in the office,' Lois said. 'And yes, you can listen in if you want.'

Derek frowned and stomped off upstairs. He dreaded Lois becoming more and more involved in anything to do with the Tresham mobs. They were small beer, compared with some, but could be dangerous, even so. Witness Haydn Nimmo. Derek would never forget the smashed-up face, the awkward twist of his neck.

'Lois, how are you?' Cowgill's voice sounded anxious. 'I've been worrying about you. You went off looking so pale and wan.'

'Thank God, then, that you stayed at the scene of the crime,' said Lois, restored to her usual stroppy self. 'Have you got the villain who did it?'

She heard Cowgill sigh. 'Not yet,' he said. 'But we have good leads, and are following them up.'

'So you've got no idea,' said Lois. 'Well, neither have I. But I've got plenty to work on. When are you coming to take a statement? I've got a busy day tomorrow, and can't waste time.'

'Lois, dear,' Cowgill said, a risky strategy, 'I know you're not heartless. Dot Nimmo worked for you, and I'd expect you to defend her. So you don't need to pretend to me. A nice young policeman will be round tomorrow morning about ten o'clock. Will that do?'

'It'll have to, I suppose. You know what I'm going to ask next . . .'

'She's hanging on,' Cowgill said quietly. 'You'll be the first to know if the worst happens. I'll see to that personally. Now,' he said in a brisker, police inspector voice. '*I* shall need to see you to ask a few questions. Formally, of course. Can you come down to the station, or would you rather I came to Farnden?'

'I'll come to you,' said Lois, thinking of the chilly reception he'd get from Derek and Gran. 'Tomorrow, I suppose? Blimey, I shall be talking to policemen all day. Can't I tell it all to the nice young policeman? No. Well, if you were a villain, I'd be deeply suspicious. All right, all right! Three o'clock tomorrow? That's the only time I can do, and it can't be for long.'

Cowgill had another appointment at that time, but he said, 'Fine. Three o'clock tomorrow, then. Goodbye, Lois.'

He put down the phone and buzzed for his secretary. 'Cancel my three o'clock appointment tomorrow, he said, 'and refix it for any other free time.'

In the intensive care department of Tresham General Hospital, a grey-haired doctor looked down at the inert figure of Dot Nimmo and shook his head. Tubes hung in festoons around her, and her face was parchment yellow. The heart monitor bleeped away her life, with alarming gaps at intervals.

A young nurse stood by. 'Sad, isn't it?'

'It's always sad,' replied the doctor. 'I've lost count of how many Nimmos I've seen in this hospital over the years. You could say they were an unlucky family, but they made their own luck. Let's hope this is the last,' he added, and walked away.

Thirty

Alice Parker-Knowle was the first person Lois telephoned the next day. It was fortunate that Dot had not as yet worked for many New Brooms clients. Alice was first because Dot had worked for her before, and was obviously a special person to her.

'Is that Mrs Parker-Knowle?' Lois wasn't sure of Alice's voice yet.

'Oh, hello, Lois. Nothing wrong, I hope?'

When Lois told her what had happened to Dot, there was a long silence. 'Alice? Are you still there?'

'Yes, I'm still here.' The voice was calm, not what Lois had expected.

'I'll be sending you another one of the team. They are all good people.'

'Not like Dot, though,' Alice said quietly. 'She brightened my life, Lois. When you get to my age, not many people can do that.' There was another pause, and then Alice continued. 'Did she tell you about the paint sprayed on her windscreen?'

'I saw it,' Lois answered. 'Dot didn't seem too bothered about it.'

'It was the second warning in one day. Somebody had clamped her car while she was having a quick sausage roll before coming on to me. She was late, by the time it was taken off. She made up the time, of course.'

Lois frowned. 'She didn't tell me that,' she said. 'In Dot's circle, threats and feuds are part of life. Most come to nothing, and she probably reckoned it would all be sorted out.' She thought privately that Dot must have been vulnerable ever since her Handy had died. Haydn had obviously been no protection, and she had been left alone to cope. Lois's anger rose. 'We don't know yet,' she said, 'that the accident was deliberate. But the car didn't stop. Not sure if anybody saw anything, but it's still rough around there and most people think it best to keep mum. You can be sure I shan't let it rest, Alice. Meanwhile, Dot is still alive, just, and we must hope and pray.'

The Bucklands were not too concerned. They said they were sorry, and asked when the replacement would be coming. Their au pair girl was not accustomed to cleaning, and her time was fully taken up with helping the nanny look after the children.

Blanche Battersby was nearly as upset as Alice. Although she had had only a brief acquaintance with Dot, she had looked forward to her next visit. The confidence of the woman made her feel better, stronger, more able to cope with Horace. It was ridiculous to think like that, Blanche knew, but she had found herself disagreeing with him several times lately, and not giving way to his blustering.

Lois wasn't sure whether she needed to ring Margaret

Horsley straight away, but then remembered the appointment, and dialed her number. A man answered.

'Joe Horsley here. Who's that?'

'Lois Meade, New Brooms. Is Mrs Horsley there, please?'

'No, she's not. But how are you getting on, Mrs Meade? Spent all your money yet?' His voice was unpleasant, and Lois bristled.

'I'll call back,' she said.

She was about to ring off when Joe said, 'Is the old bag dead?'

It was like a shower of cold water. Lois shivered. How did he know about Dot? She had said nothing, and she'd checked that the story was not in the local paper that morning.

'What old bag?' she asked quietly. 'Who do you mean?'

Joe Horsley laughed loudly. 'Oh, come on, duckie,' he said. 'You'd better stay out of all this. Too deep for amateurs. You'll cry at her funeral, I expect, but there won't be many others.'

Lois heard the click as he ended the call. She put down her phone and sat motionless, thinking. Finally she was interrupted by Gran coming in with a message.

'You all right, Lois?' she said. 'There's a policeman at the door, come to take a statement. I've settled him in the sitting room. Didn't you hear him?'

Lois shook her head. 'Miles away,' she said. 'Thanks, Mum. I'll come through.'

'Good morning, Mrs Meade.' The policeman stood up politely. He was young, but not the fresh-faced novice she had been expecting. She guessed he was about thirty, and he seemed calm and confident.

'Sit down, then,' Lois said. 'I see Mum got you a cup of coffee. You'd better drink it down, else you won't be able to write, will you?'

The policeman grinned. He had been forewarned by Inspector Cowgill. 'Thank you, Mrs Meade,' he said, and gulped it down. 'Now, I have to ask you a few questions . . .'

'I know all that,' Lois said. 'Let's get on with it. I've got work to do.'

'First I have to tell you my name,' he said. 'I'm Matthew Vickers. I've been loaned from Manchester for a few weeks.'

'Thanks,' Lois said. 'I'll try to remember that.'

In spite of her anxiety to be rid of him as soon as possible, she found him extremely charming, but steely. She answered his questions, and found that he spotted immediately her attempts at concealment. She was a match for him, of course, but had to be alert and on her guard.

Finally, he thanked her, put on his hat and walked to the front door. 'You've been most helpful, Mrs Meade,' he said. 'Oh, and Inspector Cowgill sends his good wishes. I understand you work with him from time to time.'

'And you're not supposed to know that,' Lois said tartly. 'You can tell him I said so.'

He had a faint smile on his face, and said, 'Yes, of course. I will report accurately. You can be sure of that. Good morning. And please thank Mrs Weedon for the coffee.'

Lois went back into her office and sat down, ready to telephone the hospital to enquire after Dot. She dreaded doing it, in case the news was bad. At the same time, she needed to know, and didn't trust Cowgill to tell her.

Gran appeared at the door. 'Everything all right, love?' she said. 'You still look a bit peaky.'

'I'll be fine, Mum, thanks,' she said. 'Did that policeman ask you any questions?'

Gran shook her head. 'No, only said it was a nice day. Seemed very pleasant.'

'He was, but tough with it. Did he remind you of anybody? Looked familiar to me.'

'Oh, yes,' said Gran. 'I said so to him. He said he'd rather not have it known, but he is Hunter Cowgill's nephew.'

'Oh lord!' Lois said. 'He told the wrong person, then, didn't he?'

Gran shut the door firmly, and went back to the kitchen, muttering that Lois was obviously feeling better. Quite like her old self. Huh! Wrong person, indeed!

Lois dialled the hospital and was told that Mrs Nimmo was still holding on. There was no change in her condition, but they were doing everything they could to help her.

'In other words, you don't know yet whether she will live or die?' Lois said rashly.

'Are you a relation, Mrs Meade?' The voice was icy.

'No. Dot Nimmo worked for me, and is my responsibility.'

'Did the accident happen during her working time?'

'No, not exactly. But she had just been to see me, and was on her way home.'

'Why don't you ring in tomorrow, Mrs Meade, and we'll hope to have some better news for you. Goodbye.'

Lois swore and walked over to the window. She looked up and down the village street. The sun was shining, and it looked at its best. Stone houses and garden walls. Overhanging trees and splashes of colour in the gardens. Nobody about. She could just see down to Josie's shop, and was glad to see a couple of cars parked outside. One of them was Cowgill's. She pulled on her jacket and went out, calling to Gran that she was going down to the shop for a couple of minutes. She didn't wait for an answer.

As she approached the shop, he came out and saw her. 'Morning, Mrs Meade,' he said, unable to suppress a glad smile.

'Can you tell me something very quickly, please?' she said. 'Did Dot have any close relations? She was cagey when I asked her, and I didn't press it.'

'Good God, yes,' Cowgill said. 'But only one very close. Evelyn Nimmo. She's Dot's sister, and married Handy's brother. What a foursome! She's in the phone book.'

'Thanks,' Lois said. 'And, by the way, your nephew was charming. Very like you, really, but charming.' She took the shop steps two at a time and vanished.

'Hello, Mum,' Josie said.

'What did *he* want?' Lois asked.

'The local paper and a box of matches.' Josie smiled innocently.

She's so like me, thought Lois fondly. 'No questions?' she asked.

'No, just the usual pleasantries.'

'Right. I'll just have my loaf, then. I'll be down again later.'

Gran was standing at the front door. 'Are you sure you're all right, Lois?' she said.

'Yes, of course I am. Just needed to ask Josie something. Here's the loaf. A bit crustier than usual, but it'll be good for our teeth.'

'Might be good for yours,' Gran said. 'Not so sure about mine. *Now* where are you going? I should think you'd do better to take today off work. Still, no good telling you,' she added, as Lois went into her office and shut the door.

She found the name in the phone book: J.S. Nimmo, l6 Mafeking Street. Lois dialed the number, and heard a voice that instantly reminded her of Dot. 'Is that Mrs Evelyn Nimmo?' she asked.

'What d'you want?' Oh, yes, Lois thought, that must be Dot's sister!

When Evelyn heard who the caller was, her voice changed. 'Oh, I've heard of you,' she said. 'Dot said you were all right, and that's praise from my sister!'

'I was hoping you could tell me how she is. The hospital wasn't very forthcoming.'

'Always the way,' Evelyn said. 'Especially if your name's Nimmo. I reckon if our house was on fire, the brigade would somehow go to the wrong address. Still, we're used to it. Now, you asked about Dot. I don't know no more than you. I'm going in this afternoon, but they warned me I shouldn't expect much. She's still in a coma, and very dodgy. But I'm seeing her, even if I have to go in all guns blazing! She's my sister. D'you want me to give you a bell later?'

Lois said that would be very kind, and she'd definitely be at home around five thirty.

Thirty-One

By five thirty Lois had called in to see Cowgill, answered a question or two, decided it was a ruse to get her into his office, and came home to walk her dog. She was tired, but felt restless. She couldn't settle until Evelyn Nimmo had told her Dot's chances. Although she was expecting the call, she started up from her chair in the kitchen when it came.

'Ah, hello, Evelyn. How was she?'

'Much the same. They were telling you the truth. She's out for the count, and not showing any signs of coming round. They didn't want me to stay, but I said something might get through. Might make a difference. So they let me sit there for half an hour.'

'Did you talk to her?'

'Non-stop,' Evelyn said, and Lois couldn't decide whether the choke was a laugh or the beginning of tears. 'Do you know what I told her?' Evelyn continued. 'I told her a story Handy used to tell us every Christmas Day. He swore it was true, but of course it weren't. We all enjoyed it, every year, and kidded him along. It was about when Handy was a young sprog soldier, and how his boots got stolen for a joke. Then, on Christmas morning, he woke up and found four pairs of brand new boots at the foot of his bed. We all used to chorus, "A likely story!".' She paused, and Lois laughed.

'And do you know, Mrs Meade,' Evelyn said, 'when I got to that bit, I thought I saw the shadow of a smile on Dot's face. The nurse said she didn't see it, but it was there and gone so quickly. I suppose I could have been mistaken.'

Lois felt unreasonably cheered up. 'Oh, I do hope you were right,' she said. 'Fingers crossed, then. And thanks a lot for phoning.'

'That's all right. I shall see her again tomorrow, and I'll ring you . . . And then there's another thing. Are you short-handed because of Dot?'

'Well, yes,' said Lois slowly, guessing what was coming.

'I was wonderin' if you'd like me to come and fill in until she gets better. Well, I suppose "if" would be a better word. I wouldn't want to do it permanently, but I know she'd like me to help you out.'

'Um, well, um . . . Can I give it some thought, Evelyn? Perhaps you could come into the office tomorrow, say three o'clock? We could have a chat.'

'Fine,' said Evelyn. 'I'm off now to St Joseph's to light a candle for Dot.'

Horace Battersby had come home with the Tresham evening newspaper, and looked forward to giving his wife a shock. 'Dorothy Nimmo, known as Dot, is in a critical condition,' he had read. He went through to the drawing room, where Blanche was watching the news on television. The local news would be on in a minute, and he wanted to get in first.

'Hello, Blanche, look at this!' he said, thrusting the paper in front of her. She looked at it briefly and waved him away. 'I know already,' she said, her eyes still on the screen. 'Poor Dot. Mrs Meade telephoned. I'm watching to see if it's on the local news. Have you had a good day?'

Horace was furious. He'd been to London for the day, and returned on a crowded, smelly commuter train. He should have been travelling first-class, he considered, if only his depleted finances would stand it. And now Blanche had upstaged him. She'd been doing that a lot lately, and he was in a very bad humour indeed.

'I was right!' he said, and moved towards the television set, intending to turn it off. He hesitated. Perhaps Blanche would round on him again. He'd never had to worry about such things before, and he felt frustrated and helpless.

'Right about what, dear?' said Blanche, and then added immediately, 'Oh, look, Horace, there's Dot. Gosh, that was taken a while ago!'

'Listen to it, woman! I was right about your char being Dot Nimmo.' Horace now focused on the news.

'So far,' the reporter said, 'there are no clues as to who drove into Mrs Nimmo, and the Tresham police are asking for anyone who saw the accident, or can give any information, to get in touch with them as soon as possible.'

Horace sighed with what sounded to Blanche like relief. 'Is she still hanging on, then? Tough as old boots, those Nimmos. Mind you, one less might be a good thing, though you mustn't say I said that, Blanche,' he added, seeing her shocked face. 'What's for dinner?'

Mrs Smith, sitting on the sofa with Darren, was also watching television. 'Sebastopol Street,' she said. 'Isn't that where Mrs Meade's office is? Oh, yes, look, there's the sign over her office window! Well, that's interesting. Mrs Nimmo worked for New Brooms. Mrs Battersby had a woman from them, cleaning for her. I wonder if it was the same?'

At the mention of the name Battersby, Darren stiffened. 'Perhaps we'll walk round that way, shall we? We might bump into Mrs Battersby, and you'd like that, wouldn't you? Not if she's with the Colonel, of course. We could avoid them then.'

Darren looked doubtful. 'Don't want to see the big man,' he said.

'But Mrs B is all right, isn't she? She was always very kind to you. She might be upset that you never go to see her now. Come on, Darren, get your jacket on.'

Mrs Smith's curiosity was roused and, once roused, was not easily ignored. It was a sad story. The driver hadn't stopped to help Mrs Nimmo. The telly had said there was nobody about, and she knew Sebastopol was a straight street with no bends.

She locked the house door and led Darren down the path and into the Close. There were still eyes behind the curtains every time they ventured out, but Mrs Smith was used to that. She waved her hand to the neighbours in general, and continued to walk into the High Street and along towards the Battersbys' house. Darren was lagging behind, and she waited for him to catch up. A car came towards them, a familiar car with a woman driving. It slowed down and stopped.

Darren rushed up to his mother and stood behind her. She could feel him trembling.

'Hello, Mrs Smith. And Darren? Aren't you going to say hello?' Blanche smiled with genuine fondness at the lad.

'Say hello to Mrs Battersby,' Mrs Smith said, drawing Darren out and holding his hand.

''Lo, Mrs Battersby,' he said. 'Nice evenin'.'

'Would you like to come for a drive? We could talk about the garden. I miss you, and it's getting very untidy.' Blanche smiled and opened the passenger door. Darren shook his head.

'He's still a bit shocked, I think, after that nasty time when he disappeared,' Mrs Smith said protectively. She wasn't sure she wanted Darren going off with Mrs Battersby. She had no reason to distrust her, but could not forget that they had decided so readily that Darren had had a lift home from the point-to-point.

'Has he talked about it at all? Did you find out where he went?' Blanche persisted because Horace was always asking her if she'd heard anything from the gossips of Waltonby.

Mrs Smith shook her head. 'To be honest, Mrs Battersby,' she said, 'I haven't asked him after that first day. He got so upset when the police tried to get him to talk. Anyway,' she added, 'I'm just so glad to have him home safe. He seems to be getting back to normal, so you could ask him again later. He did go for a nice drive with Mrs Meade from New Brooms.

You know her, I expect? You enjoyed that, didn't you, Darren? Talking of this and that?' He nodded, saying nothing, his eyes fixed warily on Blanche. 'Anyway,' Mrs Smith continued, 'let's try again in a day or two.'

She wondered whether to mention Darren's fear of the horses and 'the big man'. She decided against it. Hopefully he would want to go back to gardening soon. He'd really liked it, and it gave her a few hours' break with time to herself. Sometimes, twenty-four hours a day with someone like Darren was hard going, however much she loved him.

Blanche shut the door and drove off with a wave. Darren ignored the wave and began to walk away quickly.

'Wait for me!' his mother called. She was never absolutely sure that Darren wouldn't suddenly step into the road straight into the path of an oncoming tractor.

The drawing room was cool and peaceful when Blanche walked in. Then she saw Horace sitting deep in an armchair, reading the newspaper.

'Where did you go? You didn't tell me you were going out. First I knew of it was when I heard the car. Not very considerate.' He looked at her sternly over the top of his glasses.

'I felt like a drive,' she said. 'You were asleep, and I didn't want to disturb you.'

'Nonsense! I never fall asleep in a chair,' Horace blustered. 'Where did you go, anyway?'

Blanche did not answer his question, but said, 'I saw Darren with his mother. Stopped and had a little chat. I offered to take him for a spin, but he refused.'

Horace lowered his newspaper, and Blanche noticed that his hands were holding it so tightly that his knuckles were white. He frowned at her and said, 'Why? He used to come with you sometimes. Did he say anything?'

Blanche shook her head. 'No, but his mother says she thinks he is still shocked from that time he went missing.'

'Has he told her where he went? Did you ask her?'

Again Blanche shook her head. 'She hasn't bothered him, apparently. Glad to have him home safely. He got very upset when the police questioned him. Can't blame her, can you? Though if I was her, I'd want to know.'

She noticed that Horace's hands had relaxed. 'Boy's an idiot,' he said, and returned to his newspaper.

Thirty-Two

The next morning Lois was about to telephone Cowgill to give him a fact or two, but he rang her first. 'Morning, Lois,' he said briskly. 'I hope you're well?'

'What d'you want?' Lois replied.

'I'm glad you're well, because I have a job for you. And no, don't say anything until you hear what it is.' Lois said nothing. 'Lois? Are you still there?'

'Yes,' she said, 'but you told me to say nothing.'

Cowgill sighed. 'All right. Now, this is what it is. I have reason to believe that a farmer called Joe Horsley—'

'Who lives at Willow Farm,' Lois interrupted.

'Yes, quite right.' Cowgill's patience was running out. 'Well, I understand from my sources that he and his wife are looking for a cleaner. I'd like you to get in there first. You can make up some tale about a recommendation.'

'No need,' Lois said smugly. 'I've been in touch with them already – or, rather, they got in touch with me. I was sending Dot Nimmo to them, but unfortunately, as you know, she's rather unwell at the moment.'

'I see. Then you are ahead of me, Lois. Let me know when you've allocated a replacement, and I'll be in touch.'

'They don't want a replacement,' Lois said. 'They only wanted Dot. I wonder if you know why?'

There was a silence, and then Cowgill said, 'If I do, then probably you do, too. Shall we meet?'

'Where?' Lois asked. 'And when? I'm very busy at the moment.'

'Ah. Of course, policemen have oodles of time to spare. Name a time and place.'

Lois thought for a moment. Then she said, 'You know the

road between Waltonby and Fletching? Just beyond the golf club there's a small spinney. You get to it across a grass field. Tomorrow, ten o'clock sharp. I'll be watching for you. And don't look for my car. I'll be parked somewhere else.'

'Yes, ma'am. Ten o'clock sharp.'

Lois signed off. She looked down at her papers, but could not concentrate on cleaning jobs and timetables. What did she most need to know? What did she know already?

First, that Battersby and Horsley were in cahoots about something. Probably illegal. Second, Battersby and the Nimmos had fallen out at some time in the past, and the Nimmos had caused the Colonel a good deal of trouble. Third, a young Nimmo had been killed, by a stray horse in dodgy circumstances. Fourth, Dot Nimmo had narrowly escaped death, and might still die, because of a hit-and-run driver.

Was it likely that Battersby was still out for revenge? Not unless he was unhinged. From what she knew of him, he was far from that.

What had she forgotten? Darren. He might have much more to say, and so far nobody had been able to coax it out of him. She could try another trip in the car, to see if he gave her a clue. It was worth a try.

At that moment, the telephone rang again. 'Hello? Oh, hello, Floss. How are you feeling?'

'Much better, thanks, Mrs M. I can start work tomorrow, the doc says. Is that all right with you, or are you fed up with me being off sick?'

'Rubbish!' Lois said. 'Hold on, and I'll tell where to go tomorrow morning. Ah, yes. Back to the Hall for you. Mrs Tollervey-Jones has been asking, and she'll be delighted to see you. Oh yes, and by the way, have you done anything more about the Battersbys' horse offer? You could go there in the afternoon, but the horse thing should be settled first.'

'Dad's fixed it. He took over, as you can imagine. All arranged, and I can go for a ride any time I like, or if I just want to go down and have a chat with Maisie, that's all right too. *And* I'm well enough to do the mucking-out.'

'Fine,' said Lois. 'In that case, could you be there at two thirty as usual? Good girl. Glad you're better. Bye.'

So that was settled. Now, she could ring the Horsleys, grit her teeth, and suggest Evelyn Nimmo, sister of Dot. That would be neat, and might even be productive. Best to wait until after she'd seen Evelyn. She might be fine, but even though she sounded good on the telephone, you never knew. She would find out at three o'clock that afternoon. After that, she would ring the Horsleys.

Lois drove into Tresham, and was in Sebastopol Street at two. Hazel was taking details from a potential client, and Lois walked through to the kitchen to make two mugs of coffee. Then she perched on a stool until she heard the client leave with a grateful goodbye.

'Hi, Mrs M,' Hazel said, taking her coffee. 'Nice to see you here in our small but exquisite headquarters in Sebastopol Street, one of the best areas in town.'

'Ha, ha. So who was that?'

'Yet another Mrs Evans from Chapel Cornyard. The Welsh must have colonized that village a hundred years ago. Now, seriously, how is Dot?'

Lois told her all she knew, including that Evelyn would be coming in shortly to be interviewed as a temporary stand-in for Dot. 'Sounds a nice woman on the telephone,' she said, 'but I'd be glad if you'd sit in. Two heads are better than one.'

'So there's still a chance that Dot might make it? Funny thing, isn't it, but I was really sorry when I heard. Awful as she is – sorry, Mrs M – there's still something likeable about her, and I reckon if you wanted a job done she'd be solid as a rock.'

'What kind of job?' Lois asked suspiciously. Hazel sat in this office all day most days, and with her friend living next door she heard a great deal about the goings-on in Sebastopol.

'Well, you know the day Dot was run over? Nobody has come forward as a witness, have they? Yet I know of at least two people who might have seen the whole thing. Two tearaways who were hanging around the video shop opposite, lounging against that fence. They were there for quite a while, Maureen says. She was watching them out of her window next door, but had to go out before the accident.'

'And *I* didn't see anything until I heard the bugger brake. But, Hazel, surely *somebody* saw them?

'Yeah. It was one of these somebodies who told Maureen there'd been two of them in the car. But none of them would talk to the police in a million years, and they'd fix anyone who did.'

'Who's "they"?'

'God knows. There's several gangs around here. I keep my head down. It's safer that way. See no evil, hear no evil, get no evil done to you. That's why nobody comes forward.'

'But what's all this got to do with Dot being solid as a rock?' Lois looked at her watch. Evelyn would be here in five minutes.

'I reckon if she gets well, she'll take on the job of finding out who ran into her, and won't rest until it's settled – one way or another! Perhaps "ruthless as an old terrier" would have been a better description.'

The door opened, and in came Evelyn Nimmo. There was little or no resemblance between the sisters. Where Dot was blonde and flashy, Evelyn was mousey and understated. She had a neat brown skirt, with good brown shoes and a cream-coloured jersey – cashmere? – long-sleeved and with a polo neck. Ninety percent of Evelyn was discreetly covered.

Lois introduced Hazel, and indicated a chair. 'Now, first of all,' she said, 'what news of Dot?'

'No news, really.' Evelyn shrugged. 'But at least she's no worse, and still holding on. It's creepy, seeing her there, alive but not alive, if you know what I mean.' She bit her lip, and Lois said that every day she held on was more hopeful. She had no idea if this was true, but Evelyn's face brightened.

They talked for ten minutes or so, and both Lois and Hazel asked a few questions. It quickly became clear that Evelyn was more than suitable for the job. In fact, Lois was worried that she might consider cleaning beneath her. 'Are you really sure that you will like this kind of work?' she asked.

Evelyn shook her head. 'Not permanently,' she said. 'But if it helps you and Dot, then I shall tackle it with a will. You'll not find any fault with me. Nimmos pride themselves on being reliable, you know.'

'Even Nimmos by marriage?' said Hazel.

Evelyn laughed. 'Especially us,' she said. 'Dot and me have been good pupils. We know what's best for us.'

Lois looked at Hazel, who gave a small nod. 'Righto, then, I am sure you will do very well, and I'm grateful for your offer. We'll take some details now, and tell you how we work and all the rules and regs. Then you can start more or less straightaway. I've got likely clients, the Horsleys, who are desperate for some help.'

She watched Evelyn's face closely, but saw no flicker of recognition of the name. But then, as Evelyn said, she and her sister had been good pupils of their Nimmo husbands.

Thirty-Three

'Good morning. Lois Meade here. Is that Mrs Horsley?' Lois had decided to make an early start on her telephone calls. Nothing more frustrating than: 'Please leave a message, etc.'

There was a pause, and she heard a whisper. 'It's for me, Joe.' Then Margaret Horsley said, 'Hello, Mrs Meade. Have you got news of Dot Nimmo?'

'Nothing much, I'm afraid, but she is still holding on, and we're all hoping against hope. No, I'm ringing to ask if you still want some help, because Dot's sister Evelyn has kindly offered to fill in for her. She's a very nice woman, and, of course, also a Nimmo.'

'Married Handy's brother,' Margaret said. 'Yes, I'm not sure I've ever met her, but I know her name. Could you hold on a minute?'

Lois said of course she would, and waited. She was sure that Margaret was asking Joe what he thought. Was one Nimmo as good as another for their purposes? Snooping purposes? Finding out more about Lois Meade?

'Are you still there, Mrs Meade? Well, I think that would be fine. I'm sure Evelyn would do a good job, if not better! When can she start?'

Lois made the arrangements, and said goodbye. Now it was all set up. She was spying on the Horsleys, and they were spying on her – and probably on several other persons unknown to Lois.

The telephone rang, and it was the tenant of the house in Tresham that Lois and Derek had ended up buying with some of the lottery money. The woman was fuming. 'I can't stand it any longer,' she said. 'All day and every day, from five o'clock in the morning. Bloody thing crows non-stop, and it's right under our bedroom window! And don't say it's up to your agents, because they told me to ring you.'

'A cockerel? In that little back yard? No wonder you're fed up. We've got a couple over the fields from us, but we tolerate that. Nice sound at that distance. Country sounds, and all that. Have you asked the neighbours to get rid of it?'

'Several times! They say it is the old man's pet. He's had it for years, and he'd be heartbroken if they got rid of it. They're lying, o' course. It only started up a couple of weeks ago. We tried ear plugs, shutting all the doors and windows, putting on our radio to drown it out. But it pierces everything. So, Mrs Meade,' she added in a forthright voice, 'unless it goes, we do. We'll pay up any rent owing, and I reckon you'll have trouble getting another tenant, unless the agents show them round in the middle of the night! Goodbye!'

Lois looked at her watch. It was nine o'clock, and she had to meet Cowgill at ten. One more call. 'Morning, Mrs Smith. Just calling to see how Darren is.'

'He's fine, Mrs Meade, thanks. We had a chat with Mrs Battersby in the street, and he seems calmer now. Even talking about gardening again!'

'D'you think he'd like to come for another drive? I've got to take Jeems to the vet this afternoon, and could pick him up on the way back. We could take Jeems for a walk by the river.'

'He'd love that! What time?

'Three o'clock-ish. Good. I'll see you then. In a bit of a dash now, so I'll see you this afternoon.'

With the crowing cockerel on her mind, Lois went into the kitchen where Gran was ironing. 'Know anybody who wants a cockerel with a loud voice?' she said.

'Are you daft? Nobody in their right minds would want a flaming cockerel. Useless things. You tell me what they're good for? Chickens don't need them to lay eggs.'

'If you're a breeder, you'd need one.'

'Yeah, and as eggs seem to have more cockerels than hens

in them, breeders can easily hatch their own. They prefer it. Keeps the breed pure.'

'How do you know so much about chickens? We never had any on the Churchill estate in Tresham.'

'I was a girl once, y'know. Had an aunt – you remember Aunt Polly –who lived on a farm. We went there for holidays, and I helped with the chickens. So there, Miss Lois! Anyway,' she added, 'haven't you got any work to do? No idle house-wives to interview?' Gran punished one of Derek's best shirts with a twist and a shake, and then began ironing it with her usual dexterity.

'I'm here in the vain hope that my dear mother might make a quick coffee for me. I have to go out in a minute or two.'

'Then make it yourself, dear daughter. You can see I'm busy.'

Lois smiled, and put on the kettle. 'I expect you'd like one?'

Gran nodded. 'Thanks. Only one sugar. I'm cutting down.'

'It's contentment makes you fat – not that you're fat,' she added hastily. 'But supposing you had a crowing cock outside. Awake at dawn, waiting for the next piercing blast, that'd soon get the weight down. I've got to do something about the tenant in Tresham, so keep your ears open for somebody living in the middle of nowhere, with a fondness for chickens. Now,' she added, draining her coffee mug, 'I must get going. Back for lunch. Thanks for your help.'

Gran watched Lois drive off at speed, and wondered how to take her last remark. Could have been a rebuke, or the reverse. Lois always was a tricky one, just like her father.

Colonel Battersby was in his den when the call came from Joe Horsley. 'Horace? Joe here. Looks like it's going to be OK. The old bat is still alive – just – and her sister Evelyn . . . Oh, you know her? Well, she's offered to help out the Meade woman until Dot revives. What? Oh yeah, there's very little chance of that. The lads did a good job. She'll have got the message all right! So I'll get to work on Evelyn and keep you posted. What? Margaret? No, she doesn't know much. And I don't want her involved. Got that? Right.' He rang off without saying goodbye, and Horace Battersby shrugged. His affair with Margaret had ended long since, and he would have thought that fool Joe would've got over it by now. Still, as long as he did what he was told, all would be well.

Blanche came in with a request. 'When will it be convenient for Floss to clean in here?' she asked. 'Now, for instance?' That sharp little extra shocked Horace. She would never have spoken like that to him before. But before what? What had changed her into this really quite uncooperative person? Dot Nimmo. That one visit from Dot Nimmo had done it. Wretched woman!

He stood up and faced Blanche. 'Why not?' he said. 'I'll have a walk round the garden and Floss can call me when she's finished. Nice to see her back, isn't it?'

Blanche, who had been waiting for the explosion, nodded and turned to go out. One up to me, thought Horace. Then Blanche stopped, looking out of the window.

'Come here, Horace! Look – isn't that Darren? He's come back!' she said, and rushed out of the room. She called to Floss that she could clean the study now, and added that she was going into the garden to speak to Darren.

He was in the walled vegetable garden, weeding an empty bed ready for planting. Blanche approached slowly, giving him time to see her coming. He straightened up, and smiled at her. 'Doing gardening,' he said. 'Lovely morning, Mrs Battersby.'

Blanche could have wept, she was so pleased to see him, gentle and confident again. 'It *is* a lovely morning, Darren. Nice to have you back.' She knew she must tread warily. It would be very easy to frighten him away again. Still, it had not been she who had frightened him before, and so she chatted to him about the weeds, and what they would plant there, and whether he would like a coffee now or later.

As she walked back towards the house, she saw Darren's mother hurrying up the drive. 'Mrs Battersby!' she said, hoarse and out of breath. 'Have you seen Darren? He's gone missing again!'

'No, he hasn't,' said Blanche quietly. 'He's in the garden, weeding. He's humming, like he used to, always the same tune. He seems very happy again.'

'Grand Old Duke of York?' Mrs Smith subsided on to a garden seat and put her face in her hands. Blanche sat beside her for a minute, saying nothing. Then Mrs Smith gave a long sigh and looked up. 'Sorry, Mrs Battersby,' she said. 'I was terrified, I don't mind telling you. Terrified he'd gone again and this time wouldn't come back. Anything could happen to him, you know, when he's on his own. When he was little, one Sunday morning we'd left the front door open, and he went out in his pyjamas and bare feet, and disappeared. I was frantic. My husband – he was still at home then – just said he'd come back sooner or later, but I went mad.'

'What happened?'

'I rang the police, and they said, well, fancy that, there was a little boy sitting on the low wall outside the police station in his pyjamas and a policewoman was on her way to collect him. It was Darren, thank God. I'm not a religious woman, Mrs Battersby, but I reckon God was looking after him that day.'

'Maybe today, too,' Blanche said gently. 'Are you happy to leave him here, then?'

Mrs Smith nodded. 'I shouldn't say this, Mrs Battersby, but could you keep the Colonel out of his way? Darren calls him "the big man", and seems very frightened of him. I am sure there's no reason,' she added hastily, 'but if it's possible . . . you know . . .'

'I'll see what I can do, and will warn my husband to be very quiet and kind to him if they do meet. Goodbye then. We'll keep an eye on him.'

'I'll be round to get him about one o'clock, if that's all right. Mrs Meade is taking him for a drive and a walk around three o'clock.' Mrs Smith patted Blanche on the hand and added, 'Thank you, my dear.'

Tears came to Blanche's eyes, and she brushed them away before going in to use all her tact in telling Horace to keep well away from Darren.

'He seemed quite his old self,' she said to her husband reassuringly. 'But we'd better handle him with care. That nice Mrs Meade is taking him out for a drive this afternoon.'

'What time?' Horace asked idly.

'Around three o'clock. Why do you want to know?'

'No reason,' he replied casually. 'Just wondered.'

Thirty-Four

Lois sat in the vet's waiting room, holding Jeems on her knee. The little dog was always well behaved, unless there was a cat in a basket, when the red mist came down and she was frantic to get at it. No cats today, so far, but just as the nurse called her in for treatment, the door opened and a snarling cat came in. It was in an old box, carried by a boy who was not more than seven years old. The lid of the box was flapping open, and in one bound the cat leapt clear. Jeems pulled away from Lois, and was on it in seconds. Two girls behind the desk rushed out, and the noise was terrifying. One of the vets – the young, keen one – came out into the waiting room, grabbed Jeems and squeezed the end of her nose hard. A terrier will instinctively lock its jaws and its victim cannot get away, but Jeems was forced to let go in order to breathe.

Lois turned to the small boy, thinking he would be in a panic. She was wrong. He obviously thought the whole thing was great entertainment. Order was restored and she helped the boy put the cat back in the box. It was unhurt, fortunately, but Jeems had a deep scratch on her nose. Lois was forced to admit that it served her right.

When she arrived to pick up Darren, she told him and his mother the story. 'That boy,' she said, 'was laughing fit to bust.' Mrs Smith laughed too, but Darren looked anxious.

'Jeems OK now?' he said, glancing out at the van.

'Oh, she's fine,' Lois said cheerfully. 'Wouldn't hurt a fly now. It's only cats that get her going. Are you ready then, Darren?'

Lois had decided to take him to Long Farnden, park the van and go for a walk in the water meadows. The river was always interesting, and Jeems could run around off the lead. Mrs Smith had told Lois that Darren did not like enclosed spaces. He panicked and tried to escape, so the open meadows should be fine. Then they could go back to Gran's chocolate cake and a cup of tea.

Walking with Darren was oddly peaceful, Lois thought, as they strolled along the river path. He did not speak unless spoken to, and the conversation was brief. She allowed her thoughts to wander, and was pleased when she felt Darren slip his arm into hers. *He must trust me*, she thought. She began to see what a huge responsibility it was for parents and siblings to care for the Darrens of this world. Such innocence and vulnerability would be hard to protect.

When they reached the road and turned for Lois's house, she put Jeems on her lead. Darren released her arm, and took hold of the lead. 'Hold Jeems?' he said. They walked back in silence, Darren beaming with pleasure. 'Better than horses,' he said, as they turned into the gate.

Lois stood still. 'What do horses do?' she asked.

'Run away,' he said, his hands twisting on the lead. 'Run away fast, and Darren can't get off.' He began to back away, and Lois caught his arm.

'No horses here,' she said. 'Only Jeems. And Gran, with nice chocolate cake.'

Darren stopped his desperate struggle to get away. 'See Gran?' he said, so quietly that Lois could hardly hear him.

She nodded. 'Gran's waiting for us,' she said, and gently persuaded him to walk with her and Jeems into the house.

Floss had finished at the Battersbys and gone home for a quick sandwich and a lecture from her mother about not doing too much. 'I'm young and strong, Mum,' she said. 'Worst possible thing for me is to lie in bed, bored to tears. I'm off now to Mrs T-J's, and shall be back about five. She'll make a fuss of me. Don't know why, but I reckon I'm the only person she likes.'

'It's the way you were brought up,' her mother said smugly.

'After tea,' Floss continued, 'I'll be going for a ride, and a cleaning and grooming session with Maisie. Ben might join me there if he gets off early enough.'

'I suppose it's useless for me to suggest an early night?'

'Quite useless,' Floss laughed, and was gone.

As she had prophesied, Floss was immediately made to sit down and have a cup of coffee and a chat with Mrs T-J before she started work.

'Are you absolutely certain, my dear, that you're fit enough to be back at work? These flu bugs are very debilitating, you know.'

'I'm fine. Really, Mrs T-J. It wasn't that bad.' She decided to change the subject, in order to avoid an account of the various flu viruses Mrs T-J had suffered in a long and active life.

'Have you heard how kind the Battersbys have been?' Floss continued. 'They've given me a lovely horse for my own, and said I can keep it in their stables. No room in our garden! I shall be going over after tea. She's a very gentle mare, and I love her already.'

This was Mrs T-J's world, and they had a gratifying conversation about horses, horse shows, point-to-points, good and bad farriers, and the price of hay.

Finally Floss looked at her watch and jumped up. 'I must get on! Mrs Meade will be on my track. She has no time for idlers!'

Mrs T-J smiled. 'Runs a good business, your Mrs Meade. I believe my friend Blanche Battersby is very pleased, even with the cleaner who filled in whilst you were ill.'

'But didn't you know?' Floss began, about to tell her about Dot's accident. Something stopped her, and she dropped a tin of polish as a distraction. 'Shall I start upstairs, as usual?' she said.

The phone rang, and Mrs T-J went off to answer it. Floss ran lightly upstairs and began to clean the bathroom. The telephone was in the big hall, and the sound echoed up to the first floor clearly. Floss did not deliberately eavesdrop, but heard Mrs T-J say in her strong, fluting voice, 'Don't be ridiculous! I'm sure he's doing nothing of the sort. Buck up, do, and I'll be with you shortly.'

Floss raised her eyebrows. Who had rattled the old duck's cage this time? She worked on with a will, thinking of the time when she could greet Maisie with a fond pat and a kiss on the nose. And much the same for Ben, should he show up.

Tea with Gran had gone off very well. Darren had eaten two pieces of sticky chocolate cake, and had not objected when Gran presented him with a damp flannel. Lois noticed that she seemed to have established an instant connection, pleasant but not sentimental, and Darren blossomed.

'Jeems ran fast,' he said.

'Dogs love to run fast,' Gran replied.

'And horses?' Lois said. Darren darted a frightened look at her.

Gran said quickly, 'Now then, lad, if you've finished your tea, I want to show you our piano. Do you like music?' His expression cleared, and he nodded at her gratefully.

'Play the piano,' he said, and got up from his chair. Gran led him into the sitting room and opened the piano lid. Lois followed, and to her amazement she saw Darren go straight up to it and strike with both hands an arbitrary and very discordant chord.

'Wow!' said Gran. 'How about a nice quiet note?'

Darren turned and looked at her. He smiled, and struck a high note very gently, holding the key down until all the reverberations had ceased. Then he turned to Lois and said, 'Go home now, Mrs Meade. Back to Mum.'

Gran came down to the gate to see them off, and Darren said, 'Thank you very much. It was very nice cake. Goodbye.'

As they drove off, Gran went back into the house, her expression sober and thoughtful. 'If I was his mother,' she said to herself, 'I would kill anybody who laid a finger on him.'

Thirty-Five

Lois decided to go a different way to Waltonby, and turned off up a little track with high banks and overhanging trees. Before they had gone a hundred yards, Darren began to bounce in his seat. 'Not right,' he said. 'Not the right way, Mrs Meade!' He was shouting now, and Lois pulled into an open gateway and stopped.

'It's not the *wrong* way,' she said. 'This is another way of going back to Mum. It goes to Waltonby, just the same. More interesting for Darren.'

But Darren continued to protest, and Lois did not want to

deliver him back to his mother in an agitated state, so she turned in the gateway and went back to take the usual road. She was about to cross at the junction, and Darren was already settling down, when a large black car came slowly from the direction of Waltonby. Lois braked hard, and reversed to allow the car to pass. It was Mrs T-J, and she waved magisterially. She was smiling, too, and Lois reckoned Floss had as usual achieved the impossible with the old tartar.

As she continued, Lois reflected that you could never take it for granted that these narrow roads were empty. She was concentrating hard, but even so, did not notice a darkish green car in the entrance to a stretch of woodland. The first she saw of it was when she was nearly level, and then it was moving fast towards her.

The impact was sudden and explosive. Lois felt her van tipping. She heard Darren scream, and after that nothing but overwhelming pain and blessed darkness.

Thirty-Six

'Must get out,' Darren muttered. He had a pain in his leg, and his head hurt where he had banged it against Lois as they tipped over. 'Mrs Meade?' he said, and then again, louder. There was no answer, and he twisted round until he could undo his seat belt. The van was on its side, in a shallow ditch. Lois was lying underneath Darren, cushioning him. He was very frightened, and tried to open the door, which was now above him. It would not move.

'Little button,' he said to himself, and managed to pull up the lock. Then he pushed with all his might and scrambled out into the road. He started to run in the direction of Waltonby, and then stopped. He could smell smoke, and looked back at the van. 'Fire!' he said in a panic, and ran back again. 'Mrs Meade!' he shouted. 'Mrs Meade, wake up!'

Lois did not stir, and with the supreme strength of panic,

Darren managed to free her from her seat belt and drag her, painfully slowly, across the seats to the door. He was propping it open with his body, and realized he would never get her out unless he could keep it open another way. He looked round and saw a pile of sticks which had been cut from the woods. Grabbing one, he pushed it under the open door. It wedged into a groove on the floor of the van, and he tested it. It held, and he smiled. 'Darren did it,' he said, and began to heave Lois out and away from the van, which was now enveloped in smoke.

He managed to get her and himself well away just in time. With a deafening roar, the van exploded, and bits of metal and plastic flew all around.

Darren sat with Lois's inert body in the edge of the wood, and watched the van burn out to a shell. 'No good now, Mrs Meade,' he said conversationally. 'Sit here for a bit, and wait for Mum to come and fetch Darren.'

Mrs Smith looked again at the clock in the kitchen. They should have been back by now, surely? She went through to the sitting room and looked out of the window. No sign of them. She tried to ring Lois's mobile, but it was dead. Perhaps Mrs Weedon would know where they were. This time she got a reply. Gran's voice was full of alarm. 'They left here ages ago,' she said. 'Where on earth have they got to?'

'I'm going to find out,' said Mrs Smith. 'I'll be in touch.'

She ran round to her neighbour, who immediately set out in her car with Mrs Smith beside her. 'Take the Farnden road,' Mrs Smith instructed. 'I know that's the way Mrs Meade usually comes.'

It was not far to the woods, and as they approached they saw the burnt-out van, still smoking. Mrs Smith's heart lurched. 'Oh my God!' she said, and swayed in her seat. Her neighbour caught her and held her up until she gained some strength. 'Quick!' she said. 'Let's run.'

In seconds they were by the smouldering wreck, and Mrs Smith's face was ashen. 'They couldn't have survived that,' she said, turning her face away. It was totally silent. Even the birds seemed to have stopped singing.

'Mum! Mum!'

Mrs Smith shot across the road and disappeared into the

trees. Her neighbour followed, hoping that she was not imagining things. She caught up and saw an extraordinary sight. Darren was sitting on the ground, his legs outstretched, with Lois's head resting on his lap. Her head was turned to one side, and she showed no signs of life. Mrs Smith stared at them, tears streaming down her face.

'Wait there! Don't move until I come back,' the neighbour said firmly, and ran back to her car. There she phoned for ambulance and police, telling them it was very urgent indeed. Then she took a rug from the back of the car and returned to the wood. She told Mrs Smith what she had done, and they wrapped the rug as best as they could around the still form of Lois, without moving her. The neighbour silently wondered how much damage had been done in Darren's desperate tugging to get her into the wood. Still, if he hadn't done so, she would have died anyway.

'Tell Mrs Weedon,' said Darren's mother suddenly. 'Could you ring her? I remember the number. I promised to let her know.'

'Let her know what? Who is she?'

'Mrs Meade's mother. I phoned her earlier. Better not tell her . . . well . . . you know . . .'

The driver of the police car had the siren going full blast as they sped through the villages. He was already going as fast as was safe in the twisting lanes, but Inspector Cowgill shouted at him, 'Can't you go any faster, for God's sake!' The driver had never seen him like this before, tense and more or less out of control.

'We're nearly there, sir,' the driver said calmly.

'I know we're bloody well nearly there,' exploded Cowgill. 'Don't you realize a couple of minutes might make all the difference?'

When they pulled up by the neighbour's car, Cowgill rushed out and into the wood. 'I think it's this side, sir,' the driver said politely. Cowgill ran back and finally found the little group sitting quietly in a huddle. He was pale, and his hands trembled as he drew back the rug from Lois and felt for her pulse. He sank back on his heels and covered his face with his hands.

At this point the ambulance came screeching up, and the

paramedic ran to where they were. 'Stand back, sir,' he said, and Cowgill stood aside. This time the paramedic held Lois's pulse point for longer, and finally looked up at Cowgill.

'She's not dead, sir,' he said quietly. 'Pulse very faint, but it's there.'

Thirty-Seven

Cowgill insisted on travelling in the ambulance with Lois, and Mrs Smith and her neigbour set off to the hospital with Darren. He had cuts and bruises, and was clearly shocked, but his mother decided that he would feel more secure with her in the car. When she realized what he had done, she was tearfully proud.

It seemed to Cowgill that the ambulance was travelling at the speed of treacle. His eyes never left Lois's face. At one point, he thought he saw her eyelids flutter. He looked enquiringly at the medic, who nodded his head, but said nothing. 'Are we nearly there?' whispered Cowgill.

'We are going fast enough,' said the medic, in an effort to reassure him. 'Another accident wouldn't be much help, would it?'

Cowgill's eyes returned to Lois. Suddenly, her eyes opened. 'What's going on?' she said faintly. 'What are you doing . . .?'

Cowgill bit his lip. 'You've been in an accident,' he said.

Her eyes closed again, and he could see a faint colour coming into her cheeks. *Thank God*, he said to himself, and reached out to take her hand. 'Probably the only chance I'll ever get,' he muttered, and the medic smiled.

As they drew up outside the hospital, Cowgill could see Derek standing outside the big doors. He rushed forward, and was held back by one of the medics as they gently unloaded Lois. Tears streamed down his face, and Cowgill was glad he had released Lois's hand. Poor sod, he thought.

'Is she . . .?' Derek could hardly speak, and Cowgill put his hand on his shoulder.

'No, she's not,' he said. 'She has regained conciousness and asked what had happened. She was perfectly sensible, and is now sleeping.' He wasn't sure about this last bit, but it sounded optimistic. If it wasn't sleep, but repeated loss of conciousness, he knew it could be more serious. He didn't see any point in telling Derek that.

After tests had been done, it was established that Lois had no major physical injuries. Her arms and legs were grazed where Darren had dragged her across the road, but miraculously there was no bleeding. No blood from her ears or nose, and, so far, no bruising around her eyes. She had awoken again and seen Derek, who was holding on to her as if he would never let go. 'Not running away,' she had said, with the ghost of a smile, and he reluctantly stood back.

'You've laid an egg on your head,' he said, from a distance.

Lois put up a hand and felt the swelling. She winced, and the nurse said that an ice pack would fix that.

Finally, the doctor turned to Derek and said, 'We'll keep her in for forty-eight hours, Mr Meade,' he said. 'Just to be sure that there's nothing we might have missed. I think she's been very lucky – I know it doesn't look like that! But whoever dragged her out of that van saved her life.'

'It was Darren Smith,' Cowgill said, and Derek scowled at him. What was he still doing here? Then he realized that of course the police would be involved. Some vehicle had tipped the van into the ditch and then scarpered.

'He's a lad with learning difficulties, but with incredible courage. He's in Accident and Emergency right now, Derek,' Cowgill continued. 'You'd probably want to have a word with him.'

'But Lois . . .?'

'She's quite safe with us. Come back as soon as you like. We shall be taking very good care of her,' the doctor said.

Cowgill and Derek went down the stairs side by side, and found their way through the tortuous corridors of the hospital to A & E. 'There he is,' said Cowgill, 'and that's his Mum.'

Darren's scratched face brightened when he saw Derek. 'Good afternoon, Mr Meade,' he said, with his well-learned politeness.

Derek sat down beside him. 'Hallo, lad,' he said. 'I can see you've been in a fight!'

'No! Not fight,' said Darren, looking anxious. Then he saw the joke, and laughed. 'White van tipped over,' he said. 'Mrs Meade asleep. Fire in the van. Darren got out. White van no good now. Mrs Meade awake?'

'Yes,' Derek said gently, and wondered how he would have coped if he'd had to tell Darren that Mrs Meade would not wake up ever again. 'Thanks to you, Darren,' he added. 'You saved her life.'

Darren smiled tentatively, not sure what this meant, nor whether it was a good thing.

Derek tried again. 'The fire would have taken Mrs Meade away from us. But you got her out of that van, and now we still have her. Thank you very much.'

Now Darren understood. 'Fire nearly killed her,' he said, and nodded.

Cowgill, who had been standing behind Derek, came forward and said, 'I'm afraid it means more questions, Mrs Smith, but we'll see when the doctor thinks Darren will be ready to talk to us.'

A nurse came for Darren, and Derek made his way back upstairs. Cowgill walked out of the hospital and saw his driver waiting patiently. He got into the car and said nothing. After five minutes or so, as they headed for the police station, Cowgill said, 'Sorry I was out of order. You'll be glad to know Mrs Meade is going to be all right, the doctor is pretty sure.' Then he added with a deep sigh, 'God, what a day!'

Thirty-Eight

Next morning, flowers arrived at the Meades' house, and Gran pulled herself together sufficiently to put them all in water. Derek had said there was no point in her going in to see Lois, as she would be home the next day. Also, he said, the doctor had prescribed bed rest for two days, and she must be kept quiet.

'I *am* her mother,' Gran had said, but seeing the state Derek was in, she agreed to wait until Lois came home. Meanwhile, she cleaned the house from top to bottom, until it smelt strongly of polish and disinfectant, as if Lois would be so fragile that all her immunity to marauding bacteria would have been destroyed. Anyway, it gave her something to do.

Hazel in New Brooms' office had been told, and she had instantly become super-efficient, informing all the others and taking on the running of the business. 'Just give me a bell if you need anything,' she had said. 'We must do everything we can to set Mrs M's mind at rest.'

Josie had set off for the hospital the moment she was told, without consulting Derek, and sat with her mother, holding her hand and saying nothing. There was no need. Lois drifted in and out of sleep, and when she saw Josie there, she smiled. When a nurse suggested it was time for Lois to be examined again, Josie left, blowing tearful kisses as she went.

The first the village knew of the accident was when Josie put up a notice on the shop door, saying 'Closed due to family crisis'. This sent the Farnden network of gossips into a frenzy, and one hour later they all knew the details of the smash, of the van being destroyed, of Lois hanging between life and death. This last detail had become magnified as it was passed from mouth to mouth.

After a troubled night's sleep, Josie had telephoned the police station and asked to speak to Matthew Vickers. 'What is it in connection with, please?' said the receptionist.

'Just put me through,' Josie said fiercely, and Rob, standing by her side, reflected that she was definitely her mother's daughter.

'Good morning, can I help?' Matthew's voice was warm and friendly. Rob could hear every word he said. Josie breathed deeply, and felt reassured. She explained what had happened, and said she would like to be sure that the police were pulling out all the stops to catch the villains.

'So sorry about all this, Josie,' he said, in an even warmer voice. 'We shall be on to them very soon. All of us, especially the Chief Inspector, will work hard to find the people involved. Don't worry,' he added. 'I'll pop in and see you later. I enquired about your mother, and, as you will know, it

seems she is making good progress. Chin up, me duck, as
they say around here . . . Bye, Josie.'

'Why did you ask to speak to him and not Cowgill?' Rob
asked suspiciously.

'Because Cowgill gives nothing away. Ever,' she said firmly.
'Matthew has called in at the shop once or twice, and seems
very approachable.'

Rob said nothing, but thought a lot. First-name terms, and
calling in at the shop once or twice. Or three or four times?
He put his arm round Josie, claiming her. 'Let's go and open
the shop, shall we?' he said. 'Best to keep busy.' He hugged
her close, and his eyes were watchful.

Evelyn Nimmo had heard the news from Hazel, and, after
saying all the right things, had rung off and sat quite still,
thinking. She was due to go for the first time to the Horsleys,
and Mrs M had intended to meet her there to introduce her.
Hazel had said would she be willing to go on her own. If not,
she would shut up shop for an hour and be with her.

'Good gracious, no!' Evelyn had answered. 'I shall be
perfectly fine. You can't be married to a Nimmo for thirty
years without being ready for anything! P'raps you could ring
and explain to them. It'll make no difference to me. Give Mrs
M my best, won't you.'

Later, when Evelyn drove into Horsleys' farmyard, she saw
that the kitchen door was open and a woman stood there. 'Mrs
Nimmo?' Margaret smiled and came forward. 'I had a call
from your office. So sorry to hear about Mrs Meade. Sounds
as if she is lucky to be alive.'

Joe Horsley appeared behind Margaret. 'Morning,' he said
gruffly. 'Is she expected to live?'

Evelyn flinched at the blunt question, but said, 'Oh, yes,
she's tough, is the boss. Now,' she added, turning to Margaret,
'do you mind showing me what you want me to do? Where
to start, and all that? Thanks very much.'

Joe disappeared behind a barn, and Margaret led the way
into the kitchen. Evelyn looked around at the pine units and
greeny-grey slate surfaces, gadgets galore, and a ginger cat
sitting on the sunny windowsill, looking out of the window.
A place for everything, and everything in its place, thought
Evelyn.

'Oh, I love cats,' she said, and put out a hand to stroke it. Margaret laughed. 'Not very fluffy, is he?' she said, and Evelyn realized it was a perfect pottery cat, with expressionless green glass eyes. Where were the real farm cats? Outside, no doubt, in their proper place. They moved into a luxuriously furnished room, with cream leather chairs and heavy drapes drawn back with silk rope ties. 'This is the drawing room,' Margaret said.

'It's lovely.' Evelyn was impressed. 'It'll be a pleasure to work in here,' she said, silently wondering if muddy Joe would ever be allowed to sit down.

The rest of the house gave the same impression of money lavishly spent. As far as Evelyn could see, there was no dirt, no dust, the furniture shone and the silver sparkled. Never mind, she could stretch out the time along with the best. She set to work.

By lunchtime, the Horsley house was even more immaculate than before. Margaret thanked Evelyn profusely, and said she would look forward to seeing her next week.

'By the way,' she said, 'how is your sister? Has she regained consciousness yet?'

Evelyn shook her head. 'No, she's much the same. We are all very worried about her. Strange, isn't it,' she added, 'that Dot and Mrs M were both in car accidents? Makes you wonder if it was more than a coincidence.' She had no idea why she said this, except that the thought had just come into her head.

'There's car accidents every day, thousands of them,' Margaret said. 'Just an unlucky coincidence, I'm sure.'

'What is?' said Joe, coming into the kitchen and leaving black footprints all over the tiles Evelyn had just cleaned.

'Never mind, dear. Not important,' said Margaret. 'Now please go outside and take off those muddy boots! Poor Evelyn has just got the tiles looking like new.'

'Bugger that,' said Joe, not moving. 'I asked you what is an unlucky coincidence.'

Evelyn was beginning to wish she had not said it. Joe looked furious, and Margaret backed away from him. Better put it right as soon as possible.

'It was me, Mr Horsley,' she said. 'I just said it was strange that both my sister and my boss were involved in car accidents. Nothing more than that. I am sure it's nothing sinister,' she added, attempting to make light of it.

'Sinister! Of course it's not bloody sinister! Typical Nimmo . . . Quite a reputation, you lot.' He turned on his heel, and slipped on the still wet floor, going down with a crash. 'Get her out of here!' he yelled at Margaret. 'Look what you've done now!'

Evelyn left, angry and determined never to darken the Horsley door again. But Margaret followed her out to her car, and said, '*Please* don't be cross. He doesn't mean it. He knows he's in the wrong, and that's when he loses his temper. I am sure he'll apologize when you come next week. You will come, won't you?'

Evelyn glared at her. How did Dot put up with these people? She sighed. This was her first job with New Brooms, and Mrs M might think she'd messed it up. 'Oh, all right, then,' she said. 'But better keep him out of my way.'

She drove off, and saw Margaret standing disconsolately, watching her go.

'It was the sister, bloody woman,' Joe was saying into the telephone. He rubbed his backside and Margaret laughed.

'Plenty to cushion the fall,' she said, and began making sandwiches for lunch. 'Who was that?' she asked when Joe had hung up.

'Mind your own business,' he said, still in a foul mood.

'Horace Battersby, I suppose. What are the pair of you cooking up now?'

Joe ignored her. 'Don't fix up anything for tomorrow,' he said. 'I'm going to Beecham Cross point-to-point. And no, you can't come. Find yourself a chum to go shopping – spending my money is your favourite therapy.'

'You're welcome to a field full of chinless wonders, tramping up and down in ankle-deep mud. And as for money, you'd better watch it. The Colonel was always a serious gambler. But still, you know that, don't you? And as for your encouraging conversation with Evelyn Nimmo, you really put your great big foot in it. Who was it that wanted Dot Nimmo to come in the first place? And who was it agreed that Evelyn would be just as useful?'

He glared at her, but said nothing. She continued, 'Never again, Evelyn said, but thanks to me and some tactful buttering-up, she's agreed to forget it.' That wasn't quite true, but his face brightened.

'Thanks,' he said grudgingly, and stamped out into the yard, where it had begun to rain heavily.

Thirty-Nine

E arly next morning, Evelyn received a call. She couldn't believe her ears.

'Evelyn? How did you get on at the Horsleys?' It was Mrs M's voice, clear as a bell.

It couldn't be. It must be her daughter, Josie.

'Who is that, please?' she said.

'Who d'you think it is?' the voice said sharply, and Evelyn knew for sure that it was Mrs M.

'Where are you, Mrs M, and shouldn't you be resting?'

'Never mind about resting. Answer me quickly, before that bossy nurse comes round and tucks me up again. Were they all right with you?'

Evelyn hesitated, then said, 'She was. Very nice. Almost creepy. But he was foul, rude and unpleasant. I nearly said I'd not be back, not for all the tea in China. But then I thought of you, and agreed to go next week if he apologizes. He was going to the point-to-point at Beecham Cross, so let's hope he won some money to cheer him up.'

'Tomorrow? Oh, today. Bugger it. I should be going. Still, I hope to be let out today. You did right, Evelyn, thanks. Uh oh! Here she comes. See you later.'

Evelyn hung up, and sat down, feeling quite shocked. She was sure Mrs M shouldn't be back in business so soon. Perhaps she should ring Mr Meade? Or Mrs Weedon? No, probably not. If Mrs M was coming home today, they would make her take care.

Lois sat on the edge of her bed, sipping a cup of weak tea, and thinking. She remembered nothing about the accident, but was assured that her memory of that would return. But she did recall that she had been intending to get Derek to take her to Beecham Cross. It was coming back to her, something that Mrs Smith had said about the Battersbys taking Darren to a point-to-point a couple of times.

So what was their ulterior motive? Horace always had an ulterior motive. One of the last things she remembered before the accident was her intention to ask Darren if he liked point-to-point racing, and to suggest that he might like to go to one with her and Derek. She looked at her watch. After the doctor's round, she would ring Derek to fetch her at once. They might just have time, but even she realized they could not, under the circumstances, take Darren. No, she would talk to Derek right now.

'What!' he said. 'Are you mad?'

She spent the next five minutes persuading him, and then the doctor came into the ward, and she said she'd ring him back as soon as possible.

'We are very pleased with your progress, Mrs Meade,' the doctor said kindly. 'You will be able to go home this morning, if your husband can fetch you? I expect you're anxious to get back and see what kind of a mess he's made of the house!'

Lois shook her head and tried to smile. 'No, my mother lives with us, and she keeps everything tickety-boo. They'll have the red carpet out!'

The doctor nodded. 'Jolly good,' he said. 'And just take it easy for a week or two. Sometimes problems arise, small ones, and you have to be sensible.'

'Oh, I'll be sensible,' said Lois. 'And thanks very much for all you and the nurses have done for me.' She stood up, and began to collect her things together.

'Hey, slow down!' said the bossy nurse, and the doctor laughed.

'She's right, you know. Just watch it, Mrs Meade!'

Derek was in the ward about an hour later. 'What kept you?' Lois asked.

'You'll see,' Derek said, and took her bag from her. 'Take my arm, and we'll walk slowly. And just do what you're told,' he added as she set off at a good pace. 'Do you need to thank anybody?'

'All done,' said Lois. 'And what do you mean by saying I'll see why you took so long?'

'You'll see,' he repeated firmly.

When they emerged from the hospital and began to walk to the car park, Lois felt as if her legs had turned to jelly. 'Can we stop for a minute?' she said. Derek looked anxiously at her, then he shouldered her bag and picked her up as if she was a sickly child.

'Blimey!' said Lois, snuffling into his ear. 'Talk about a knight in shining armour!'

He got her safely to the van, a temporary replacement since the crash, and set her down. First he opened the rear doors, and she said she hoped he didn't think she was travelling in the back, however comfy he had made it.

'Come and look,' he said, pointing. She peered in, and saw it. A wheelchair!

'Where the hell did you get that?'

'Borrowed it from Ivy Beasley,' he said. 'She still had it from when she broke her leg. She sent you a couple of caustic messages I won't repeat. Anyway, I'm not taking you to Beecham Cross unless you go in that.'

'What, all the way? I'll not make the last race.'

'Ha ha. No, I'll push you around, and you can do whatever it is that makes it so important to disobey everything that's been said.'

'I do love you, Derek,' Lois said. 'In spite of what might seem to the contrary.'

He laughed, and helped her into the passenger seat. 'Gran put some stuff together for a picnic, so we can go straight there,' he said. 'I might say she nearly went on strike at the thought, but I said that you'd probably get there somehow, so it might as well be with me. So relax, me duck, and enjoy the show.'

The sun had come out from behind dark clouds, and Lois took several deep breaths. She had been told she was lucky to be alive, and looked with new eyes at the green and pleasant landscape as they drove along at a circumspect speed. If only she could remember what happened. But she had been told not to worry about it. She settled back in the seat, and tried to recall the last time she had been to a point-to-point. That was easy. Her father had taken her, when she was about fifteen. She had been reluctant to go, but he'd said it would be fun. She'd be surprised. And there'd be plenty of young farmers about, whooping it up.

Dad had been right. It had been fun, and the horses and
hounds had been wonderful, exciting, dangerous creatures.
They didn't see many horses on the Churchill Estate in
Tresham. Plenty of dogs there, but not all matching, and some
that were quite difficult to love. They were not ones that
obeyed a man on a horse.

Beecham Cross was in the heart of Buckinghamshire, and
enclosed in a great curving stretch of wooded hills. In the
other direction, the fertile Aylesbury Vale stretched out to the
horizon, quintessentially English, with its small fields and
hedges, dignified beech trees and farms nestling among modern
farm buildings. The Meades could see rows of parked cars in
a field on the right, and the race course with a clutch of
marquees and other cars on the left. Through Derek's open
window they could hear the public address system making
blurred announcements, impossible to understand as always.

They were there in good time, and looked at the parking
charges. 'Twenty pounds to be near the course, twelve pounds
for the field,' read Derek out loud. He turned into the left gateway.

'Hey, that's the wrong turning,' Lois said. 'Twelve pounds
is over there.'

'I'm not pushing a wheelchair over a hayfield,' said Derek.
'In any case, there'll be special parking for the disabled.'

He was right, and Lois felt a complete fraud. They sat for
a while, eating Gran's picnic. She discovered she was hungry,
and set to work on ham sandwiches in new bread with plenty
of mustard, homemade sausage rolls and bananas. They shared
the big flask of coffee, and then Derek got out and repacked
the basket. He opened up the back and assembled the wheelchair, and then put out a hand to help her out. She did her best
to look frail, and sat down with a thump in the wheelchair.
Derek put a small rug over her knees, and she began to push
it off. 'More convincing,' he whispered in her ear, and pulled
it up again. The grass had been well-flattened by feet beating
a path from the ring to the bookies, and they joined the crowd.

Standing in a queue by the row of bookies with unlikely
names like Tim Fruit, Joe Winalott, and Reg Champion, Lois
saw a tall, slim young chap in cavalry twill trousers and tweed
jacket. His field glasses were slung over his shoulder, his
tobacco-brown felt hat, a little battered, was pulled forward
over his eyes. 'Young farmer,' she said to herself.

'What did you say, me duck?' Derek said, leaning over her. She would have to get used to turning her head round so that he could hear. 'I said there's a young farmer. I met one once. They all look the same. Mind you, I fancied him. My dad introduced me.'

'Your dad wasn't a farmer,' Derek said.

'Oh, never mind,' said Lois. 'Will you wheel me along up to the ring? I want to hear what people are saying.'

'I expect there's a special place reserved for wheelchairs,' Derek said.

'Not for me,' said Lois. 'I want to be among the crowd.'

The horses were pacing round the ring, led by an assortment of lads and girls, one of them having difficulty controlling an excitable horse. Lois thought again of how she felt that time with Dad. Here was power – shiny, rippling muscle power – and she had a sudden wish to be up on that dark bay, knees gripping its sides, hands holding reins that controlled the bit in its mouth and kept it steady. Moving up and down with the powerful creature beneath her.

She laughed out loud. Of course, that was what it was all about. Power, the excitement of danger . . . and sex.

'Can you see all right, duckie?' An elderly man, short and bent, with a silver-topped stick, looked down at her. 'Is hubby going for a race card? Here, borrow mine while he goes. Over there,' he added to Derek, pointing to a trestle table with cardboard boxes full of booklets.

'Thanks,' Lois said, smiling up at the man. 'Is this the first race?'

He nodded. 'D'you want a tip from me? I'm a dab hand at this, y'know. Been going to all the races for years. Not much else to do at my time o' life. Now, let me show you.' He pointed out the lists of horses, showed her the names of owners and trainers and, on the right-hand side, the jockeys. He pointed to the tiny print at the end of each entry. 'That's its form,' he said. 'Won ten points at Hunter chase; beat Hot Socks at Fakenham. That's what the horse has done.'

'Is that good?' Lois asked, twinkling at him. He had very blue eyes, and a kindly face. He reminded her of someone.

'Not bad,' he said. 'Hubby's in a long queue, I'm afraid. Would you like me to put a bet on that one for you?'

'How much?' said Lois.

'Five pounds. Don't go mad!' said the man, taking her money. He limped away, chuckling.

Derek returned with the race card and handed it her. 'I hope you can find your way around it,' he said. 'Looks like double Dutch to me.'

Lois smiled a superior smile. 'I'll explain it,' she said. 'I've got a bet on already. Nice old man has gone to do it. Says the horse is a dead cert.'

'Did you give him money?' said Derek, looking alarmed.

'Yep, a fiver. Kind of him, wasn't it.'

'You'll not see that fiver again, even if the horse wins,' Derek said gloomily.

Forty

B y the second race, Derek was beginning to find his way about. He had been wrong about the helpful old man. He had returned with Lois's winnings – 'Got you four to one,' he'd said proudly – and continued to show them around. There were small marquees for ice-creams and strong-smelling burgers, a large marquee where the jockeys went in and out, an enclosure labelled 'Owners, Riders and Officials Only', and a mysterious betting agency that inexplicably announced it did not take bets for point-to-points. 'Betting on other races in other places,' explained the old man, adding, 'Hey! I'm a poet and don't know it!'

'My dad used to say that,' said Lois. Funny, she thought, how her dad kept surfacing today. Must be the bang on the head. Derek asked her about every five minutes if she was feeling all right, and of course she said she was fine. But she had to admit to herself she had a strange floating feeling, as if she was a couple of feet above the ground. Well, come to that, she was! Sitting in a wheelchair was exactly that. She settled for this, but knew it wasn't the whole reason.

'Push me up to the bookies, will you?' she said to Derek. 'I want to have a look.'

It was while they were waiting in the queue that she saw them. Joe Horsley and Horace Battersby, in close conversation with the bookie right at the end of the line. Lois peered through people's legs. She could just see the bookie's name for a second, in firmly chalked letters: Trusty Clarkham. He was shaking his head and waving them away. They moved on to the next, and this time money changed hands, and they received tickets. Then they walked away, grim-faced.

'Did you see them, Derek?' she said, remembering to turn around to face him.

'See who?'

'Battersby and Horsley,' she said.

'Sounds like a gents' outfitters,' said Derek with a chuckle. 'Oh yeah, I can see them over there now. Standing by the ring, watching the jockeys mount. Miserable-looking pair.'

'Can we keep an eye on them?' Lois said. 'Watch to see if they go to collect winnings after the race?'

'Sure,' said Derek. 'At your service, Mrs M.'

Lois wanted desperately to stand up. She couldn't see much once the race started, except horses' legs flashing by. She and Derek had both bet on the same horse, Good Start, number four. The old man had said it did well at Cottenham, and had a chance. The odds weren't very good, and just before the race started, it was favourite to win.

They decided to have a splash, and put on ten pounds each.

For Lois, it was a case of listening to the commentary, which was good, once you got used to it. Good Start seemed to be going well. It cleared the fences ahead of the field, and was coming up to the last jump. Suddenly the crowd chorused 'Ahh!' and the commentary told her that Good Start, number four, had fallen. Apparently the rider was not hurt, at least not seriously. He was running clear of the horses, but Good Start was lying still on the ground, and the trailing jockeys were steering their mounts clear of him.

'Sod it!' shouted Lois, causing heads to turn in her direction.

Derek was more philosophical. 'Better luck next race,' he said. 'Mind you,' he continued, 'punters who backed the winner will be pleased – an outsider at twenty to one! Good Start was the favourite.'

'It's dogs next,' Lois said grumpily. 'The dogs are racing, it says here. Look, it says Hound Race, winning owner will receive a purse of four hundred pounds.' She continued to read, and then laughed.

'What's funny?' Derek said, glad she had cheered up.

'Listen to this: "Dolly, five years, dozy old girl, but wakes up in time." There's several like that. Looks like it could be fun.'

Derek could see that a vehicle had arrived next to Good Start, who had not moved. Derek decided not to tell Lois he'd overheard someone say the horse was dead.

After an interval, while Derek went off to buy ice-creams and Lois got into conversation with some children who had a small terrier just like Jeems, the hounds had come into the ring, kitted out with coats bearing their numbers, and led by the huntsman carrying a hunting horn. Lois held out her hand as they passed by her. One stopped, number three, and sniffed her hand, then moved swiftly on as the huntsman called her name: Snowdrop.

'Derek!' she said loudly.

'I'm watching out for you-know-who!' he yelled back.

She didn't answer, but reflected he'd not be much good as a discreet Dr Watson. Finally the hounds left the ring, led by a blast from the horn, and disappeared off to their start, halfway round the course.

Lois decided to try wheeling herself up to the bookies. She was determined to back Snowdrop. The old man materialized out of the crowd, and began to push her. 'I can manage!' she said sternly. He was too old to push a heavy wheelchair.

Then Derek turned up with ice-creams and took over. 'Very kind of you,' he said.

'Fancy any of the hounds?' the old man said to Lois.

'Number three, Snowdrop,' she said confidently.

'Good choice,' he said, nodding. 'She knows what she's doing. Alert. Good choice,' he repeated.

'I saw those two miseries,' Derek said to Lois. 'Collecting a fistful. They saw me, but I don't suppose it matters.'

'I don't want them to see *me*!' said Lois. 'Can I borrow your cap?' She pulled it down well over her eyes. 'Bit of a headache from the sun,' she said to the old man, when he noticed.

'You look very pretty, even in that old cap,' he said gallantly, then turned to Derek. 'Don't worry,' he said. 'I'm too old to be a danger to Mrs Meade.'

Finally Snowdrop was declared the winner, after the pack had milled about, lost the scent and gone the wrong way, raising guffaws from the crowd. 'Told you, didn't I ? the old man said. 'She knew what she had to do,' he crowed, and disappeared.

After they'd collected their winnings, Lois said she'd like to go home. 'But it's the ladies' race next,' said Derek. He had looked forward to seeing the girls in their bum-hugging britches.

'I'd rather go now,' Lois said. 'I think I've done enough.'

Derek agreed instantly, and pushed her over to the van. 'In we go,' he said, and when they had gone a mile or so, Lois turned to him.

'Derek, did you tell that old man our name?'

He shook his head. 'No, why?' he said.

'Because he said he was too old to be a danger to Mrs Meade. So how did he know my name?'

About five miles from home, Derek slowed and stopped. 'What's up?' Lois said.

'I need a pee,' he said, and got out of the van. He disappeared through a gateway into a field, and Lois idly switched on the radio. She sat back and listened to soothing music, and just as Derek emerged again from the hedge, a familiar four-by-four drove slowly by. It was a narrow road, and the vehicle almost scraped the van. Lois had a good view of the occupants, and saw that the Colonel was driving, by his side was Joe Horsley, and in the back – she gasped – was surely the nice old man? He saw her, too, and a look of horror crossed his face. Then they were gone.

'Derek! Did you see that? Did you see the old man in the back of Battersby's car?'

He shook his head. 'Too busy avoiding the nettles. Are you sure?'

'Dead sure,' said Lois. 'Mystery solved. He knew my name from his dodgy friends, Horace and Joe. But why?'

'Wasn't that Meade's van?' Colonel Battersby's question was addressed to Joe, and his voice was sharp.

Joe nodded. 'He was just coming out of the field gate, and she was sitting in the passenger seat. Arthur, did you see them?' He turned round to the old man, who shook his head. 'Not really,' he said nervously.

'More importantly,' said the Colonel, 'did the woman see you?'

'I had my head turned away,' Arthur lied. 'She wouldn't have known it was me.'

'I hope not,' Battersby grunted. 'To get to business,' he continued, 'what did you find out? Did she mention us at all? Had she seen us?'

Arthur had liked Lois a lot. He'd liked Derek, too. He made a quick decision. In for a penny, in for a pound. 'No, don't think so. Neither of them said anything about either of you. She couldn't see much, anyway, from that wheelchair. I took them to a bookie up the other end of the line.'

'So what did you find out?' Joe sounded more conciliatory. 'Was she badly hurt? Did she mention the accident, or say if she knew who'd done it?'

'She'd lost her memory, or at least couldn't remember anything about the accident. She'd been told that sometimes it never comes back.' Lying was easy, he found, in these circumstances.

'The boy, then,' the Colonel said to Joe. 'He's the dangerous one now. Didn't lose conciousness, apparently. He's dim, but not that dim. So you know what to do.'

Forty-One

' Well, Dad,' said Margaret, 'did you enjoy the races? Win anything?'

Arthur shook his head. 'Mug's game,' he said. 'Stay well clear of it, Megs.'

'Still, it was a lovely afternoon, beautiful horses, very jolly hounds race, wasn't it, Arthur?' Joe did his best to put a smile on his father-in-law's face. 'And Horace and me won enough to cover the outing. Now then, have we got the kettle on? Your father and me are desperate for a cup of tea.'

Arthur brightened. 'And a piece of that jam sponge we had yesterday,' he said.

'You can take the rest back with you tomorrow, if you like,' Margaret said with a fond smile. 'Unless you want to stay a few more days? You're very welcome.'

'No thanks, Megs dearie,' he said. 'Got a big bridge match at the club on Monday, so I have to be back.'

Margaret's mother had died five years ago, and her father had insisted on staying in the bungalow on his own. Neighbours were kind, and he was in good shape himself, apart from being a little bent over – widower's hump, he called it. They'd lived in Tresham for years, so he had plenty of friends. He could have stayed a few more days. The bridge match was not, in fact, until Friday. But he couldn't stand Joe. Never could, not from the day Megs had brought him home to meet them. He didn't trust him, and with good reason. One or two dodgy racing deals involving the Colonel and Joe had also involved him, though he'd never been told the full details. Just as much as he needed to know to be useful. Why hadn't he said no? Why? Because of Margaret. He knew she wasn't one hundred percent happy with Joe, and he didn't want to make it worse.

If he had known it was something criminal, of course he would have refused. He didn't ask himself how he would have known. Then there was this thing with the Meades. He knew there had been an accident, and that Mrs Meade had been hurt. The Colonel had said he wanted Arthur to find out as much as possible from that nice woman, as she was the boss of the cleaning agency that his wife used. They were wondering if the whole business would fold, if the boss was badly hurt, and then Blanche would be desperate for cleaning help.

Arthur thought privately that it would do the woman good to do it herself, instead of swanning about doing good works. Megs was a different matter. She was a farmer's wife, and was always saying she worked as hard as Joe on the farm. She really needed the help. By the time he'd arrived yesterday, the Nimmo woman had gone, but he'd gathered she'd be coming again. Something had happened, but he didn't ask what. Megs and Joe had been cool with one another, but that was nothing new. No, he'd be happier back in his own home.

He wondered who the dim boy was. The one they said would be the danger. Danger to what? And what was Joe deputed to do to fix it? He suddenly had a compulsion to be away from the farm, back in Tresham. Away from Joe, really. He loved his daughter deeply, and would do anything to help her. But he'd had enough of all this cloak-and-dagger stuff, with meaningful looks and cryptic conversations. He had no time at all for that Colonel. It must have been hell serving under him.

'I'll be getting along after tea,' he said firmly. 'Got a bit of watering to do in the greenhouse. You won't mind, Megs?'

He saw from her face that she did mind, but she said, 'Of course, Dad, it's up to you.'

Next day, Sunday, Joe went off early, saying he'd be out all day. Fishing, he said, though Margaret noticed he had left most of his fishing gear in the tack room. 'Will you be home for supper?' she'd asked, and he had grunted. It could have been yes or no, and she couldn't be bothered to ask. She decided it would be a good day to visit her aunt over at Waltonby, and, with any luck, bump into Horace and humiliate him in front of his wife. She knew now that she could never undo the hold he had over Joe, but that wouldn't stop her sticking pins into him as often as possible. She stacked the dishwasher, rang her aunt, and was ready to set off by half past ten. 'I'll be there in time for coffee,' she had said, 'and don't worry about lunch. Dad's gone home early, and I've got stacks of food left. D'you fancy shepherd's pie and apple crumble?' Her rheumatic old aunt had enthused over this plan, and Margaret drove off down the track feeling cheerful, glad that *someone* would be pleased to see her.

Auntie Eileen was a nice old lady, not at all the stereotypical bitter spinster who had never managed to catch a man. She lived next door to the school, and claimed she'd known more children than anyone else in the village. Every afternoon, when the children came out of school, now always accompanied by an adult, she stood at her gate with her small Yorkie dog, and greeted them as they danced by, pleased to be released from school. In the old days, of course, the children were unaccompanied, and she'd had a tin of boiled sweets by the gate for those who looked miserable or bullied. Couldn't do that now, she reflected as she stood waiting for Margaret. I'd probably be arrested.

It wasn't often her niece remembered her, but her visit was no less exciting for that, and when the car drew up, Eileen opened the gate and walked stiffly out to meet her.

Conversation was never difficult with Auntie Eileen. Margaret was fascinated by her encyclopedic memory of the family history, and when that topic was exhausted, goings-on in Waltonby and all the villages around kept the two of them happily occupied until Margaret dished up the shepherds pie.

'So what's the hot gossip from Battersby Towers?' Margaret asked, with a conspiratorial grin. Her aunt had been the only one to know about Margaret's affair with Horace, and she had strongly disapproved. But when the Colonel had been so cruel in ending it, she had swung round to defend Margaret in private and deny all rumours in public.

'Much the same as ever,' she answered. 'They've sold most of the horses, but kept one for a girl who comes to clean. She comes of a reasonably good family, and apparently loves cleaning other people's houses. I often see her on a very nice mare, ambling round the village. Pretty girl.'

'From New Brooms?' said Margaret, suddenly interested. 'You know, the agency run by Mrs Meade from Long Farnden?'

'That's the one,' Eileen said. 'Lois Meade was in a car accident recently, with that simple boy Smith who lives in the council houses. He apparently saved her life, so his mother is saying. Nice lad, but frightened of his own shadow. Does a bit of gardening for the Battersbys, and likes Blanche. But folk have seen him turn tail and run away from the Colonel, and I can't say I blame him. You'd have done better to run away, Margaret,' she added with a sly smile.

'That's as may be,' she said. 'But tell me more about the boy. If he's that scared, how did he manage to save that woman's life? Didn't her van go up in smoke? Don't tell me he fetched buckets of water from the stream and quelled the fire!'

Auntie Eileen didn't smile. 'He dragged her out of the van, and away into the edge of the wood, where they would be safe,' she said. 'Neither you nor I, Margaret, know how much that cost him. He was bruised and cut, and has lost what little self-confidence he had.'

'Sorry,' Margaret said. 'Don't mock the afflicted, as Frankie Howard used to say. So what else is going on? No, don't tell me until after I've fetched the apple crumble. I made it with ground almonds, specially for Dad, but yesterday he couldn't get away fast enough. He and Joe don't get on, though Dad does try. They'd been to a point-to-point, and Dad was upset when he came back. God knows what had been going on.'

'Arthur was always a good soul,' Eileen said. 'Your mother was a lucky lady, and she knew it. How's he managing without her?' She began to tuck in to her pudding with gusto.

'He keeps going, joins things and helps people out when he can. But the light's gone out of his life, and it feels like he's just coasting along until they meet again.'

Eileen nodded. 'At least I'm used to living alone. Always have, so it's nothing different. And . . .' She stopped and pointed to the window. 'Look,' she said, 'there goes Darren Smith, with his mother. He's carrying gardening tools, so they're probably going up to the allotment. Best one on the field, so they say. At least the lad's got green fingers, if nothing else. I wonder what'll become of him? His mum won't last for ever.'

Margaret got up and peered out of the window. 'He's thin, isn't he? Looks like a puff of wind would blow him away. Sorry, Darren,' she added quietly. 'I didn't mean to be unkind. It's too easy, isn't it, Auntie, to be cruel?'

Forty-Two

If Joe had wanted to divulge his real destination that Sunday, he would have been mildly surprised by the coincidence. A family day for both of them. He had in fact gone into Birmingham to visit his sister. He hadn't mentioned it, because Margaret loathed her. She was an unmarried mother of twin boys, and, as Auntie Eileen would have said, no better than she should be. Joe's sister was an ageing woman with a long career of prostituting herself. She had few clients now, and regarded herself as retired. The two boys had been the result of a temporary liaison with a local bank manager, who had kept her in reasonable comfort for about five years, and things had been going well until his wife found out. So that was the end of that, and she'd had to bring up the boys herself, keeping all three of them with what she could earn on the streets. A monthly cheque had also arrived in the post from the bank manager, until she saw in the local paper that he had died on the golf course. Heart attack, the report said, and she had thought wryly that he'd clearly found his nightly exercise somewhere else.

It was a run-down part of the city, and in spite of a few spindly trees and vandalized tubs of wilted flowers put there by the council in an attempt to bring beauty into the lives of its residents, it was no place to bring up two lively lads. Inevitably they fell foul of the law, and were old in the ways of gangs before they were out of junior school. Now seventeen, they were seldom at home and totally out of what little control their mother had attempted.

They liked their Uncle Joe. He brought them gifts, and also jobs for them to do for him. These were well paid. They were told never to ask questions, and to keep their mouths shut. That meant not telling their mother, or Auntie Margaret, though they protested they'd never set eyes on her.

'Hi, boys,' Joe said, walking into the living room with a smile. 'Where's your mum?'

'Next door, gettin' the ole man his breakfast,' Jim said. 'He's bedridden, poor ole bugger.'

They were not identical twins. Jim was the tallest and took the lead, while Stephen was smaller and quiet most of the time. He allowed Jim to make decisions for both of them, but occasionally lost his temper, and on those occasions could be terrifying.

'I'll go and get her,' Stephen said now, but his uncle shook his head. 'No, don't bother her,' he said. 'It's really you two I've come to talk to. A little job I want done, and you're the experts. Now listen carefully, and don't interrupt.'

By the time his sister returned, greeting him fondly, Joe had made a satisfactory deal with the twins, and they had disappeared in the way they had perfected. Nobody ever saw them go, and they never told anyone where they were going.

'It was their birthday on Wednesday, wasn't it?' he said. 'I brought them new mobile phones and they seemed pretty chuffed. Better late than never, Jim said, cheeky bugger! So how are you, you old bag?'

Not in the least offended, his sister nodded and said she was fine, healthy and broke. A wad of notes changed hands, and she went off to make coffee. 'Don't bother,' he called. 'Can't stop. Got an appointment to keep, so I'd better be off.'

'Well, that was a flying visit! Can't you stay and talk for ten minutes? Tell me how your lovely wife is, an' all that?'

Joe said that ten minutes was all he could spare, and reluctantly sat down.

Auntie Eileen suggested to Margaret that they should go for a stroll round the village after lunch. 'I'm not very quick on my pins these days, but if you don't mind going at my pace . . .'

Margaret assured her that it would suit her fine, and they set off, Eileen with her stick, limping cheerfully along. As they passed the driveway into the Battersbys' house, the big car came down and had to stop to let the pair walk slowly past. Margaret could see both Horace and Blanche were in the car, and took her chance.

'Hi, Horace!' she shouted at the closed window. She waved at his scowling face, and blew him a kiss. The expression on Blanche's face was a wonderful combination of disapproval and curiosity. Horace ignored Margaret completely, and they drove away with a squeal of tyres and revving engine.

'Really, Margaret,' Eileen said, 'that was not very dignified.'

'It wasn't meant to be,' Margaret said. 'If he'd had the window open, I'd have made even more mischief. Horrible man!'

'But his wife is thought to be a really nice woman. Don't you mind upsetting her?'

'She should keep him on a leash if she wants a peaceful life. Anyway, she's welcome to him. I bet he's murder to be married to.'

They wandered on, and came to the gate in the allotment field. 'There's Darren,' Eileen said. 'Working hard as always.'

'Could we go in and speak to him?' Margaret asked.

Eileen considered. 'I don't know,' she said doubtfully. 'We usually leave him alone when he's happy. Still, my friend Charlie is over there, on his patch, and we could go and say hello to him, then have a word with Darren on the way out. If we approach the lad first, he'll probably vamoose. Come on then.'

They walked through the trim, neatly planted allotments, each with its rows of vegetables and the occasional patch of flowers for cutting. Charlie's, said Eileen, had an area stuffed full of wild flowers. 'Time you got rid of those weeds,' Eileen said, as they approached, and Charlie bristled.

'They're not weeds! It's my wild flower garden. You should see the butterflies when all the flowers are out. And bees too. Doin' my bit for the environment, I am.'

Eileen and Charlie were obviously very old friends indeed, and were soon deep in local gossip. Margaret said quietly that she'd just have a walk round and look at the other allotments. Eileen nodded, and returned to her conversation.

Darren was at once aware of a strange woman walking towards him. His mother had gone home, promising to fetch him in an hour's time. He kept his head down and continued to pull out every weed that dared to show its head. Soon he saw the woman's legs approaching. He still did not lift his head, but then a nice voice said hello to him, and he looked up. The woman was smiling, and saying something about the weeds always win in the end. He wasn't sure what she meant, but her smile was friendly and he nodded.

He remembered what his mother said about being polite, and stood up, holding out his hand. 'How do you do,' he said. 'My name is Darren.'

'And mine's Margaret. It is a lovely afternoon. Just right for gardening. Do you enjoy gardening?'

'It is a lovely afternoon,' echoed Darren, not looking at her. Eileen had said that he seemed unable to look people in the eye, which gave him a reputation for being shifty. But Eileen had thought that it was fear. Looking people in the eye was a connection too terrifying for him. Margaret respected Eileen's judgement. After all, she'd been talking to children over the gate for fifty years or more.

'Your garden looks very neat,' Margaret said to Darren, who was now looking over at the entrance gate, as if considering his getaway.

'Yes. Very neat.' He put his hand over his ear, as if to shut out her voice.

'You were a very brave boy, I hear. Rescued Mrs Meade from the fire. That was very well done, Darren.' Margaret meant well, but his reaction was a disaster. He threw his fork to the ground, turned around and ran swiftly towards the gate. But it was blocked by two people: Colonel and Mrs Blanche Battersby, getting out of their parked car. Blanche had forgotten her handbag, and they were on their way back to collect it, much to Horace's annoyance. It had been Blanche's idea to stop for a minute and see how Darren's patch was getting on, and maybe have a word with him. She had tried to persuade Horace to stay in the car, but he was angry, suspected her motive and insisted on accompanying her.

Darren stopped dead in his tracks. He put his hands up to his face and began to hum loudly, shaking his head from side to side. Eileen had seen it all before, knew he was in a state of unbearable terror, and came hobbling as fast as she could down the narrow grass path to reach the lad.

'It's all right, Darren. Auntie Eileen here,' she said, and she let her stick fall to the ground. Her arms went around him tightly. 'Hold on,' she said. 'Mum's coming to take you home. Hold on to me and you're quite safe.'

The humming quietened and his head was still, but Eileen could feel him still trembling violently. 'Anything I can do?' Margaret asked, joining them.

'Go and fetch his mother,' Eileen said, and looking towards the gate, noted that the Battersbys had disappeared. Then another figure appeared, and Eileen said, 'Thank God. Here's Mum, Darren. Now you're safe as houses.'

Darren did not fly into his mother's arms. He stood quite still, thin, white-faced and heartbreakingly vulnerable. He looked up, at an angle away from anything happening, and stayed like that, motionless, until his mother took his hand and led him gently away.

Margaret looked at Eileen, and was shocked to see her wiping away a tear. 'What was all that about, Auntie?' she said.

'That bloody Battersby!' Eileen replied, and the expletive was powerful, coming from an old lady who, as far as Margaret knew, never swore.

'Tell me what it was about,' she said, anxious to help her aunt.

But Eileen shook her head. 'Another time, dear,' she said. 'We must get back now and have a cup of tea before you have to go.'

'Was it my fault?' Margaret persisted. 'Something I said to him? I certainly didn't say anything to frighten him. I was just congratulating him on rescuing Mrs Meade.'

Eileen said, 'Ah, might have been that. Perhaps remembering the fire was too much for him. That might make him run away, but his total panic was much more likely the appearance of the Colonel and his lady. Blanche is fine, but the sight of the Colonel would be enough.'

'They didn't stop to help, did they?' Margaret said. 'Scarpered, like a couple of rabbits.'

'Just as well,' said Eileen. 'Now, come on, we must get the kettle on.'

Forty-Three

Floss Pickering knocked at the Meades' door and Gran admitted her, warning her that Lois was tired from her foolish outing to a point-to-point when she was just out of hospital. Three days had gone by, and Lois still looked pale, with dark circles under her eyes. Derek had privately cursed himself for not standing up to her and forbidding the plan. But Lois was so persuasive, and had, in fact, looked much healthier the day he picked her up than she did now.

'Her son Douglas is coming home this afternoon,' Gran said, 'and I had hoped to make her rest this morning. But she's in her office now, staring at the computer screen. Perhaps you can at least take her mind off all that for a bit.'

'I haven't come with any problems, Mrs Weedon,' Floss said. 'I just wanted to see how she was and wish her well . . . and to offer help.'

'Hazel has more or less taken over in Sebastopol Street, and is trying not to consult Lois unless it is really urgent. Now, in you go, and make it a short visit.'

Floss knocked softly on the office door, and went in. Lois looked round and smiled when she saw who it was. Floss was shocked to see that Lois had lost weight. She was a shadow of her usual bonny self, Floss thought.

'Hello, Floss, come and sit down,' Lois said.

'I've just popped in to see how you are and offer help of any kind. Anything at all.'

'How nice of you,' Lois said quietly. 'But unless you can help me unfreeze this sodding computer, I think everything's been taken care of. Gran's gone into stern caring mode, and Derek stands guard over me in case I escape.'

'Well, you're in luck,' Floss said. 'Computer studies was about all I was good at at school, so let's change places and I'll fix it for you.'

'Wonderful!' said Lois, and got up from her chair, wincing as she walked round the desk. 'I'll get Gran to make us some coffee.'

'Oh, I'm not sure I can stay long,' said Floss quickly, remembering Gran's strictures.

'Take no notice of my mother,' Lois said. 'It'll do me a power of good to chat to you. Catch up on the gossip and news from the outside world! My Douglas is coming this afternoon, and he'll want to know what's happening in Farnden. He hasn't been home for quite a while.'

'I expect he's worried about you. I've never met him, but Josie talks about him quite a lot.'

'He's a good lad. Works hard. He's just finished with his long-time girlfriend, and probably wants some mothering. Or grandmothering!'

Floss laughed. 'Well,' she said, 'let me think of some news. Your accident is high on the list, of course, and Darren Smith's brave rescue. But what else? Oh yes, I fell off my horse yesterday.' She bared her arm and showed a badly grazed elbow. 'She shied away from a barking dog, and I wasn't concentrating. Still, that's not really news, is it?'

'What did the Colonel say?' Lois asked. Her voice had sharpened, and Floss saw a flash of her old boss.

'He was more anxious about the mare than he was about

me,' Floss said ruefully. 'But Mrs Battersby was very kind, and made me go into the house and have a cup of tea – very sweet, it was. Ugh! We chatted, and then old Horace came in and said the mare was fine. She made him some coffee, and he sat down and asked me lots of questions about you. How you were, and had you recovered your memory, and was it going to affect New Brooms, and all that sort of thing. I was surprised, actually, that he was so interested.'

'Did he mention Darren?' Lois said. 'After all, he works for them, and he was the hero of the whole nasty business.'

'No, he didn't ask about him at all. I suppose he knows that I've not really had anything to do with him. I have taken him a mug of coffee in the garden once or twice, but he doesn't speak. Doesn't seem to want to, so I've never bothered.'

Gran came in with a tray, and looked at Floss. 'I expect you'll want to be getting on with your job soon,' she said. 'Where are you working today?'

Floss looked at her watch. 'Yes,' she said quickly. 'I must get over to Mrs Tollervey-Jones. I'll just finish this drink, then I'll be off.'

Gran vanished, and Lois laughed again. 'She prides herself on being able to put the frighteners on,' she said. 'Go when you're ready, Floss. I'm very glad you called. Thanks for fixing the computer, and for the chat.'

When Floss had gone, Lois sat back in her chair and closed her eyes. She did feel tired now, but her mind was buzzing. As soon as she could, after Douglas's visit, she would get in touch with Evelyn Nimmo, and see if they could get some ideas together. And that reminded her of Dot. Poor old Dot. No change apparently. If she didn't make it, that would change things!

It would be a perfect day to go for a ride on her lovely mare, thought Floss as she drove to the Hall, with the morning sun dappling the drive under the trees. But she had her job to do, and reminded herself that she was saving up to get married. Ben was on a short list for a job in Tresham, but competition for jobs in computers was fierce. She knew her parents would stump up for all the money she needed, but she did not intend to allow that. After all, she had a job, and should be able to save enough to contribute. She was afraid her mother would want a grand wedding with all the trimmings, and her father would hear of nothing else. The least she could do was insist on contributing. And then she and Ben would want a cushion of money behind them when they set up house together.

Dreaming of fitted kitchens and pale cream drapes, she parked in the Hall stable yard and went across to give her usual greeting to Victoria, Mrs T-J's stately mare. The horse whinnied and Floss held out the expected mint. Then she made her way across the cobbled yard to the open kitchen door.

'Yoo hoo! I'm here! Morning, Mrs Tollervey-Jones.'

This familiar approach would not have been allowed by Mrs T-J from anyone else but Floss. But she had become fond of the girl, and on the subject of horses they talked the same language. She appeared in the kitchen, and smiled. 'Morning, Floss,' she said. 'How are we this morning? I hear you had a tumble?'

'Oh dear,' said Floss. 'Has the word got around?'

'Not far. Blanche Battersby told me. She hoped you would be able to continue working.'

'Good heavens, it's only a graze,' said Floss. 'Takes more than that to stop me.'

Mrs. T-J nodded approvingly, and said, 'Oh, yes, and by the way, Blanche is coming over for coffee this morning. Could you be a dear and make it for us? We have something important to discuss.'

'Of course. Just tell me when. Or would you like me to open the door to her, usher her into the drawing room, and announce her name? Would it be fun?'

'Well,' said Mrs T-J, with a modest smile, 'if you insist, dear. Now, we must get on.'

Old bag, thought Floss. But she was mildly fond of the autocratic old woman, and knew exactly how to please her. Won't hurt me to play the game, she thought. And I can have a listen to the discussion on the really important thing. Maybe the Battersbys had run even shorter of money, and felt they had to sell Floss's mare. But that would have nothing to do with Mrs T-J. Well, she would just have to wait and see.

When the big door knocker sounded, Floss downed tools and went to answer it. I should really have a frilly cap and apron, she thought.

'Good morning, Mrs Battersby,' she said. 'Will you come this way, please?'

'Floss?' answered Blanche. 'What on earth's got into you?'

Floss winked, and led her across the black and white tiled hall, larger than four of the Pickerings' rooms put together, and knocked on the drawing-room door.

'Come in,' called a firm voice.

Floss opened the door and stood to one side. 'Mrs Blanche Battersby, madam,' she said, with a straight face. But she couldn't maintain it, and suddenly burst into roars of delighted laughter. The two eminent ladies stared at her, and then slowly smiled. Finally they too were amused, in a restrained way, and the gloomy house was filled with unaccustomed merriment.

'I'll go and make coffee,' spluttered Floss, and disappeared.

'What would we do without her?' said Mrs T-J.

'Not very well,' replied Blanche, suddenly serious.

Floss tiptoed with the coffee tray until she was very close to the drawing-room door, which she had been careful to leave ajar. The conversation continued, and Floss stood motionless, sure they had not heard her.

'But where do you think your money's gone, Blanche?'

'There is only one person who can get at it. Horace. I trusted him absolutely, but I am sure now that he is still gambling. And although he claims to win more than he loses, I am not convinced. I do hope you don't mind my talking about this? Nobody knows better than I that it is bad form to talk about money. But I am desperate, Evangeline. I really have no one else to turn to. I cannot mention it to our girls, of course. Horace would never forgive me!'

Mrs T-J frowned. Her long experience as a magistrate made her suddenly suspicious that Horace might have been having a bash at poor Blanche. But no, surely not. She had never seen any evidence – bruises, fear in her eyes, that sort of thing. He was too much of a gentleman to hit a woman. Then she thought how ridiculous that was. How many wives of so-called gentlemen had she seen in court, beaten and cowed?

'You're not frightened of him, are you, Blanche?'

'Of course not! He has never harmed me! Why do you ask, Evangeline?'

Methinks she doth protest too much, thought Mrs T-J, misquoting the bard.

Floss had cramp. Her calf muscle had seized up, and she reluctantly took a step forward. She pushed open the door, and said, 'Here's coffee. I've put out those chocolate Bath Olivers you like, Mrs Tollervey-Jones. Shall I pour?'

She watched Mrs T-J's discomfort with a touch of guilt. Those were the old thing's favourite biscuits, and nobody else was allowed to touch them. But she could hardly withdraw them now!

'No thank you, Floss. I can manage. Off you go.'

On her way out, Floss glanced at Blanche, and saw her sitting slumped in her chair. She seemed miles away, deep in thought. So the Colonel was gambling her money away, was he? Oh well, she supposed her mare would soon be on the way out. The Colonel would soon forget he had conditionally given it to Floss. Maybe her father would buy . . .? But not at the price Horace's horses commanded.

'Please let me know when you're going,' Mrs T-J said, as Floss reached the door. 'Blanche will be staying to lunch, and it will be a signal for me to do some preparation. No, I insist, Blanche. We will have a cold collation,' she added, silencing Blanche's protest.

Floss left them to it. She finished her work, told them she was going, and drove off down the drive. She wondered if she should warn Mrs M about the Battersbys' finances. They would probably regretfully dispense with Floss's services next. It would do no harm to keep Mrs M informed.

Forty-Four

Lois looked at her watch for the umpteenth time. Douglas was due some time around the middle of the day, and Gran had prepared a special lunch, just in case he made it in time. Otherwise, there was a perfect chocolate cream sponge in the larder for tea, and one of Gran's stalwart steak and kidney pies for supper. It was twelve thirty, and they had agreed to give him until half past one before sitting down themselves.

An hour to pass, then. Lois closed her computer down, and went into the sitting room. She would just shut her eyes for ten minutes, and then help Gran to put the finishing touches to lunch. She slept. She was driving along the road to Waltonby, and Douglas was in the van with her. He was much younger, about twelve, and was grinning at her with his lovely open face. The shabby dark-green car came out of nowhere, at speed, heading straight at her. She screamed, and felt someone shaking her gently.

'Mum? Mum, wake up. It's me, Douglas, the prodigal son.'

She shot to her feet, flinging her arms around him and fighting back tears. 'Douglas! You're all right?'

'Course I'm all right, Mum. You were dreaming. Come on, Gran sent me to get you for lunch. I've been here for a while, but didn't want to wake you up.'

Douglas had grown from a pleasant, amenable lad, with sandy hair and freckles, into a well-built young man, still freckled, and with his sandy hair cut very short into a golden fuzz. He was still pleasant and amenable, and Lois was especially partial to her first-born son.

'How are you, Mum? And don't give me the usual "I'm fine", because I can see you're not.'

Derek nodded in agreement. 'Perhaps you can persuade her to rest. She takes n'notice of me,' he said.

Lois bristled. 'What do you think I was doing in the sitting room? Resting, I was. And, as a result, having a nightmare. It was the crash all over again.'

Derek put out his hand and took hers. 'You're doing well, me duck,' he said. 'And don't worry. The doc said you'd be bound to have bad dreams for a while, but they'll fade. Now, Gran, let's try and forget all about it, and get going on this fantastic nosh.'

To lighten the atmosphere, Douglas had a joke or two at the ready, and soon they were all laughing at his account of people in his office. 'Mind you,' he added, 'sometimes they're not so funny, and I could happily ditch the lot of them. Maybe it's time I looked for another job. Nearer home, Mum, d'you reckon?'

'You must do what you think is best. Your Dad and me have always said that. I cut the apron strings long ago.'

Gran did not agree. 'It would be lovely, Douglas,' she said, 'to have you nearer. And don't take any notice of your mum – she's still clinging on to mine, you know. Not that she would admit it!'

Lois had no energy to argue, and just smiled.

Derek patted his son on the back, and said, 'We're always here to help, lad. You know that. Young James never hesitates if he needs help – mostly financial! And we try to treat you all the same.'

'Our Josie's doing well, isn't she?' Douglas said, running his finger round the pudding dish and licking up every creamy drop.

'Very well,' Lois said. 'She and Rob are coming up tonight, and Gran has killed the fatted calf for supper. You *are* staying tonight, aren't you?'

Douglas said he certainly was. He wanted to make sure Lois could be trusted to get better sensibly, and he intended to help his father put on the pressure. 'After all,' he said, 'if you're the target of some local tearaways, I mean to find them and give them a good kick up the arse.'

Hunter Cowgill, lifting up his office phone to ring Lois, was planning a much more draconian punishment for the culprits, when he found them. He had followed up various leads, but they'd come to nothing so far. If only the boy Darren could give them more details of the incident – and Cowgill was sure he had them locked away in his head – then they'd be on the track in no time.

'Hello, is that you Lois? This must be a bad line. You sound very faint.'

'I'm feeling very faint,' Lois said, winking at Douglas. 'You haven't forgotten I've had a bad time?'

Cowgill was instantly contrite. 'Of course not,' he apologized. 'Are you up to a short conversation?'

'Shorter the better,' Lois replied, her voice back to the one Cowgill was used to . . . and loved.

'Believe it or not,' he said, 'I am ringing to ask how you

are and checking that you're doing just as the doctor ordered. Not that I have much hope of the latter.'

'I'm fine. Really fine. And even more fine because Douglas is here, and is staying until tomorrow. But don't ask me to believe you rang just to enquire after my health. As a matter of fact, I was going to get in touch. I've remembered something – at least, I've dreamed something.'

'Sure you want to talk about it?' Cowgill asked anxiously.

'Anything to help our brave boys in blue. I dreamed the crash, but this time Douglas was in the van with me, and the car coming straight at us. It was old, dark green, and dirty. Maybe I'll dream it again and see the number plate.'

'Please don't do that,' Cowgill said. 'Not even in the interests of police investigations. The details you dreamed might just be a big help, but no more nightmares, Lois, and that's an order. Take care, and I'll be in touch. Bye.' He looked at the receiver, and blew it a kiss. 'Silly old fool,' he said quietly.

Derek's face was thunderous. 'I told that idiot not to telephone any more. Much good it did! Next time, Lois, put him straight on to me.'

'He was only asking how I was. Harmless old policeman, really. But I did need to pass on my dream about the car. It might help.'

Douglas got up from the table and put his arms around her. 'Did you really dream it was me in the van, Mum?' Lois nodded. 'I wish I had been,' he said darkly, and there was silence among them. Then Douglas shook himself. 'Now,' he said briskly, 'all hands to the sink. Then a stroll down to the shop. We'll catch Josie gossiping with the customers. Come on, Dad, you too.'

The dirty old green car haunted Lois. She dreamed about it again the next night, and this time, before she blacked out, she saw the back of it as it skidded round and away at top speed. And this time she was sure there were two people in it.

'Still no number plate,' she said to Douglas, as he packed his overnight bag and kissed his mum goodbye.

'Don't try to remember,' he said. 'If it comes back, fine, but if it doesn't, the police will have other ways of finding those thugs. Or do you still fancy yourself as a part-time gumshoe?'

'What's a gumshoe, Douglas?' Gran said.

'You're a telly addict, so you know perfectly well,' Douglas said, giving her a hug. 'Thanks for all the lovely food. See you again soon.'

Derek gave his son a manly shake of the hand, and they waved him off in his car.

Lois sighed. 'That went quickly, didn't it?'

'You could've been more encouraging for him to settle round here,' Gran said, and Derek added that it wouldn't be long before he'd be back. Their boy was worried about his mum.

They were all quiet for a minute, then, 'Boys!' Lois said suddenly. 'They were boys in the car in my dream. Two of them, two boys. It just came back to me. I'll just run in and give Cowgill a call.'

Derek groaned, and Gran shrugged her shoulders. 'I give up,' she said.

'I don't,' said Derek. 'I'll tell him. Give me his number and I'll give him a call.'

Forty-Five

Margaret Horsley hesitated at the entrance to the hospital. She bought a bunch of strange, thornless roses from the kiosk, and went into reception. After all, as one of Dot Nimmo's clients, she had every right to visit her, she was sure.

'Are you a relative?' the receptionist asked.

'No, but she worked for me before her accident. I was fond of her,' she lied, 'and would really like to see her, even if she doesn't know I'm there.'

'Just take a seat, Mrs . . . er . . . What is your name?' The receptionist then had a long conversation with someone Margaret presumed was either the doctor or a senior nurse. When the woman said, 'All right, then, love, see you later,' she realized she had been foolishly optimistic. The conversation had had nothing to do with Dot Nimmo.

Eventually, Margaret was called over. 'You can go to the ward,' the receptionist said sniffily. 'But you must stay only five minutes. And make sure you report to staff before and after you go in. Now, if you take the street along there – it's a corridor but we call it The Street – follow the yellow line until it turns into a green one, then turn first left, then right, and left again, and look for signs to Beddington Ward, you'll find it easily.'

Head spinning, Margaret set off. She was quickly lost, and in the end a young porter took pity on her and accompanied her all the way. She thanked him profusely, and looked around for a nurse. Not a soul about. She took a step forward to Beddington Ward, and a voice said, 'Just a minute! You can't go in there without permission.'

'I'm sorry, but I do have permission,' Margaret said meekly. You have to creep to these people, she thought. 'I'm Mrs Horsley.'

The nurse frowned. 'Well, I suppose you'd better go in. You're not another sister, are you?'

'No. Evelyn is her only sister. I just wanted to be by her side for a moment, and to bring these flowers.'

The nurse took away the flowers, and Margaret walked towards Dot's bed. Margaret's first thought was that she was a horrible colour. Looks bloodless, poor old thing. And her ghastly blonde hair is showing all the grey roots. She wouldn't like that. Margaret felt an overpowering urge to giggle. She sat down and looked at her hands, at her wedding ring and the flashy diamond Joe had given her for their tenth anniversary. How had he managed to afford it? She was only too well aware of the state of their finances. She waggled her fingers. Five minutes doing nothing seemed endless. Her thoughts began to wander, and she saw again the boy Darren, humming and trembling, held tight in Auntie's arms. What had Horace done to him? Nothing would surprise her. Had Joe been involved, too? She would pluck up her courage and ask him. She would ask him if he'd been there when Darren had been so frightened that he ran off and hid for a whole night by himself. The thought of it made her blood boil. 'Wicked sods!' she said aloud.

'Sods,' repeated a very faint voice.

'What!' Her heart was thumping. Maybe it had been an echo in this sterile room.

'They're all sods.' It was a whisper, a breath exhaled with difficulty.

'Nurse!' yelled Margaret. 'Come quickly, quickly!'

Two nurses came running. '*Please*, Mrs Horsley! We must have absolute quiet in here!'

'She spoke, you stupid bitch!' Margaret said, completely out of control. 'Dot spoke!'

The nurse who had cautioned her stiffened. 'You must leave now,' she said frostily, 'and I suggest you pull yourself together. You'll do no good here.'

The other nurse was bending over Dot, monitoring displays and checking tubes.

'Bye, missus,' whispered the voice.

'Bye, Dot!' said Margaret loudly. 'See you soon.' She marched out, her heels clicking on the hard floor, her nose in the air.

After that, hospital staff went into action, and were puzzled that Dot Nimmo said nothing more. Evelyn Nimmo had been sent for, and had said she would come at once. After much gentle encouragement from staff had produced nothing but the blank, apparently unconscious face of Dot, they agreed to wait until Evelyn arrived. Surely she would be able to reach her sister, when a woman who had merely employed her to clean the house had clearly got through. The nurse who heard Dot's farewell to Margaret was adamant. 'She definitely spoke. It was very faint, but it was there,' she said firmly.

Evelyn telephoned Lois straightaway to give her the news. 'They said she spoke. Mrs Horsley was with her, and it wasn't much. It was when Mrs H was talking to herself really. She said "sods" loudly, and Dot said "They're all sods". Then she said goodbye, so this nurse said.'

'Sounds like Dot all right,' said Lois, feeling ridiculously excited. Dot recovering! She really was an old bag, who would lie through her teeth if necessary, but Lois had respect for her. After all, to survive at all in the underworld she inhabited was an achievement.

A tough old bird, was Dot, and it looked as if she'd won another battle.

'Well, looks like very good news! Let me know how you get on. I'll be here most of today.'

Evelyn put down the phone, emptied the fruit bowl into a

paper bag and set off for the hospital. This time the visitor –
a relative, yes – was whizzed up to Beddington Ward.

'Come in, please, Evelyn,' said the young nurse. 'Do sit
down, and I'll fetch you a cup of tea. Milk? Sugar?'

Blimey, thought Evelyn, this is a bit different from usual.
The tea was brought, and the nurse said she would leave the
two of them together. Dot might well respond if only her sister
was listening.

Evelyn sipped her tea. 'Dot?' she said. 'It's me, Evelyn.
How're you feeling?'

Nothing. Evelyn thought she might just as well read a maga-
zine, and was reaching for one, when a faint whisper reached
her. 'Bloody awful. What d'you expect?'

Evelyn rushed round to the other side of the bed and knelt
down so that her face was close to Dot's. 'Was that you, Dot?'

'Who d'you think? God?'

'Can you see me?'

'Eyes are shut, y'fool. An' they're stayin' shut.'

Footsteps approached, and the doctor came in. 'Any luck,
Mrs Nimmo?' he said.

Evelyn looked hard at Dot, and one eye clearly winked.

Evelyn turned to the doctor with a sorrowful face. 'Nothing,
I'm afraid,' she said. 'But I'll stay here for a while, and see
if my darling sister is able to say anything to me. We were
so close, you know.'

'Fine. Just ring the bell if she shows any signs of communi-
cating.' Wishful thinking is a wonderful thing, he thought as
he retreated.

His footsteps died away down the corridor, and Evelyn
turned to Dot. 'You old fraud,' she said. She heard the shadow
of a cackle. 'I suppose it suits you for some goddam reason
to stay here? Well, I'll not give you away. Mind you, you do
look bloody awful, so I suppose you are still pretty rocky.
Look after yourself, Dot.'

The whispery voice said one more thing. 'Goodbye, *darling*
sister.'

Evelyn chuckled all the way out of the hospital, ending up
in radiology, surgical, eyes, teeth and numerous other irrele-
vant departments, until with relief she found her way out.

'Might have some of those roses for meself,' she said to
the kiosk girl, 'by way of a celebration,' she added. Another

bereaved wife, the girl thought, and handed over the flowers with a sympathetic smile.

Forty-Six

L ois laughed when she heard that not only had Dot spoken to her sister, however faintly, but was up to something from her hospital bed. 'Wicked old thing!' she said. 'But still, there's not much she can do at the moment, except pretend to be still in a coma.'

'Don't you be so sure,' said Evelyn. 'My sister is as crafty as a cartload of monkeys. Anyway, when you are feeling well enough yourself, you could go in and see if she favours you with a word or two.'

Assuring Evelyn that she was quite better, Lois looked at her desk diary. Tomorrow was a good day. She would go to the hospital tomorrow. If Dot had any ideas about who had knocked her down so disastrously, Lois very much wanted to know.

Alice Parker-Knowle had been very concerned about Dot, but was too disabled herself to risk the hazards of the General Hospital. In any case, she could see no sense in wasting time visiting an unconscious woman. If Dot recovered, then would be the time to make sure she was looking after herself, and perhaps help her out financially.

A series of New Brooms cleaners had filled in for Dot, and this morning it was her sister. 'Good morning, Mrs Parker-Knowle,' Evelyn's cheery voice called from the front door. She came in to where Alice was sitting, and the old lady replied, 'I do wish you would call me Alice.'

'I would feel uncomfortable, I'm afraid,' Evelyn replied. 'Not respectful, somehow.'

Alice sighed. 'Your sister Dot had no such qualms,' she said. 'I do miss her, you know. Not that I'm dissatisfied with

New Brooms' service,' she added hastily. 'It's just that Dot was special.'

'She still is,' said Evelyn. 'She spoke to me this morning. Very weak, of course, but she definitely spoke. I don't think the doctor believed me, and Dot made it clear she wouldn't speak to them. I don't know what the old thing is up to, but it looks like our Dot is on the mend.'

Alice's grin was broad. 'Oh, I'm *so* pleased,' she said. 'D'you know, I think I *shall* go and visit her tomorrow. I can take a taxi, and there'll be wheelchair access to the ward. I've got a wheelchair tucked away in the shed, if you would kindly get it out for me.'

'Are you sure, Mrs Parker-Knowle? Wouldn't you like me to come with you?'

Alice rapped her stick on the floor. 'I order you to call me Alice,' she said, smiling. 'Think how many minutes it will save. And no, thank you for offering, but I'd like to go by myself. There are always people to help, and if Dot decides not to speak it would be a waste of your time.'

'Would it be in the afternoon? I could go in the morning, and tell her you're coming. I shall also tell her that it's not easy for you, and she should make an effort to speak! Of course, she may pretend not to hear but I reckon it'll get through.'

'That's settled then. Now, why don't we have a coffee before you start? This thundery weather makes me thirsty.'

It was almost dark, although still in the middle of the day, and thunder rumbled around threateningly. Heavy cloudbursts sent streams of water rushing down the gutters, and when Evelyn went to put rubbish in the bin, a shower of ice-cold water hit the back of her neck.

'Bugger it,' she said. It was unusual for her to swear. Unlike Dot, whose language had started off reasonably well, but had deteriorated after years of living with Handy, she spoke well and had tried to maintain a respectable exterior in the face of her Nimmo relations. But this morning she was driven to swear. The shock of the shower was the final irritation in the saga of Dot and her accident. Now she, Evelyn, had to bear the burden of dealing with Dot's emergence from the coma. How typical of her sister to be plotting from her hospital bed! Of course, she'd get found out. They must have ways to look at her brain and see she was actually conscious. She shrugged. Ah well, she could only wait and see, and in the meantime keep this nice old lady happy.

Alice struggled out of her taxi, and the driver helped her into her wheelchair. 'I'll take you into reception, me duck,' he said kindly, and pushed her through the automatic doors up to the desk. 'Will you be okay now?' he asked. Alice nodded and joined the queue. She had been practising and had become quite adept at manoeuvring in a wheelchair.

As it happened, she did not need to wheel herself. A porter was summoned, and Alice was wheeled directly to Beddington Ward. She explained that she was Dot's friend and employer, in that order. The nurse was welcoming, but said sadly that Dot had not shown any signs of speaking since the alleged conversation with her sister.

'But who knows, Mrs Parker-Knowle, you never know.' The nurse offered a drink, but Alice refused, and settled herself in close to Dot's bed. She looked at the colourless face. She could be dead, thought Alice. But she was still breathing. It was shallow, but definitely regular and steady. Alice smiled. This was her Dot, holding on to a life that to another would seem hardly worth living. Husband dead, only son dead, short of money and living in a dump. Cleaning other people's houses when she hadn't the heart to clean her own. The victim of a hit-and-run driver. What must it feel like to know that someone hated you so much they could come out of nowhere and take your life – a life which, in spite of everything, you wanted to hold on to?

Alice felt tears, but sniffed them back.

'Got a cold, dear?' said the whispery voice.

Alice stared at Dot's motionless figure. 'Dot? Did you say something? Dot? It's Alice here.'

'I know it is. How did you manage to get here?'

'Taxi, wheelchair, helpful porter. D'you think I should tip him, Dot?' Alice was determined not to be shocked into anxiety by Dot up to her tricks.

Dot's eyes flicked open, and a faint smile appeared. 'Don't waste yer money, dear,' she said. 'Save it up for me when I get back to work.'

Alice sighed. 'I hope it will be soon. Anyway,' she added,

leaning forward and speaking briskly, 'before nurse comes back, tell me what you remember. Who knocked you down, Dot? I've useful contacts in Tresham who can sort this out – rough justice if necessary.'

Dot's eyes opened wide this time. '*You,* Alice?

'Yes, me. So tell me quickly what you saw.'

Lois had trouble finding a parking place, as usual, but now walked quickly through the automatic doors and up to reception. There was nobody there. 'She's gone down the Street for a few seconds,' a porter said. 'Why don't you take a seat?'

Lois shook her head. 'No,' she said. 'I'm expected, and I know my way.'

She sped through the reception area and into the Street. Anxious not to show any hesitation, she took a turn and half ran towards the lift. She was lucky. She had chosen the right route, and was soon on her way to Beddington Ward. As she approached, she heard a voice she recognized. Surely that was Alice Parker-Knowle? She slowed up, and stood unseen outside the ward door, which was ajar. She very quietly pushed it open so that she could hear clearly. No one about at the moment.

'What did you say, Dot?' Alice was saying. 'I couldn't quite hear that. Oh, you said you were minding your own business when . . . what was that? No, of course I'm not deaf. Well, not very. Go on then . . . Two in the car? Did you see them at all? What did the car look like? Oh, very dirty, was it. And what colour? Green, you think?'

'Now, now, what's going on here?' A brisk nurse stopped in front of Lois, who said smoothly that she wasn't sure if Mrs Nimmo was allowed two visitors at once, and so she was waiting until somebody in authority came along. 'Oh, I see,' said the nurse, somewhat mollified. 'Well, just wait here, and I'll see what the situation is.'

She returned after a couple of minutes, shaking her head. 'There seems to be no change. I don't suppose it would matter if you went in to see her too. It's not as if conversation is going to exhaust her, is it?' With the ghost of a smile, the nurse passed on to the next ward.

Alice smiled broadly when she saw Lois. 'Bring up a chair, Lois. I've been having a nice chat with Dot. She's much improved.' Her last few words were in a stage whisper, and Lois sat down and looked closely at Dot. Once more the shutters had come down.

Lois took the limp hand. 'Dot! Open your eyes at once, if you know what's good for you. I expect you're hoping for your job back in due course? Well . . .'

'Blackmail, Mrs M,' said the hoarse voice, and now Dot had fully opened eyes and a grin for Lois. 'I just told Alice all I can remember. I ain't got much brain workin' yet, but with a lot more rest I am sure it'll improve.'

'Dot, you don't think they'll keep you here in luxury until you decide to wake up for them, do you? They'll have your number, duckie, probably by tomorrow. Then you'll be out on your ear.'

'Oh, I don't think so, Lois,' Alice said quickly. 'She'll need a good convalescence, and I am sure we can find her a nice home to go to.'

'Mmm, perhaps,' said Lois. 'Mind you, she'll probably be expelled for stirring up trouble amongst the inmates. Now then, Dot, just concentrate. Did you see their faces? Old or young? Male or female? Strangers or people you knew? Rival gang – that kind of thing?'

'Yes, young, male, a bit familiar. Oh yes, and they were laughing.'

Something clicked in Lois's head, and she said, 'Laughing? So were the two who mowed down me and Darren . . . Blimey, Dot, what's going on?'

'God knows,' Dot said in an ever stronger voice. 'An' are you better, Mrs M? Sounds like you were on the list, too. Get old Cowgill on to it. Oh lor'!' she added. 'I can hear the bloody doctor's voice. Time for his round. Night night all.'

Her eyes closed, mouth slightly open, and Lois rose to go. 'I'll take you down, Alice,' she said. 'We need to have a chat.'

Forty-Seven

'There's a café over there,' Lois said, pointing to a newly set up coffee and snack area. 'This hospital's improved a lot since my Derek was in here. Mind you, that was a while ago. Hit-and-run, just like poor old Dot. Our local villains must reckon it's an easy way of solving problems.'

She settled Alice into a space by a table, and went to collect coffees. Soon back, she unwrapped a packet of two shortbread biscuits, put one in front of Alice and began to munch the other.

'Now then, Alice, what do you mean by telling Dot you have contacts in Tresham? What sort of contacts?'

'You were eavesdropping!' Alice said, annoyed.

'Naturally. It's my job. Well, my unpaid, dangerous and sometimes useful job. I'm hoping to find out who nearly killed Dot – and me and Darren.'

'And what do you do when you know the answer to that?' Alice was suspicious. Was this nice Lois part of Tresham's underworld? Dot had told her some entertaining stories about dodgy goings-on in her family.

'Tell the police, of course,' Lois replied. 'Didn't you hear Dot mention Cowgill? He's the detective inspector I work with. I'd appreciate it if you'd keep all this to yourself. Are you happy now to tell me who your contacts are?'

Alice hesitated. 'Well,' she said slowly, 'it was when my husband was alive. He had some friends in the Conservative Club, and the Round Table, and amongst them were the great and good of Tresham. Wheels within wheels, Lois. You know the kind of thing. Like the Freemasons, they took care of their own.'

'So did your husband need to be taken of?'

'No, no. Not John. It was his so-called friend, Horace Battersby. I think I told you before that there was trouble between Horace and the Nimmos. A building contract and non-payment of a bill. Horace was let off lightly in the end. John's contacts saved him from a court case, and – even worse – being blackballed from the clubs!'

'But now that your husband has passed away . . .?'

'Oh, I still keep in touch. They look after me now. And, of course, I was very friendly with several of the wives. Helped with their charity events, that sort of thing. I think I've told you all this before, so you must forgive an old lady.'

Lois drank her coffee, and looked around. 'A good place to meet, this,' she said. 'People coming and going all the time, and a good chance that you'll see nobody you know. Would you like another coffee?'

Alice refused, saying the taxi would be here shortly to take her home. 'Another five minutes, though, if you want to ask me anything else,' she said.

'Do you know anything about Horace and racing and gambling, sailing close to the wind? Has he ever been in trouble in that direction, or near to it?'

'Horace?' Alice laughed. 'He likes to think he's Mr Big in the gambling world. It's all horse racing, of course. Poor old Blanche knows something's going on, but can never get it out of him. He and that Horsley. Joe Horsley – do you know him? Another nasty piece of work.'

Lois did not answer, and Alice continued. 'Yes, of course you know the Horsleys! Dot told me she was cleaning at their farmhouse. Putting poison in their coffee, probably,' she added, chuckling.

The taxi driver approached their table, and Alice gathered herself together. 'I'm ready,' she said. 'Goodbye, Lois. Anything else I can do to help, you know where I live. Off we go then,' she added to the driver, and they disappeared through the automatic doors.

Lois fetched herself another coffee and sat down again. Strangely enough, it was easier to sit and think amidst all this noise and bustle, and nobody taking any notice of her. She turned over in her mind all that she had heard. Most important, of course, was Dot's conversation. It had been a dirty green car with two people in it, and they had been laughing. Snap. An exact copy of what had happened to her and Darren. Surely it shouldn't be beyond the wits of the Tresham police to locate them? A number plate? She should have asked Dot if she had ... Wait a minute! Another snapshot of the crash. The car was so dirty round the lower half that the number plate was totally obscured. Deliberate, or just a filthy car? She shut her eyes and tried to picture the laughing faces. Of course she had had only a lightning glimpse of them, side-on. But Dot had seen them coming straight for her. She must talk some more about that.

Then there were the Horsleys. Joe Horsley was a nasty piece of work, Alice had said. The stuff about Horace and the Nimmos was not new, but the fact that the Colonel had faced a possible court case for not paying *was* new. And confirmation that he and Joe Horsley were deep into gambling on horses – serious stuff – and probably other similar pastimes as well, was new. It was serious enough for them to be very anxious not to be found out. So Dot's poor son must have known something, and of course Dot herself, and now she, Lois, was a threat to them, with her association with Dot, and poking about in matters that did not concern her. No doubt they had noted her presence at the point-to-point, and would know that she had not heeded the warning, and was not giving up. Which meant that she had to be very careful. The jokers in the green car might not bungle the job next time.

It occurred to her that perhaps they had not meant to kill any of them, not Haydn, nor Dot, nor herself and Darren. Perhaps the orders had been to frighten them off, making it quite clear that next time they would finish the job? If so, then they had obeyed orders and added evil intent themselves. That lad of Dot's had not stood a chance. His reactions might have been a bit slow, of course, or they could have miscalculated the actions of the terrified bolting horse. Lois shook her head. That one didn't make sense. But one useful conclusion emerged. If the intention had been to kill, then whoever was behind this, the one who carried out the master plan was not very bright in choosing his hitmen. Bungling from beginning to end. She and Darren could easily have died, and so could Dot, but they hadn't.

So, now, which of them was not very bright? She drove home still sorting it out in her head, and vanished into her office to see if making notes would help to clear her head.

* * *

Derek came home late for supper. Gran had refilled the kettle a couple of times and put it back on the hob. She looked at her watch as he came through the door.

'So what kept you?' she said.

'What d'you think?' he replied, an unusually grumpy greeting from Derek to his mother-in-law. 'Work, Gran, earning us a living.'

What's eating him, she wondered, but said nothing more.

'Where's Lois?' he asked.

'In her office. Sorting papers, she said. Will you call and tell her supper's ready.'

'When I've had a wash,' he replied, and walked through to the hall. Gran heard Lois's door open and shut with a bang. *Oh dear*, she thought, *what's happened now*? This wasn't the most peaceful family to live with. Still, it was hers, and she loved them all. She peeped into the oven, and everything seemed to be ticking over nicely.

Lois looked up from her notes, and said, 'Hi, m'love. Goodness, Derek, you look cross,' she added, seeing his gloomy face. 'What's up?'

'The sodding lottery, that's what's up. I wish we'd never won it.'

'Well, I don't,' Lois said, shrugging her shoulders. 'We can make very good use of it, and have already. Rent from our little house coming in, and some improvements round this house. What's happened?'

She got up and came round her desk to give him a hug. He sighed. 'Those Horsleys,' he said. 'Typical farmer, Joe Horsley. He'd asked me to give them a quote for more work in the kitchen. I got a call on my mobile this morning. Says I'm far too expensive and that after winning the lottery, I don't need the money anyway. They got lower estimates, he says, so would I like to re-quote? I told him to get lost. Depressed me, though.'

Lois was furious. 'I've a good mind to take New Brooms away from them,' she said. 'Leave them in the lurch, rotten sods. Well,' she added, 'it's him, really. She's not too bad, Dot reckoned.'

They were silent for a second or two, and then Lois brightened. 'I know,' she said, 'we'll put up the cleaning charges. That'll fix him. He'll need a good win on the gee-gees even more urgently!'

'They might just do without,' Derek said gloomily.

'Oh no, they can't wait to get Dot back. They need her for what she knows. Far more to it than meets the eye with the Horsleys.'

Derek groaned. 'Oh, Lois, can't you leave it alone? Isn't it enough to get yourself nearly killed, and a young lad into the bargain? Aren't we enough, me and Gran and the kids?'

Lois said nothing. Derek turned her towards him and looked closely into her face. 'All right, all right,' he said sadly, 'you don't need to answer.' He turned away and went to the door. 'I'll get a quick wash before supper,' he said. 'Gran's about to explode.'

Forty-Eight

Early next morning, Evelyn received a telephone call, and was stunned to hear Dot's voice loud and clear.

'They've rumbled me, Evie,' Dot said, chuckling. 'Kicking me out this afternoon. Well, not exactly kicking, but they made it plain they needed the bed for more deservin' patients.'

'But they're not sending you home?' said Evelyn, genuinely shocked.

'Good God no,' Dot said. 'They wanted to know if I would like them to arrange a convalescent home. I said not bloody likely, as you can imagine. Not ready to be dumped in a home yet, I said.'

'So where are you going?' said Evelyn, with a sinking heart.

'To my *darling* sister, o' course! I knew you wouldn't hear of nothing else. So when can you come and collect me? I'll need some clean clothes an' that.'

While Evelyn reeled from this news, Dot gave her a list of things to do and to bring. 'I'll need to come back for tests and things,' she added, 'but I told them you'd be happy to do that, 'aving a car yourself. I made it quite clear I couldn't wait to get home. Liar! Still, I always was, and when it matters

I tell the truth. An' this is the truth: I'm very grateful to you, Evie. I'll do the same for you one day. See y'later.'

Evelyn sat without moving for several minutes. Then she sighed, and picked up the phone.

'Hello? Mrs M? I've got some good news . . . I think,' she said. She told Lois about Dot, and was amazed to hear a shout of laughter.

'Wicked old thing!' Lois said. 'So when are you picking her up? Do you want me to get one of the girls to cover for you today?'

They rearranged Evelyn's day, and Lois offered help with collecting Dot. 'No, I'll be fine, thanks,' Evelyn said. 'You should be taking it easy yourself.'

'Don't worry about me. It might not be much fun for you, but Dot's news has cheered me up no end! I feel stronger already. She's one of those characters you're always pleased to see coming through the door, awful as she is . . .'

There was a pause, and then Evelyn said, 'I hate to say it, Mrs M, but you're right. I wouldn't change her for a win on the lottery.'

'Derek might agree with you there,' Lois said, suddenly serious. 'But let me know how it goes, and I'll be in touch.'

When Derek came home to lunch, he dumped his bag on the kitchen floor and went straight through to Lois's office. He walked straight in, and found her with young Floss, both busy with pens and notebooks.

'Oh, sorry,' he said, backing out.

'No, it's OK. We've finished, more or less.' Lois put down her notes and saw Floss out of the front door. 'Things not too good at the Battersbys,' she said on returning. 'Apparently old Horace swore at Floss when she dropped a newspaper in a puddle of dog pee in the kitchen. Poor kid was very upset. You'd think their rotten dogs would be house-trained, wouldn't you? I shall have to have a word.'

Derek sat down in the chair opposite Lois, and said, 'Their sort are always the worst. Especially them with corgis. Still, no doubt you'll put it right with a diplomatic complaint. Now,' he added more briskly, 'I've got an idea. And don't interrupt until I've finished.'

Lois widened her eyes, settled back and listened. This was more like her old Derek.

'I know you'll say you got quite enough to do already, but I think it would be good for you to have some interest outside New Brooms and snooping for Cowgill. No! I said don't interrupt! What I'm suggesting is that although I love our garden, and it's always been my territory, I can't seem to find the time to do it all these days. It would be good if you could take on the flowers, and maybe the whole of the front garden. I'd still cut the grass, because that's not woman's work—'

At this point, Lois could keep silent no longer. 'What d'you mean, not woman's work!' She then listed all the dirty jobs and heavy tasks she had managed quite easily from the day they were married. 'I'm a big strong woman, and cutting the grass would be child's play to me.'

'So you'll do it then?' said Derek, taking a step in the right direction.

'I haven't said I would. I'm just pointing out that I could.' Lois looked at him and smiled. Then she got up and came round to him. He stood up and put his arms around her.

'To please me?' he whispered in her ear.

'To please you, I'd do anything,' Lois said, and added, 'Well, nearly anything.'

'*Anything*,' said Derek firmly, and grinned in triumph.

By evening, Derek had visited their nearest garden centre, collected up packets of seeds, a pair of ladies' gardening gloves, and a new trowel and fork. 'I'll clear a space in the greenhouse for you,' he said enthusiastically, 'and anything you want to know, just ask me. With any luck, we'll have some prize blooms to put in the horticultural show this year. Bet you'll get a first easily.'

Derek knew exactly what he was doing. At the mention of a challenge, Lois's expression changed. 'Ah, now you're talking,' she said. 'I bet I can beat those boring old men on the allotment any day. I'll show 'em. By the way,' she added, 'the front hedge needs clipping. I'll start on that straight after tea.'

'Blimey!' said Gran, who was listening open-mouthed. 'Now I've heard everything.'

*   *   *

Hunter Cowgill, cruising by in the early evening, could not believe his eyes. There was Lois, in tattered jeans and a beaten-up old hat of Derek's, up a step ladder, clipping the golden privet hedge.

He stopped on the opposite side of the road, opened the car window, and leaned across. 'That's what I like to see,' he called. 'Toning up the muscles. Soon be ready for anything. But seriously, Lois, isn't that too much for you so soon after the accident?'

Her face told him he'd said just the wrong thing, and he flinched in anticipation. The sharp retort was muted. Lois carefully came down the steps and looked across at him. She walked over and said seriously, 'You know, my Derek is not stupid. Never has been. He has just given me the perfect opportunity to gather information. You are the fourth person who has stopped to talk. None of the others in a car, of course, but just walking by. I don't need to tell you this could be very useful indeed.'

'Well done Derek! Anything you'd like to know from me?' Cowgill said, and wished his heart would stop thumping in that frightening way.

'On your way, Hunter,' Lois said. 'I'll be in touch.'

As he drove on, he began to hum quietly to himself. She'd called him Hunter, for the first time ever! Wasn't that the sun coming out, after a dull and rainy day?

Forty-Nine

Dot was waiting, ready dressed and clutching her few belongings in a plastic bag, when Evelyn arrived to collect her. In spite of her protestations of being absolutely fine, she looked thin and pale. But the twinkle in her eye was strong enough, and she refused help in walking out and into the car park.

'Blimey, Evie,' she said 'I was 'aving my convalescence in there, until they sussed me out. Mind you, I'm glad to be going. It's like being let out o' prison. The air's never really fresh in there, with air conditioning an' that. 'Ere, before we start, I'm dying for a fag – you got one in your handbag?'

Evie was speechless. She shook her head and remembered her resolution not to argue with Dot. If they were going to live together for a while, a short while, the only way to keep the peace was to agree with everything Dot said. And anyway, the old thing looked so fragile that Evelyn was determined to handle her gently.

They were halfway home, just entering Long Farnden, when Dot said, 'Slow up, Evie, I'll just nip in and see Mrs M about starting work again.'

'Don't be ridiculous!' said Evelyn, already forgetting her good intentions. 'Starting work? You'll not be doing that for several weeks yet.'

'Stop here,' said Dot, as if she had not heard. 'I shan't be long. You can read the paper or summat.' She opened the door and clambered out with difficulty. Evelyn was around the car to help her at once, but Dot shook her off. 'I can manage,' she said, and proceeded up the garden path.

Lois, standing at her office window, stared. It couldn't be! But it was, and Gran was answering the door. Lois rushed out and took Dot by the arm. 'You dope!' she said. 'Here, Gran, I'll take her into the office and you can make coffee. Is that Evelyn out there? She'd better come in too.'

'No!' Dot said sharply. 'She's all right out there. I just want a quiet word, Mrs M. And don't bother with the coffee, Mrs Weedon. I'm not stoppin' long enough.'

Gran withdrew huffily. Well, Dot and Lois could get on with it. Then she had an idea. She would go out and talk to Evelyn in the car, keep her company. Brightening, she opened the front door and walked down the path.

'How are you, Mrs M?' Dot said, settling herself with relief in a comfortable chair.

'Fine, thanks, but if you don't mind my saying so, you still look poorly. Why don't you go back with Evelyn and I'll call in and see you later?'

'No,' Dot said firmly. 'I need to tell you something important, and then I can rest easy.'

Lois sighed. 'Carry on, then,' she said.

'It's about the accident,' she said. 'Well, two accidents really. Mine and yours. Two too many, don'tcha think?'

Lois nodded. 'Let's hope there won't be another. They say these things go in threes.'

As if Lois hadn't spoken, Dot said, 'And then there was Handel, my husband. I expect you remember that. Fell into a gravel pit. Did he fall, or was he pushed? Now, Mrs M, while I was in hospital I had plenty of time to think. Whatever way you look at it, the person most likely behind it all was that sod Battersby. He nearly come a real cropper that time he wouldn't pay up, and it was only his toff mates who covered up for 'im.'

'But that was ages ago, wasn't it?'

'These things are never forgotten. Not in the Nimmo Mafia. That's what I call 'em. But the more I thought about it, the more I reckoned that Battersby's not bright enough to organize all that on his own. So what did I do? I remembered about that Joe Horsley. He was deep in debt, and Battersby got him out of it. Then, o' course, Horace began the gamblin' and went the same way. But Horace . . . he isn't a real colonel, by the way . . . honorary title, you might say. Anyway, he got a hold over Horsley, and now it's a two-way thing. Locked together in crime, they are.'

'Sounds like something on the telly,' Lois said rashly.

'It's the God's honest truth, Mrs M! We're talking about life and death here. I lost a husband and a son, and you and me nearly bought it as well. It don't get much worse than that!'

Lois was contrite. But she had felt excited at the possibility that Dot might come up with some new piece of information, and now it seemed not. She knew it all already.

'Sorry, Dot.' Lois was contrite, and endeavoured to put it right. 'But do you know what crime the two of them are up to? I know they've got petty gambling scams, but that's not enough to be prepared to attempt murder to keep it quiet. What else do you know?'

Dot was quiet for a few seconds. Then she closed her eyes, and put her hand over her forehead. 'Sorry, Mrs M. Feeling a bit wambly. Dizzy . . .' What little colour she had had drained away, and Lois got up.

'Right, that's it,' she said firmly. 'You're having a nice cup of tea, and then we'll get you safely to Evelyn's. And no arguments! I'm still the boss.'

A faint smile crossed Dot's face, and she said she was feeling a bit better, but yes, a cup of tea would be nice.

After Evelyn and Gran had returned to the house, and some stern words had been said to Dot, they rested for a while and then made their way back to the car. As Dot settled into the passenger seat, she beckoned to Lois, who leaned into the open window. Then Dot whispered, 'There's more, Mrs M. I'll tell you later.'

It had begun to rain, and in the chilly wind Lois and Gran hurried back to the house. 'Your hedge looks nice,' Gran said grudgingly, 'but you left a lot of clippings on the path. Folks could slip on those.'

'Glad you approve, Mum,' Lois said absently and disappeared into her office. She wanted to think about Dot's revelations. Was there anything lurking there that she'd missed? She had noticed that Dot could talk in a kind of code. What was not said was as important as the spoken words. Battersby and Horsley were locked in crime together. She had asked Dot what the crime was, but she'd not answered. Did she know? She had implied that she knew. Lois thought for a minute or two, and then said aloud, 'But does Margaret Horsley know?' Was she in it too, whatever *it* is? She went to see Dot in hospital. Was that an act of friendship, or a scouting-out visit, to see if the comatose Dot had said anything? Or was likely to say anything?

And then there was Blanche. A posh lady if ever there was one. And yet fond of Dot. Was it fondness, or a need to keep the widow of Handy Nimmo sweet? She seemed gentle and kind with young Darren, but there had been some upset there. Some reason why the boy had disappeared for twenty-four hours and couldn't explain where he'd been. And why *was* Darren so scared of Horace? A list, Lois said to herself. I need a list of all these things and then perhaps I'll see what common thread runs through. She took a pen and began to write, but crossed it out again and chewed her pen. Something else. Something I've missed or forgotten. Then she remembered how it all started. Saddle thefts – Battersby and Horsley?

Darren horse riding with Blanche. Battersby's empty stables, and Floss's mare . . . The point-to-point, and a bookie refusing to deal with the Colonel and Joe. Four attempts at murder – one successful? A loose horse . . .

Horses, horses, horses. More attempts to come? Lois shivered. She thought of her gardening project and her intention to put all her spare time into it, and almost regretted ever having met Cowgill. Almost.

'Dot is a very foolish woman,' Gran said, frowning at Lois as she came into the kitchen. 'And if I dared, I'd say the same about you. Two of a kind, if you ask me, as my friend Ivy Beasley says.'

'Your friend!' Lois laughed. 'She's an old dragon, and you know you've met your match with old Ivy. Anyway, what do you mean about me being a foolish woman? A *very* foolish woman?'

Gran shrugged. She said that if she remembered rightly, a certain daughter of hers had come straight out of hospital after a serious accident and gone straight off to a point-to-point, been wheeled about on bumpy fields by her husband, and come home exhausted. 'Who does that remind you of?' she ended up, her face rosy with indignation.

Lois was silent for a moment, considering the injustice of this attack. Then she realized that it wasn't unjust at all, that her mother was perfectly right. All she could think of to say was, 'But I'm younger and stronger than she is, poor old Dot.'

'Mmm,' said Gran. ''Nuff said.'

Lois sat down at the kitchen table and waited for her mother to put a frothy coffee in front of her. Josie had given them an Italian cream-maker, and Lois had become addicted to the delicious froth on top of her coffee. Gran did not hold with it. 'Instant is good enough for me, and should be good enough for you,' she said. 'Made with hot milk in a saucepan, couldn't be bettered. All this foreign *latte* and *express* stuff – it not only makes me choke, but makes twice the washing up. Here you are, here it is.'

'If that's meant to put me off, then hard luck. Mmm, delicious! Did we finish your flapjack? Could do with a piece to give me strength. As you say, I'm still an invalid and need building up.'

'Always the last word!' Gran exploded. 'I don't know what your dad would've said.'

'I do,' said Lois, who had been unable to do wrong in her father's eyes, even when she'd spent the night in a prison cell for shoplifting from Woolworth's in her teens, refusing to speak to the police. 'Anyway,' she continued, 'tell me what Evelyn and you talked about out there in the car.'

Gran sat down with her Nescafe and pursed her lips. 'It was a private conversation,' she said huffily. Lois said that if Gran would tell her, she would fill her in with the latest from Dot. She had no intention of doing so, but thought a severely edited version would do no harm.

Gran considered the offer, and began to speak. 'Well, we naturally talked about Dot and how she was a foolish, stubborn woman, and a trial to her sister. And then I said you'd been much the same, and we agreed that somehow both of you seemed to come up smelling of roses.' She expected a retort from Lois, but none came, and so she carried on. 'Evelyn was worried, o' course, as are we all, about what all these accidents are about. Apparently the police have said they want to talk to Dot as soon as she gets home. You'd think they'd have sorted it out by now . . . What's your Cowgill doing about it? Wasting his time talking to people clipping hedges, I expect.'

Lois merely raised her eyebrows, and said nothing.

'Anyway, Evelyn said she reckoned it was all to do with that Colonel at Waltonby. Old Battersby. She says she's discovered that Margaret Horsley – you know you sent Evelyn there instead of Dot – well, Margaret once had a passionate affair with Horace Battersby. Can you imagine anybody wanting to go to bed with him? Like going to bed with a dead stick . . .'

'Mum!' Lois said at last, in mock shock. 'Fancy you two discussing such things. But I agree that it's a funny business. They're still friends, aren't they? Perhaps there were no hard feelings?'

'Oh, yes there were! The Colonel's lady was furious, and said the Horsleys were never to be seen anywhere near her house again. Blanche Battersby is a gentle soul, but when she's roused, she's like a tigress.'

Lois said suspiciously, 'How did Evelyn know all this?'

'Margaret told her. Seems that Evelyn found her crying into a cup of tea the other day, and it all came tumbling out. Evelyn said she was really sorry for her, and reckoned that Joe was no better than Horace. Wife-beaters, the pair of them.'

'Did Margaret say that?' Lois said sharply. 'Actually say wife-beaters?'

'I'm just telling you what Evelyn said. Interesting, don't you think? I expect you'll want to be off now to your office to phone your friendly cop. The sooner those two get put behind bars the better.'

Fifty

The twins were awake early. They frequently woke at the same time, and now Jim, always the leader, looked at his watch on the bedside table. The grubby curtains were drawn across smeary windows, but rays of watery sunlight found their way through to the small room, where there was just enough space for twin beds, an old commode serving as a bedside table, and a narrow, gimcrack self-assembly cupboard. There were piles of clothing everywhere, mostly on the floor.

'Time to get up, Steve. We got a job to do today, if you ain't forgotten.'

Steve peered out from under the bedclothes at his brother. 'It's too early,' he said. He'd been awake for some time, but loved to lie in and think his thoughts away from his brother's domination.

'Nearly seven,' Jim replied. 'Get up, lazy sod!' A sudden burst of temper sent him across the room, where he tugged an ancient duvet off the curled-up Steven and dragged him roughly out of bed.

Downstairs their mother was frying sausages. 'Get up, you two!' she yelled. 'You got to make an early start!'

They appeared together, and sat down at the kitchen table. A strong smell of burning meat filled the room, and Jim groaned. 'Not burnt bangers again! God, what a mother! 'Ere, Steve, give us yours. Do a swap. I know you like 'em well done.' He sniggered, and Steve obligingly sank his teeth into a charred sausage.

Before they disappeared, their mother said, 'Give my love to your Uncle Joe and Auntie Margaret. Well, maybe just to Uncle Joe.'

'Shan't see 'im,' Jim said shortly. 'We go there, do the job, and beat it as fast as we can. Come straight back.'

'We'll see you when we get back. Shouldn't be too long,' said Steve mildly, smiling at his mother.

'We have other things to do, Steve,' Jim reminded him. 'Meetin' the lads in the city.'

'I'll expect you when I see you, then,' said their mother. 'Do a good job for Uncle Joe. We need to keep on the right side of him.'

Jim grinned and flexed his arm muscles. 'We'll do a good job all right. Come on, Steve. Look lively.'

So today's the day, thought Horace Battersby, liberally buttering his toast. Let's hope they do a better job than last time. 'Blanche,' he said loudly, and she came obediently in from the kitchen. 'I've been thinking about Floss and the mare. When she was so clumsy – Floss, that is, not the mare – I almost revoked the deal. Wretched girl is getting much too familiar. But I've had a better idea.'

'But we're very fond of Floss!' protested Blanche. 'She's not just a cleaner, Horace, I regard her as a friend. I thought you felt the same way . . .' Her voice tailed off. She was feeling depressed, and wished that Dot Nimmo would soon be back again. That odd woman always cheered her up, and she knew Alice P-K felt the same way. Floss was fine, of course, and Alice was happy with Evelyn, but they both agreed there was nobody like Dot. It would be awkward, of course, explaining to Mrs Meade that she would like to have Dot as often as possible, without hurting Floss's feelings. Oh well, perhaps she would ring the hospital today, and find out how Dot was.

Horace was still speaking, and Blanche's attention was wrested back when she heard him explaining his better idea. 'I shall tell Floss that she must share the mare with you. I know you miss your riding, and it will give the horse more exercise. Floss doesn't ride her enough, spending most of her time scrubbing floors. In fact, you can take her out this morning. I'll saddle her up for you and see you off. I'd like to check Maisie, see how she goes. Lovely day. Just right for a jog around the countryside. Or,' he added, as if it had just occurred to him, 'you could ask the barmy lad if he'd like a ride. Time he got back on a horse.' He knew this would appeal to Blanche, and waited.

'But . . .' Blanche had planned to go shopping in Tresham, but knew it was a waste of time trying to change Horace's mind. She supposed she could go this afternoon. She knew that Darren was due to be gardening this morning, and she might persuade him to have a walk round the village on the mare. Horace was right. It was time he got his confidence back. He had enjoyed riding so much. Yes, that would make it worthwhile, if she could persuade him.

'Very well, dear,' she said. 'I'm sure you're right.'

'There's a good girl,' smiled Horace. 'More coffee, please.' And he lifted the newspaper in front of his face to put a stop to the conversation.

As Blanche made fresh coffee, she thought about Horace's proposal. Floss would be upset, she was sure. She would see it as criticism of her care of Maisie. There must be a more tactful way of doing it. Perhaps if she asked Floss's permission to ride the mare when Floss was busy? That would be fine. Floss might even be flattered to be asked. She took the coffee to Horace, and told him how she would put it to Floss. She endeavoured to make it sound like a firm decision, and Horace looked up from the newspaper.

'Good idea, Blanche,' he said curtly. 'I was going to suggest it myself.' And then up went the newspaper again. As soon as she had left the room, he picked up the telephone.

Floss arrived soon after breakfast, and Blanche tentatively said to her that she might – with Floss's permission – take out the mare when Floss was working. Would Floss mind? Blanche would take great care of her, and of course would never want to ride her when Floss was free.

A small doubt entered Floss's mind, but she shrugged it off and said that she wouldn't mind in the least. On the contrary; it was a very good idea.

'Then would it be all right with you if I took her out this morning? Perhaps a little later on? Horace thinks *I'm* not getting enough exercise!'

So it was Horace behind the new arrangement. Floss's small doubt had been justified. The old sod was still angry with her about the dog pee, and this was his petty revenge. For two pins she would walk out and leave them to it. She was sure Mrs M would understand . . . But would she? This was just the kind of thing she had worried about, when the gift to Floss was suggested. Ah, well, better forget it. She was not one to bear grudges, even if horrible Horace was.

She assured Blanche that it would be fine, and even gave her permission for Darren to be walked around the village, if he would agree.

Halfway down the motorway, Jim pulled in to a service station. 'What are we stopping here for?' Steven said.

'Just need to check the tyres,' Jim said. 'Steering is a bit one-sided. We don't want anything to hold us up on our way back. No, don't get out. Can't trust you to do it properly. Just keep your eyes open.'

'What for?' said Steven.

'Anything, you idiot,' said Jim. 'Anything and everything.'

Quickly and efficiently Jim checked the tyre pressures, got back in the car and sped out of the service station.

'I didn't see nothin'' said Steven.

'I did,' Jim said sharply. 'I saw my idiot brother grinning at a bimbo in the car at the next pump.'

'What of it?'

'Just the kind of thing that's remembered,' Jim said. 'We don't want nobody remembering they saw a lecherous idiot grinning at them from a dirty green motor at a service station on the motorway.'

'You're paranoid,' said Steven, not quite sure what the word meant, but it sounded good. 'We're just two young lads out for a bit o' fun. Dozens like us.'

'Don't say that! We're special,' snapped Jim, and put his foot down hard on the accelerator, forgetting that a speeding ticket would bring them to the notice of the very people they were trying to avoid.

Floss had finished upstairs at the Battersbys, and Blanche suggested she had a coffee break before tackling the drawing room. 'Horace has scattered papers everywhere,' she said apologetically. 'He takes a newspaper apart as thoroughly as he does everything else,' she added. 'I'll have a coffee with you, and then I'll be off. Horace wants to see how she goes.'

Floss felt a pang. Maisie was hers, and they were used to each other. Still, she supposed Blanche must have ridden her before, and Darren was known to be really good with horses. 'I hope you have a nice ride,' she forced herself to say, and changed the subject. 'Did you know Dot Nimmo is out of hospital?'

'No! Is she really? How marvellous!'

Floss thought Blanche's reaction was a bit over the top, but continued. 'Mrs M told me on the phone. She says it'll be some while before she's well enough to start work, but the old thing is apparently keen to be back in harness.'

The news had lifted Blanche's spirits already. As she walked towards the stable, she heard the mare snickering. Probably thought she was Floss. What a nasty man Horace could be! He always knew the way to make people suffer. Had he always been like that? Probably. Love is blind, and she was certainly deeply in love with him at first. She stopped. She had forgotten Darren, and walked on to the kitchen garden. It was beginning to rain, more mist than real rain, and she wondered if Darren would be there. Yes, there he was, wheeling the new barrow between the vegetable beds.

'Darren! Come here a minute, please!'

Darren walked slowly towards her. Had he done something wrong? No, Mrs Battersby was smiling her lovely smile. It was all right. Quite safe. He greeted her with his usual, 'Lovely morning, Mrs Battersby,' though misty rain was still falling.

'I'm taking the mare out for some exercise, Darren. Would you like to come? Just sit on her and hold the reins? I'll be with you all the time, so you'll be quite safe.'

Safe, thought Darren. Mrs Battersby says I'll be safe. Nice horse. Gentle. Nice for Darren before Mum comes to take him home.

He nodded, and followed her to the stable. Blanche was glad that there was no sign of Horace. When Darren was up on the mare's back, he had the old feeling of being in close touch with a friend. He knew she was excited, looking forward to going out. He patted her neck, and made a gentle purring noise. The horse immediately quietened. Blanche took a leading rein and they began to leave the yard and walk down towards the road.

Jim and Steve were parked a few yards away from the Battersbys' entrance, the car windows open. The village was quiet. Rush-hour traffic was long gone, and the children were in school, not yet ready to emerge into the playground in a noisy throng.

'I can hear somebody,' said Steve quietly. 'I can hear hooves on the gravel, and a woman's voice.'

'If it's them,' Jim whispered, 'hold on to your seat.'

The rain had stopped, and the skies were clearing. Blanche talked soothingly to Darren, and he was relaxed and smiling. The mare hesitated, pricking her ears, but Blanche urged her on, and they came to the gates, which Horace must have opened.

Jim revved up the engine suddenly, as loudly as possible, and drove straight at the emerging trio. He turned sharply at the last minute and was gone. The mare reared up, and tore the leading rein out of Blanche's hands. She screamed and clawed at the flying mane.

As the mare twisted round in terror, Darren was thrown off. He too was screaming, and as he hit the ground with an unbearable thud, the high-pitched cry ended, suddenly and with a terrible finality. Then there was no sound except for galloping hooves fleeing along the road in fear, and Blanche stumbling back to the house, shouting fruitlessly for her husband.

Fifty-One

Horace had heard the screams and Blanche shouting for help. He'd heard the squeal of tyres as the twins made their getaway, and he'd heard the galloping hooves. He got up from his desk and looked out of the window. He saw Blanche limping up the drive, but the rest of it was round the

corner of the curving gravel. So Blanche was all right. Thank
God for that. They seemed to have done well this time. He
went over to his desk and dialled for an ambulance, told them
there had been an accident, and gave details. 'The lad might
need urgent attention,' he said. Then he walked slowly to the
front door, immediately breaking into a run as he stepped
outside.

'Horace! Quick! Send for an ambulance!' Blanche collapsed
to the ground, and Horace knelt beside her. 'Leave me!' she
said. 'Darren, by the gate. Terrible accident. Go now!'

'I have already sent for an ambulance,' he said. 'I heard the
screams and the terrified mare, and knew something dreadful
had happened. They should be here soon. Let me get you into
the house . . .'

'No! Go and see to Darren. He's not moving.'

'Probably concussed,' Horace said calmly. 'Now, come on,
Blanche, let's get you up.'

'Go!' she screamed, and Horace recoiled. Her face was
twisted with pain and hatred. She struggled to her feet and
limped on towards the house. 'I'll phone his mother,' she
yelled back at him, and made it to the front door.

By the time Horace reached the gate, the village network
had gone into action and there was a small crowd surrounding
the prostrate Darren. Horace recognized the vicar, standing
over him and keeping the others at bay. A silence had
descended on the little group as they stared at Darren. 'So
still,' muttered an elderly woman to her neighbour.

'Ah, Colonel, is the ambulance . . .?' The vicar turned to
greet him.

'Yes, the ambulance and police are on the way.' Horace
looked at Darren, and was overwhelmed with a feeling of
nausea. Surely he wasn't *dead*? Oh my God, he thought,
desperately trying not be sick, have those two . . .? At this
point he made a dash for the other side of the hedge and threw
up. Everything was spinning, and he sat down on the grass
with his head between his knees. He heard sirens approaching
and made a huge effort to stand up. Reaching the gate, he
leaned against a pillar and took deep breaths.

Mrs Smith, hurrying down the street, saw only the back of
the crowd and the approaching ambulance and police car. She
pushed her way through, saw her son motionless on the ground,

and let out the most blood-curdling cry that Horace had ever heard. It was as if she had been physically pierced to the heart.

Then there were ambulance men dealing with Darren, lifting him on to a stretcher and into the ambulance. They helped his mother in beside him, closed the door and drove off, the siren blaring. Horace watched dully. Everything had slowed down, and the moving figures seemed vague and unfamiliar. He was aware of someone speaking to him, and he blinked, trying to clear his vision. It was a policeman, who took his arm and escorted him back to the house.

Blanche stood swaying at the door, and next to her was Floss, dumb with shock and looking frighteningly pale. The policeman held both their arms, helped them into the drawing room and into chairs, and then went back for Horace. Floss got immediately to her feet again, and said shakily, 'Shall I put the kettle on? Mum says hot sweet tea is best,' and then she burst into tears and ran from the room.

'Let her go,' said Hunter Cowgill, coming through the door. 'She'll recover better on her own. Now then, let's all take a breath and try to sort out what has happened here.'

Lois received the call when she was in the shower. She had been gardening early in the morning, and after Gran came back from the shop she decided to clean up and go off to visit a new client.

Over the sound of spraying water, she heard Gran's voice shouting to her and, wrapping herself in a towel, she emerged. She took the phone and retreated. It was Cowgill, and Lois began to joke, saying she was in the shower and thank God he didn't have a video screen on his mobile. There was no response, and she knew at once that something serious had happened.

'Derek? Has something happened to Derek?' she said anxiously.

'No, Lois dear, not to Derek.' He paused.

Lois said again, 'Has something happened?'

'Yes, I'm afraid so. There's been an accident at Waltonby. Young Darren . . . came off a horse.'

'But . . . What d'you mean? Is he badly hurt?'

'I'm afraid he hasn't made it, Lois.'

There was such a long silence that Cowgill thought maybe they'd been cut off. 'Lois?' he said. 'Are you still there?'

'What kind of an accident?' Lois said quietly. 'Tell me what happened. *Exactly* what happened.'

Cowgill reflected that he was the policeman and the one to ask the questions, but Lois was special. He knew she had been fond of Darren Smith, and had been the one who had found him, distressed and lost. She was entitled to know as many details as he had so far gleaned. And, more importantly, the whole thing seemed undeniably linked with the other hit-and-run accidents, and so with Lois herself.

He told her what he knew from questioning Blanche, who was apparently the only witness. Floss and Horace were in the house, but could not see the gateway from any of the windows. Blanche had collected Darren from the garden and was to take him for a walk on the leading rein around the quiet village. The intention was to give him confidence to ride again. He hadn't been anywhere near a Battersby horse since his disappearance. They had reached the gate and were just hesitating to make sure it was safe to go, when the car came from nowhere, accelerating fast and aiming straight for them. At the last minute it had swerved violently, nearly overturning, and continued until it was out of sight.

'Did Blanche see anything of the car?'

'Unfortunately no,' Cowgill replied. 'She was knocked to the ground by the rearing horse, and when she crawled across to Darren, the car had long gone. Her ankle is broken, apparently, but she managed to get to the house to phone Darren's mother.'

'Brave woman,' muttered Lois. 'And Horace?' she added, suddenly angry. 'Where the hell was bloody Horace? He must have heard the row – a terrified horse screams, you know. He couldn't miss it! Didn't Floss hear something?'

'She was using the vacuum cleaner upstairs at the back of the house, and it's a noisy old thing apparently. She didn't know what had happened until Horace called her.'

'Where is she now? I must come over straight away.'

'I think she's gone home, and I'm on the way back to the station. There's a great deal to do, Lois, but I wanted you to know first. And I'm going to ask a favour of you . . . I wonder if you're up to making a quick visit to Mrs Smith some time? I'll let you know when she's back from the hospital. She thinks a lot of you. As do I. I must go now, but get in touch whenever you need to, day or night. Are you all right? Is Gran there?'

'Yes. I'm all right, Gran or no Gran. Bye. I'll be in touch.' She ended the call, and slowly towelled herself dry. She knew she ought to be crying for Darren and his mum, but she couldn't. Her anger was too great for tears. If she had had the strength, she would have gone straight to Waltonby and strangled Battersby, and laughed at his pleas for mercy. As it was, she dressed slowly, her thoughts churning, and went downstairs.

Gran took one look at her and asked, 'What's happened?'

Lois told her the bare details and then, asking politely for a strong coffee, went into her office and closed the door.

Fifty-Two

Joe Horsley was out on the farm, enjoying himself on his quad bike. With no speed restrictions on bumpy field tracks, he roared joyfully as he took off into the air on an especially hard, dry rut in the set aside margin of a maize field. When he slowed down to open a gate, he heard his mobile ringing.

'Hello? What d'you want, Margaret? I'm really up against it to get this job done before it rains . . . What? Are you sure? Bloody hell, they've done something right for once . . . No, no, of course I don't know who was in the car! Just *listen* for a minute, will you!'

But Margaret had signed off. When the mobile began to ring again, Joe had a good idea who it was. 'Horsley! Have you heard?' Battersby said. There was then a tirade so loud that Joe held the mobile a couple of feet away to avoid ear damage. He had had just enough warning and thought quickly.

'Hang on a minute, Horace!' he said. 'The boys did as they were told, as far as I can tell. Put the frighteners on. It can't be helped that the ruddy horse went spare, can it? And the idiot boy shouldn't have been riding if he couldn't control the thing. What? Blanche holding it with a leading rein? That's not nearly enough if a horse is in a panic. For God's sake, calm down, man! The lads always get away at speed. It's one of their eerie twin things – you don't even see them go. Take it from me, Horace, we're in the clear. What? Oh, don't worry, she'll get over it. A broken ankle soon mends. Must go. Bye.'

Joe opened the gate, drove through, and left it open as he revved up the engine as fast as it would go, taking off with a whoop along the grassy track of the next field.

In a noisy bar in the seamier quarter of Nottingham, the twins were celebrating. 'Did you see that bloody horse? Like something out of a wild west movie!' Jim was high on success and a lot of something more substantial.

Steven said nothing, but drank deeply to the bottom of the glass.

'Hey, steady! I don't fancy carrying you home. What's the matter with you, anyway? We done a good job, and Uncle Joe'll stump up the cash and maybe a bonus for excellent performance. He wants that dope out of the way. He told us.'

'We killed 'im,' Steven said dully. 'We killed that kid on the horse. I looked back. He was dead.'

'Shh! For Christ's sake keep your voice down. So what? Anyway, he was probably knocked out from the fall. Why d'you always spoil things? You'd better go 'ome. Get a bus. Go on, bugger off. And don't tell Mum *anything*, d'you hear?'

Steven looked at Jim blearily. 'You wait,' he said. With his face very close to his brother's, he stuck his thumb in his mouth and sucked. Then he turned away and disappeared through the crowds. Jim shrugged his shoulders, and turned back to his mates at the bar.

Margaret was waiting for Joe when he finally came back. His sense of triumph ebbed when he saw her face. It was streaked with tears, and her eyes were red. As he walked towards her, she slapped his face as hard as she could, first one side and then the other. Then she began to yell.

'You bastard! You bloody bastard!' She thumped his chest, and he stumbled backwards.

Grasping her fists, he forced her into a chair. 'Shut up! Shut up and *listen*!' he shouted. She was shaking violently now, as if in a convulsion. Slowly she quietened down, and was limp, her head hanging down. He released her hands and sat down on a chair next to her.

'Margaret, just listen and try to answer some questions. I know you're upset, but you've obviously got hold of the wrong end of the stick. Tell me what you've heard, and who from.'

She raised her head and looked at him. He was nervous, she could tell. He was as nervous as hell. So it was true. Perhaps she should play along, and see what he said. While she had waited for him to come back from the fields, she had made a plan, a last-ditch plan that would end all her unhappiness one way or another.

'Your charming sister phoned,' she said in a quiet voice. 'Wanted to know where the twins were. Urgent message, apparently. Seems she thought they were down in this part of the world. Something about a job they were doing for you?'

'Ah,' said Joe. 'What did you say?'

'I said I hadn't seen them and didn't know anything about it. I was not anxious to prolong the conversation.'

'So what else?' Joe was chewing his fingernails now, and Margaret grimaced. They were already bitten down to the quick.

'Do you have to be so disgusting?' she said.

'Get on with it!' Joe put his hands in his pockets. He was losing patience.

'I thought I was supposed to be listening?'

'Answer the questions first, you stupid woman.'

'Take that back,' Margaret said, moving as if to stand up.

He reached out and pushed her back into the chair. 'What else have you heard?' he shouted. 'A call from my sister wouldn't get you in this state . . .'

'I had another phone call. This time it was anonymous. Difficult to tell whether it was a man or woman. Disguised, I suppose. It told me a tragic story, Joe. About a horse and a young lad who fell off and was killed. There was a car, apparently, driven fast, straight at the horse, by two men. They did not stop and the car will never be found. That's what the voice said. Then he warned me to take care, even with nearest and dearest, and then he rang off.'

She stopped there, and watched him closely. He was visibly shocked, and made a great effort to pull himself together.

Margaret continued. 'So I'm listening, Joe. What did you want to tell me?'

'All rubbish,' he croaked. 'Take no notice. You get calls like that from perverts, getting their kicks from putting the fear of God into women. Take no notice.'

'Right,' she said, meekly obedient now. 'And what was it you wanted to tell me?'

'It'll keep,' Joe said. 'I need to go out now. Shan't be long. I'll tell you then. Now don't you worry, Margaret. Put the whole thing out of your mind. Ring your dad and have a chat. He always cheers you up.'

She said nothing. How could he do it? After all these years of marriage, he still thought he could soothe the little woman with a few kind words, and all would be well. She watched him drive out of the yard, and then went upstairs to splash her face with cold water and bathe her sore wrists. After that, she would settle down in the sitting room and think out the sequence of moves in her plan.

The first thing she decided was that she couldn't do it on her own. And the only ally who would be of any use was Blanche Battersby. This was going to be tricky, since Blanche was no friend. Although it was a long time ago, Margaret's affair with Horace had caused Blanche a great deal of heartache. But was it because she was so in love with her Horace, or because of the humiliation she would suffer if the affair became public? Margaret knew perfectly well that, like her own, the Battersbys' marriage was a bit of a dead duck.

How could she coax Blanche to help? Was there any common ground where they could meet and maybe mend the split? It came to Margaret like a blessing from above. Dot Nimmo. Dot was valued by both of them, and with any luck would soon be returning to work. That could be it. Blanche could be approached on the subject of Dot, and then it would be up to Margaret to work a diplomatic miracle.

What was it Joe said? Ring Dad. Well, maybe she would do just that. He always loved to hear from her, and she could sound him out on one or two things. She got up from the chair and walked to the window. Down towards the bottom of the lawn there was a small lake that Joe had made for her, years ago. She saw a flash of colour, and, holding her breath, watched a kingfisher alight, the first she had ever seen. She remembered how Joe had promised her that one day a king-fisher would come, and felt a pang of sadness at how he had changed. After a while, she went out into the hall and dialled her father's number.

Fifty-Three

The next morning, Cowgill called again, saying that Mrs Smith was back home in Waltonby, and had said she would like to see Lois any time. The funeral would be on Friday, at two o'clock in Waltonby church. Mrs Smith was calm, but Cowgill had the feeling she could collapse at any time and would need support. There were no relatives, and she had no idea where Darren's father was, nor did she want to find out.

'I'll go this morning,' Lois said. 'How's Mrs Battersby? I shall call on her, too, to arrange for someone to fill in for Floss. Poor girl is heartbroken. I've told her to have a day or two off.'

At this moment, the doorbell rang, and Lois put down the phone and went to answer it. It was Floss. 'Can I come in, Mrs M? I have to talk to someone, and Mum's . . . well, she's Mum. You know . . .'

'Come into the kitchen, Floss,' Lois said, taking her arm. 'It's warm in there, and there's nothing secret from Gran, even if I try to keep it secret!'

Floss was shivering, though it was not particularly cold outside. 'It's a mackerel sky today,' Gran said by way of a greeting. 'Means we shall have a change in the weather. Come and sit down and I'll make us some coffee.'

'Sorry to bother you, Mrs Weedon. It was just that . . .' Floss burst into tears, and Lois put her arm around her. She was sniffing hard herself, and Gran pulled a tissue from her apron pocket and dabbed her own eyes. After a minute or two, Floss sighed deeply and turned to Lois. 'He was a nice lad. Seemed to belong somewhere in another place where the rest of us couldn't go. He was lost here. Never felt safe. Except in Battersby's garden – provided the Colonel wasn't about – or on the allotment.'

'How is your mare?' Lois asked. 'Did you catch her?'

'Oh yes, after a while. She went into one of those meadows out towards Fletching, and I talked her into standing still. I rode her home, and she was trembling all the way. When I got her into the stable, old Battersby came down to see if she was all right. Couldn't have cared less about me. He looked ten years older. Really shaken up. I heard Blanche shouting at him, and no wonder. He had apparently told her he would help with saddling up the mare and getting them on their way, but he was nowhere to be seen. *I* knew where he was, of course. He was in his study. It looks out down the drive, but he wasn't that quick off the mark even after all the yelling and neighing. I didn't hear it with that old vacuum cleaner going. Did you know Blanche has broken her ankle?'

'Yeah. I'm going over there in a while. I said I'd send somebody else in until you felt better.'

'I'd rather go to work, and I don't mind going over there. I might be able to help more, knowing where everything is. Poor Blanche won't be able to get about. I don't want to stay at home, Mrs M, just thinking about it. I'd be better doing something.'

After she had gone, Lois telephoned the Battersbys and of course Horace answered. 'How is Mrs Battersby?' she asked, and the Colonel grunted that she would be fine in no time.

'Is Floss coming in this afternoon?' he said. 'I can't do it all on my own.' He sounded sorry for himself, and Lois bridled.

'I'm sure you're very capable,' she said, 'what with organizing armies, an' that. Anyway, Floss will be with you as usual. I am sure you will respect the fact that she was and is very upset. Thank you.'

She rang off, and then dialled Mrs Smith to tell her she would be with her in half an hour. The poor woman's voice was weak, but she assured Lois she would be very pleased to see her.

'Give her my condolences,' Gran said. 'He was a good lad. That time he came and had tea, d'you remember? He was very partial to my chocolate cake . . .' Then she reached for the tissues again, and Lois tactfully went out to her van.

*   *   *

In the shop, Josie fielded a number of questions about Darren. News between villages travels fast, and several of the older women had been full of sympathy and understanding for Mrs Smith. Others had not been quite so understanding. 'A blessing in disguise,' said one, and, oblivious of Josie's frown, continued, 'There was no future for him. Nothing but worry and disappointment for his mother. No, the Almighty knows when to take his own.' Josie fumed, but said nothing.

'Stupid old bag!' she burst out, as soon as the woman had left. But there were others with the same sentiments, and Josie felt like putting a bulletin on the door. 'Darren Smith has died, and IT IS NOT A BLESSING IN DISGUISE!' Rob had not gone in to work today, and he calmed her down. 'People always say stupid things at such times,' he said, 'mostly because they're embarrassed and don't know what to say. They like a happy ending, and this is the only one they can think of.'

Josie thought privately that this was just about the most useless way of looking at it, but then her mother came into the shop, and she went to greet her. 'Sorry, Mum, about Darren. What a sodding thing to happen.'

'Don't swear, Josie,' Lois said mechanically. 'But yes, it is a sodding thing to happen. I'm just going over to see Mrs Smith. She wants to see me.'

'Oh, Mum. Would you like me to come too? You look very tired. Shouldn't you still be resting?'

Lois shook her head. 'No, I feel like poor little Floss. I'm better doing something. I thought I'd take a gift for Mrs Smith. Are those yesterday's flowers?'

'Certainly not!' said Josie. 'They're fresh this morning. Here, take a couple of bunches from me. Though what good are flowers when you've lost your only son?' She bent down to pick out the best bunches from the bucket, and was able to hide her tears. 'Mum,' she said, when she straightened up, 'do *you* think it is a blessing in disguise?'

Lois stared at her. 'Good heavens, no! Do you?'

Josie shook her head, and began to wrap gift paper around the flowers. 'There's some as does,' she said quietly.

'They should talk to Mrs Smith,' Lois said. 'Bye-bye, duckie. Don't let 'em upset you.'

*   *   *

Mrs Smith opened the door, and although Lois thought she had prepared herself for what might be, she was taken aback by the deathly pallor of the woman's face.

'Come in, please,' Mrs Smith said, and stood aside to allow Lois to enter the narrow hall. 'Go into the sitting room, please. The kettle's on. Would you like tea or coffee?'

Lois wanted neither, but she said tea would be fine, thinking it might help. In the few minutes while she was alone, she looked around the room, seeing all the photographs, neatly framed, of Darren. Darren in a paddling pool, Darren on the beach, Darren on a tricycle. And Darren on a donkey, his head thrown back in laughter.

'Thanks,' she said, taking the tea. 'It was kind of you to let me come and see you. My mum sent you her sincere condolences.'

'He liked her,' Mrs Smith said blankly. 'He said he liked Mrs Weedon. He said so several times. But then, he said most things several times.'

It was like watching an old factory chimney crumble under explosive. Lois took Mrs Smith's hand, as she seemed to get smaller and smaller, hunching up into a tight ball of grief. No sound came from her. It would be easier, thought Lois, holding on, if Darren's mum could yell and shout and drum up a storm.

Then Lois did it for her. Her eyes filled with tears at last, and she yelled out loud, 'It's not fair! It's not fair! Where were you, bloody Horace!'

Mrs Smith slowly uncurled and looked at Lois. 'Yes, dear,' she said in a whisper. 'He was supposed to be helping. Where *was* Horace Battersby?'

Fifty-Four

As Lois opened her car door, after a good hour with Mrs Smith, she heard a voice calling her name. She turned around and saw an old lady walking with difficulty towards her.

'Hello? Can I help you?' Another client for New Brooms?

'Good morning, Mrs Meade.' The voice was breathless with effort. 'You don't know me, but I am Margaret Horsley's aunt. Everybody calls me Auntie Eileen. Have you got a minute to spare? I just wanted to have a word.'

Lois looked at her. A nice face, with a wise expression. 'Why don't you sit in my van for a minute or two, while we talk?' she said, and helped the old lady into the passenger seat. 'Now, what was it you wanted to ask me?'

'Nothing,' said Auntie Eileen firmly. 'I didn't want to *ask* you anything. I've something to *tell* you.' Lois nodded and waited. 'It's about Darren. I've known him since he was very small. He was happy in this village. Everybody knew him, and he was so anxious to please that you couldn't help liking him. Nobody made much fuss about it, but we all supported his mother where we could. A village was the right place for him. His farmer friend over the fields taught him to ride, and he was really good with horses.'

Lois looked surreptitiously at her watch. She knew all this already, and wondered how she could shorten the chat. She was still planning to call on the Battersbys before going home.

'You'll know most of this, I expect,' Eileen said, not missing the glance at the watch. 'But there is something you probably don't know. You might wonder why I'm telling you. Well, I've heard about you and cases you've helped the police with. That's why, and what I'm going to tell you might help Mrs Smith. Somebody's got to pay for Darren's death, which I'm pretty sure was not an accident.'

Lois sat up straight, startled into close attention. The object of her talk with Mrs Smith had been to comfort and support, but the poor woman had been too distressed to reveal anything of incidental use. Now, either the old lady was wandering, dramatizing in the way of village gossips, or she really did know something. 'Go on, Auntie Eileen,' she said. 'Take your time.'

Eileen did not need to take time. She had mulled over the facts for so long now, determining all the while to reveal them to the right person, and now she spoke fluently and clearly.

'Blanche Battersby knew all Darren's difficulties, and as she is a Christian woman, she did her best to help. He loved working in their garden, and then began to ride the quietest

of their horses, always with Blanche by his side. The Colonel
kept well out of the way. I heard him one day, out by the
gate, saying loudly that Blanche was wasting her time. The
boy would never be any good.'

'Where do you live, Auntie Eileen?' Lois hesitated, and
then added, 'Do you mind if I call you Eileen? It seems more
natural . . .'

'Call me what you like, dear, as long as you don't call me
early in the morning. Oh yes, I forgot to tell you. I live just
around the corner, next to the school. I spend a lot of time at
my gate, talking to the children. They know me, and I know
most of them.' She tut-tutted and added, 'Except for the ones
that are hustled into four-by-fours at the school gates, that is.
They love to chat, do the children. Amazing what they know,
what they pick up from school.'

'And what were you saying about Darren?'

'It's not unconnected, dear. Have patience! Well, one day
the Colonel saw Darren riding in the paddock, jumping a nice
old horse over some low jumps that Blanche had fixed up.
There were a couple of the children there as well. Blanche
used to give them lessons after school. It was them that told
me what happened. Seems the Colonel shouted across to
Darren, "Well done, lad!" He was smiling, and seemed
surprised, they said. Then he went into a huddle with Blanche,
and the children's mother was cross because they were late
having their lesson. They were indignant, and said it wasn't
their fault!'

'And after that?'

'Darren was often round the village. I used to see him,
always up on a horse, going by with Blanche. One day she
stopped at my gate and had a word. Darren was very shy, you
know, but he was excited, and suddenly said, "Going to a
point-to-point tomorrow! Lots of horses. Maybe Darren have
a ride!"'

'But how could . . .?' Lois stopped sharp. She had seen in
her rear-view mirror the tall figure of the Colonel approaching.
'Um, Eileen,' she said. 'Colonel Battersby is coming this way.
I'm going to drive off now, and I do have a good reason. I'll
bring you back straight away. Fasten your seatbelt.'

Starting the engine, she drove off quickly before the Colonel
could see who was in the van with her. He might know the

van, but couldn't possibly see Eileen. 'Sorry about that,' Lois said, when they were out of sight. 'I'll explain.'

'No need,' said Eileen. 'He's dangerous. And now it's all gone wrong, he's probably desperate.'

Then she finished her account of Darren and the point-to-point. Apparently he'd been taken, but of course had not ridden a horse. 'But when he came back,' Eileen continued, 'he told his mother, who told me, that the Colonel had said that one day Darren would ride in the races, if he was a good boy and did what he was told. Mrs Smith was really proud, poor woman. After that, Darren was always there, riding horses, and some of them were not quiet at all. His mum said Darren was so good with them. He could ride a bucking bronco, she told everyone in the village. Sometimes Margaret's Joe was there as well, and he told her the same.'

'So what happened? Did he get to ride in a race?'

Eileen shook her head. 'Good heavens, no. After that they took him to one or two more races, and then that one when he went missing. I reckon there's a lot more to find out.'

Lois pulled up outside the school. 'Thanks for listening,' Eileen said, smiling. 'Sorry I can't tell you anything else, but you'll find out. Bless you, dear.' She hobbled into her garden and shut the gate.

'Bye,' Lois said, 'and watch your back!' She made it sound like a joke, but she meant it.

Lois decided she would postpone her visit to the Battersbys. She needed to think around what Eileen had told her. Her own instinct about the point-to-point had been on the right track, it seemed. The Colonel had promised Darren he would ride in a race, if he was a good boy. How could he possibly do that? Surely there would be all kinds of rules and regulations about something as dangerous as horse racing? She needed to know. Perhaps Cowgill could help there? Time to get in touch. When she was back home, she checked her messages and saw one had come in. Mrs Horsley – would Lois ring her back? What did she want? Well, she could wait.

Gran had followed her into the office. 'If you don't come into the kitchen and eat something, my girl,' she said, hands on hips, 'I am going to chain you to a bedpost and throw away the key.'

Lois frowned at the interruption, then relented. 'I'm starving,' she confessed. 'Lead on, Macduff.'

Margaret Horsley telephoned again about an hour later, and asked if she could come over and see Lois. 'Would you be at home for a while now?' she said. She sounded odd, as if she had been crying, or shouting. Her voice was muffled, and when she heard that Lois would be available, she rang off straight away.

'I'll be in my office for a while,' Lois said to Gran. 'Mrs Horsley is calling in, quite soon, I think. Then I do have to go out again later.'

Gran made a face, but decided to say nothing more. At least she had fuelled Lois for another few hours. She set up the ironing board near the door into the hall so that she would hear the doorbell.

Margaret arrived half an hour later, and Gran was there to open up. 'Yes? Can I help you?' she said, perfectly well aware who the woman was, and what she wanted.

'I have an appointment to see—'

Lois appeared from her office and took over. 'Thanks, Mum,' she said. As Gran stalked off, Lois stood back to allow Margaret to go ahead of her. As she passed, Lois was aware of a strong whiff of alcohol. Oh, grief! What now? She sat down at her desk and prepared to listen.

'It's about the cleaning,' Margaret said, and her words were faintly slurred. 'I was wondering if Dot would be back soon? Evelyn's all right, but not as good as Dot, and I really would like her back soon.'

Lois looked at her hard, and knew that this was not the reason she had come. A casual telephone call would have given her the answer. She began to feel uneasy, as if something dangerous was round the corner. On the several occasions that this had happened before, she had always been right. She wished devoutly that it hadn't struck her just at this moment.

'It'll be another week or two, Mrs Horsley,' she said. 'But Dot is determined to get going as soon as possible, so I'm sure you won't have to wait much longer. I am sorry you don't find Evelyn satisfactory . . . is there any particular thing you'd like to mention?'

Margaret shook her head. She seemed to have nothing more

to say, and half rose from her chair. Then she sat down again, and looked waveringly at Lois.

'You know, don't you?' she blurted out finally.

'Know what?'

'About Darren and the horse, and my husband and that bloody Horace, and their pathetic little scams at the races? And then the sods involved my father. I couldn't stand that. My old dad. The last straw. Now a defence–fence–fenceless lad has been killed.'

'Why are you telling me this, Mrs Horsley?' Lois wished she had already telephoned Cowgill, and alerted him that something was very wrong and could become scary.

Margaret looked surprised. 'So you can help me do something about it, of course!' she said. 'You do that sort of thing, don't you? Everybody knows. Joe knows and the Colonel knows, and even that stuck-up bitch Blanche knows. Why else d'you think you nearly snuffed it?'

'Ah,' said Lois. 'Now, Mrs Horsley, I'm going to get Mum to make us some nice strong coffee, and you can tell me all about it. Everything you can remember.'

'No!' Margaret said violently. 'Don't need coffee. Head's as clear as a bell. And I've told you most of what I know. Now, I want you to come with me. I'll pay. I need a witness, and you're the best person I can think of. I tried asking the lovely Blanche, but she put the phone down on me. So that's that. Are you ready?'

'Where are we going?' Lois said, thinking it best to humour her.

'You'll see,' Margaret said. 'Not far. Now, are you coming or aren't you?'

'I just have to make one call. Message left for me, and it sounds urgent.'

'No calls,' Margaret said. 'This is urgent. If you can't come now, I'll do it myself. God knows what'll happen, but . . .' She blinked hard, and took Lois's arm. 'Please,' she said, and Lois followed her out of the room, yelling to Gran that she'd be back soon, and not to worry.

They got into Margaret's car, and took off on an erratic course up the High Street. Lois fumbled for her mobile in her bag on the car floor, hoping that Margaret would not notice that without taking it out, she found Cowgill's

number, made sure it was ringing, and then quickly closed
it down.

She pulled out a packet of Polo mints and offered one to
Margaret. 'Take it,' she said as sternly as she could. 'Wherever
we're going, it would be better if you didn't stink of drink.'

Fifty-Five

Lois knew very soon where they were going. They were
on the Waltonby road, and she said, 'Are we going to the
Battersbys'?'

Margaret nodded. 'Joe's there. He told me for once where
he was going. Two birds with one stone,' she added and
laughed.

Lois did not like the laugh, nor the imagery. *Kill* two birds
with one stone? She looked over into the back seat, but there
was nothing there but a small handbag.

'Nothing in there,' Margaret said, pleased with her own
sharpness. 'I'm not drunk, you know, just had enough to give
me courage. Look in the pocket at the back of your seat, and
you'll see a flask. Have a slurp, go on! Then give me one.
Go on! I thought you were supposed to be so tough? It's
whisky. Good for you, Joe always says.'

Lois reached for the flask, pretended to drink, and said, 'Are
you sure you should have more? After all, you are driving—'

Margaret snatched the flask from her and took a long
swallow. 'Trust me,' she said expansively. 'Passed my driving
test first time, you know. Now, here we are. You get out and
I'll lock the car.

'Why?' Lois said. 'It's not likely to be stolen here.'

'In case they decide to make a quick getaway,' Margaret
replied, and laughed again. It was a mirthless laugh, and Lois
shivered. Whatever Margaret had in mind, it was not going
to be a pleasant reunion.

*   *   *

Horace Battersby and Joe sat on opposite sides of the Colonel's desk, and their conversation was drying up. Horace had not believed Joe when he said they were in the clear. He'd had some very harsh words to say about the twins. He considered that Darren's death was extreme carelessness. He had instructed Joe that they should frighten them, scare them off, but not kill. He began to wonder what exactly Joe had told them.

Dot and the Meade woman narrowly escaped death – well, they might just get away with that, though the police had been round asking more questions. Blanche had gone in to Tresham that afternoon, and they'd had a row before she went. She'd said she was fed up with all this and was thinking of leaving for good.

'It seems your Margaret rang her,' Horace continued. 'Blanche wouldn't speak to her, but is now convinced the affair is on again. God, it's trouble every way you look! I heartily wish you'd never got me in to this.'

'What d'you mean? If I remember rightly, you were the one who got me—'

'Oh well, it's no good going over it now,' Horace interrupted. 'We have to decide what we're going to do and say. It's serious *now*, but if our aborted master plan for Darren leaks out, then we'll be up against the firing squad. Just a minute!' he added, getting up from the desk. 'Is that a car? Blanche is not due back yet – if ever!'

The doorbell rang. Both men froze. 'You go,' said Horace.

Fifty-Six

'Well, fancy seeing you!' Margaret said as the door opened a fraction. 'Let me in, Joe. I am sure Horace will be pleased to see me. And my friend Lois here.'

She put her foot in the doorway so that he couldn't close it, and smiled at Lois. 'You don't mind my using your first name, do you? S'more friendly . . .' Lois said it was fine, and waited in some trepidation.

Joe slowly opened the door and stood aside. 'Come on, Lois,' Margaret said, and, just saving herself from tripping on the step, marched in. 'Where is he?' she asked.

Joe led the way to the Colonel's study and walked in, followed by the two women. Horace began to bluster, ordering them to knock before they interrupted him when he was working, but Margaret ignored him. She pulled two chairs up to the desk and motioned to Lois to sit down.

'And you, Joe,' she said. 'And you can shut up, Horace,' she added rudely. 'We've got a lot of talking to do. Where's the lovely Blanche?'

'Gone shopping,' Joe said quickly. Horace was looking apoplectic, and Joe was anxious that he should not reach for the paper knife, or worse. 'I apologize for Margaret,' he said. 'She looks as if she's been on the bottle again. Best if we just hear her out, Horace. God knows what this cleaning woman is doing here, but if you ask me, we should listen to what they have to say and then get rid of them.'

Margaret burst into raucous peals of laughter. 'Hold on a minute, Joe darling,' she said. 'I think you'll find that more difficult than you think. And you, Horace,' she said, turning to him in sudden sobriety, 'are going to be doing some talking. Though Lois and me will have some questions, of course. I'll start, shall I?'

Horace glared at her, but shut his mouth like a rat trap.

'First question: would you like to hear what I know already? I'm sure Lois would be interested.'

Lois nodded. Horace did not respond, and Joe said sharply, 'Make it snappy, woman!'

'Right, then,' Margaret began. 'We have two idiots involved in racing scams. Minor stuff, and so far undiscovered. Then they get ambitious, and try something bigger. It goes wrong, and in their charming way, they decide to put the frighteners on anybody who might know about it. Unfortunately, as they couldn't organize a piss-up in a brewery, they make a mess of it. Our old friend Dot Nimmo, down on her hands and knees scrubbing our kitchen floor, overhears an incriminating conversation between you two and gets knocked down in the road by a hit-and-run merchant. Never been too fond of the Nimmos anyway, have you, Horace?'

By now, Horace and Joe were stupefied into silence, and

Lois contented herself with waiting. Thunder rumbled around outside the house, and an eerie twilight filled the room. Nobody got up to switch on a light.

'So these two idiots consider who else they have to silence,' Margaret continued. 'Police are becoming a nuisance, and they've heard that Mrs Meade – the cleaning woman – is on the snoop. So another so-called accident is arranged. Mrs Meade is lucky to escape death, and a dim lad is frightened out of his wits. Well, you'd think they would be content with that, but they are still not sure about the lad. Difficult to know what he thinks or knows. And as he was in the van with the potential snout, he could have seen the twins. Oh yes, I know about the twins,' she added, as Joe's eyebrows went up. 'Your stupid sister is not very discreet, I'm afraid.'

She paused and looked at Lois. 'Now, why don't you tell them about Darren? And about his mother?'

Lois had listened with mounting anger. She needed to know now exactly what scam had been so dangerous, even when it went wrong, that so much violence had resulted.

But how were they to be persuaded to talk? Margaret seemed to know exactly what she was doing, and had handed over to her, so she began to talk, in the hope that inspiration would come to her.

'Right,' she said. 'Now, what can I tell you about Darren Smith? Well, actually, quite a lot. *You* think he is – was – useless, hopeless and a burden to his poor old mum. Wrong! Darren was a valuable person, a loving son and a trusting villager. People liked him. No malice or jealousy – no greed. Not many like that, are there? He didn't understand the world around him, though he tried. He was scared by change, and acted like a dimmie to escape into himself. *And* he loved horses. But you know that, don't you, Colonel Battersby?'

Horace stood up, shoving his chair back with a loud thud. 'That's enough!' he shouted. 'You can get out, both of you! Everything you've said is a lie, and I shall not listen to another word! Get them out of here, Horsley, and be quick about it!'

Lois stood up too. 'I haven't finished,' she said, certain now of what more she had to say. 'So you'd better sit down again, and listen. And if you try any violence on either of us, I am in immediate contact with the police.' *At least*, she thought to herself, *I hope to God I am*. Cowgill should have been alerted by her aborted call. He would know something was wrong, and she trusted him to go into swift action. She glanced out of the window, but could see no hopeful signs.

Joe put a restraining hand on Horace's arm, and both sat down.

'Good,' said Lois. 'Now I have to tell you about Mrs Smith. You don't know much about her, do you? But she knows about you. She is floored with grief at the moment. Can't eat anything, can't sleep. She looks like a ghost, she's that pale. Darren was her only son, and her life. Husband left. No support for her. She's scraped and saved to give Darren all the help she could get. She loved him, Battersby; she loved him more than you could ever love anybody. She understood everything about Darren, everything that happened to him and everything he tried to tell. And she'll get you. And so will I, and so will Margaret. So now, the best thing you two can do is tell us whatever you decide is the truth about that last scam. Tell your version first, before Mrs Smith gets angry, forgets about squires and council houses, and tells all *she* knows to the cops.'

Horace's thoughts were whirling. He couldn't let Joe speak, because the idiot would give away the whole thing. These two women could run rings round Horsley. So now he had to tell them something. He had to think quickly. Just tell them enough to make it sound convincing, and then, if necessary, deny it all later. After all, it would be his word against theirs . . . and that wretched Smith woman. But, as so often before, he underestimated Joe Horsley. Just as he began to speak in a conciliatory tone, Joe interrupted.

'Margaret,' he said, 'if I tell you what the bloody stupid idea was, will you agree to keep it to yourselves? If I promise to give up gambling, and get us out of debt . . . and be nicer to your dad? And can you keep *her* quiet, too?' He gestured towards Lois, then pointed at Horace. 'Take no notice of him,' he added. 'I'll tell the truth, I promise, if you'll do what I said . . .'

'Tell us first, Joe,' Margaret replied, managing to look soft and pliant. How could he be so stupid as to think she – and Lois! – would agree? But she could see he was desperate and nudged Lois to go along with her.

Without looking at Horace, Joe began. It was a sorry story, and a cruel one. Horace had begun to see how well Darren could ride and control horses, even frisky ones, and had come up with a plan that would earn them real money. They would train the lad to ride so well, with practice sessions over the fields, that they could enter him in a point-to-point. But there were strict rules and regulations about races and jockeys, including point-to-points, so they decided to apply for a rider's qualification certificate, but not in Darren's name. Even in his racing gear, with goggles and helmet, they knew he might just be recognized by someone.

'Horace said to put him down as his son. It would be OK for Darren to ride then,' Joe said, avoiding Battersby's eye. 'Said he could be his long-lost son. He laughed about that. Said the hunt secretary was a nincompoop and would never question it.'

'And Darren was thrilled,' Lois said scathingly. 'Keep going.'

'I told Horace that I doubted if Darren could get past officials an' that. He was unpredictable and could do anything. Go into one of his trances.'

'But Horace knew better?' Margaret asked soberly.

Joe nodded and continued, 'Said not to worry; that he could deal with Darren. Get him to learn the right things to say. It'd be a doddle. Battersby thinks he's God,' Joe added, looking at Margaret. 'Can do anything he wants.'

Margaret got the message, and smiled. 'A long time ago, Joe. So what happened?'

'Bloody disaster, that's what happened. Battersby planned it all. Member of the right hunt, horse was registered, hunted it the right number of times. It was a dozy old horse, and had never come anywhere in a race when Horace rode it. But Darren could work miracles on it. Unbelievable! You could see him up there smiling and saying things to it, and the old nag went like the wind!'

'So, then what happened?' Lois looked out of the window again. Still no sign of Cowgill. Best to spin this out as long as possible.

'We'd have a big bet on Darren and his snail-type nag, and get great odds. Bingo! We'd have a share out and nobody the wiser. Nothing illegal, Horace said. I reminded him about the false identity, but he laughed again and said he would claim a one-night stand with Mrs Smith. I knew it would never work, and we'd be in trouble.'

Now Margaret was getting impatient. 'And it didn't work. Why?'

'Because Battersby is not God, and Darren was never in a million years going to be able to cope with it all and make us rich. The actual race day, with all the rituals and rules, would crucify him – and us. I tried to tell him it was no good and we'd better drop it. But Colonel bloody Battersby was all-powerful, and then he pushed Darren too far.'

'Shut up, Horsley, for God's sake! D'you know what you're doing, man?'

'Yes, I do,' Joe replied quietly, looking steadily at Margaret. 'He couldn't believe there wasn't a way of making the lad talk like a parrot. So we carried on, and all seemed to go well. Darren knew he was going to the point-to-point and would have a ride, but not in a race. That was all he knew, and that's what we told his mother. The rest of it would be masterminded by Horace once we got there.'

'I can't believe this,' said Lois, shaking her head. 'How could anyone be so . . .?'

'It gets worse,' Joe said. 'We got him up on the horse, just for the feel of it, a while before the race. Horace was giving him instructions, and I could see the lad didn't understand. Then he started his warbling and twiddling his hands.'

'Horsley! If you say another word, I'll . . . I'll . . .'

'You'll what, Horace?' Margaret said. 'Shut up, and let Joe finish.'

Joe passed his hand over his eyes, as if trying to blot out the memory. 'Horace lost his temper,' he said. 'He'd got his silver-topped stick – always carried it – and whammed the horse on its backside, yelling at Darren that he was a bloody moron. Even *he* couldn't lash out at Darren, and the horse was the next best thing.'

Silence followed this.

'And the horse bolted,' said a quiet voice. They turned around swiftly, and saw the door pushed open. It was Blanche. She calmly took another chair and Lois and Margaret made a space for her to sit down.

'The horse bolted,' she continued, 'right out of the race-track and across the fields. Horace had the presence of mind to withdraw it from the race officially, and spread the word that a nearby vehicle backfiring had caused it to bolt. Sometimes Horace has the luck of the devil,' she added wryly. 'Nobody was about to see what happened. Only me . . . and

Joe. But Horace's luck was running out, anyway. One of the race officials knew him from way back, and was very suspicious of this so-called son. They were looking for you, Horace. There was no chance Darren was going to ride. I heard they'd decided to let it rest, after you withdrew him. Wheels within wheels, I expect. Lucky old Horace.' These mild words were said with such venom that Horace winced.

'So what happened to Darren?' Lois asked.

'By the time we got to where the horse had come to rest, Darren was nowhere to be seen. Horace wouldn't wait. I was sent to look for him, and then find my own way home. Such a gentleman, our Horace,' she said, looking at him coldly. 'I couldn't find him and in the end allowed Horace to persuade me that Darren had been given a lift home by a friend. I left it there, when I should have checked with his mother. I can't forgive myself for that . . . You know the rest, Mrs Meade. As for Mrs Horsley, I have no idea of her part in it, and I don't care. She's welcome to *him*,' she added, nodding towards Horace.

None of them spoke for several seconds, and then Margaret reached into her pocket and brought out a small instrument. 'It records,' she said smugly. 'It has recorded everything that's been said. So me and Lois will be going now.'

Joe looked beaten by Margaret's betrayal, and said nothing, but Horace jumped to his feet. 'Give me that thing at once!' he shouted, and rushed round the desk towards Margaret. Joe came to life and grabbed Horace from behind. His hands were round the Colonel's throat, and Margaret screamed.

At this point, there was a thunderous knock on the door.

Fifty-Seven

The group sat motionless until finally Lois stood up. 'I'll go,' she said, and opened the door, hoping against hope it would be Cowgill. It was. And by his side, a triumphant-looking Dot Nimmo, who walked straight in towards Horace's study.

'There they are!' she yelled. 'Don't any of you do anything stupid! We got a posse of cops out 'ere in the yard!'

Cowgill looked acutely embarrassed, and said, 'If you would just stand to one side, Mrs Nimmo, I do want to talk to these people.' Then he said in an aside to Lois, 'Gran suggested Dot, who knew exactly where you'd be. Are you all right?' She nodded, and they followed Dot into the study.

Dot sat herself down on a stool by the big bookcase that she had polished with such care, and folded her arms. She looked around with a satisfied smile on her face, and Margaret began to speak.

'Before you start, Inspector,' she said, picking up her recorder, 'I think you'll find most of the answers to your questions are in here.'

Cowgill looked across at Lois, and she said, 'True, if it worked.'

'May we try a sample, Mrs Horsley?' Cowgill suggested politely.

Margaret switched it on, and sat back, waiting for the incriminating evidence to start. They all waited. Nothing. Margaret shook it, and pressed buttons. Still nothing. Lois frowned, and shifted uneasily in her seat. Surely . . .

Suddenly Horace laughed. 'She forgot to switch it on!' He laughed until he choked. Blanche picked up a glass of water from his desk, and threw the contents at him. 'Do be quiet, Horace,' she said.

'Ah,' Cowgill continued, not in the least perturbed, 'well, never mind. It was a very good idea, Mrs Horsley. Well done.'

'I'll say good day to you then, Inspector, and I hope that's the last we'll see of you,' said Horace, standing now. He brushed off the water and quickly recovered his old bombastic self.

'I think not, Colonel Battersby,' Cowgill said, more firmly now. 'Whatever has been said here will have been recorded in several good memories. Mrs Horsley and Mrs Battersby and, most usefully, Mrs Meade, who is an independent witness.'

He looked across at Lois, but she was staring with unabated dislike at Colonel Battersby.

'Even so,' Cowgill resumed, 'I shall be asking all of you a number of questions. I have, of course, had information from other sources. We have not been idle, Lois,' he added quietly, then continued, 'For a start, I need to ask you, Mr Horsley, about anonymous calls I have received from a young man in Birmingham, who is not as anonymous as he thinks.'

'Little sod!' said Joe. 'What did he say? And what else did he tell *you*, Margaret?'

Margaret was not allowed to speak. Cowgill immediately wound up the meeting, and issued instructions to his 'posse' of men waiting outside. When all was quiet, only Dot Nimmo and Lois were left in the house with Cowgill.

'Fancy a drink, Mrs M?' Dot said cheerfully.

Lois looked at her garishly made-up face and remembered the prostrate Dot with tubes suspended over her unconscious form. 'You're on,' she replied. 'The pub round the corner is good, according to Derek.' She turned to Cowgill. 'I expect I'll see you later,' she said.

'Most certainly,' Cowgill replied, and watched the two women walk down the drive, wishing he was Dot Nimmo, who had taken Lois's arm and was laughing with her.

It was not far to the pub, and as Lois and Dot reached the door, the storm broke. Rain fell in sudden torrents and the two women were glad to walk into a cheerful atmosphere of light and warmth, and the heady smell of hops and malt barley.

'So now you can get back to work and family,' Dot said, looking fondly at Lois.

'Derek will be pleased,' Lois said. 'And so will I, Dot. I must say that spell in hospital really shook me up. I haven't told anyone else, but there were moments when I thought of giving up.'

'Do you mean New Brooms?' Dot asked cunningly.

'You know exactly what I mean,' Lois said. 'Anyway,' she said, lifting her glass, 'here's to us, and a bit of peace and quiet.'

Dot clinked glasses, and said seriously, 'There is one thing I haven't told you, Mrs M. It's about Haydn.'

'Oh, don't worry, Dot. I'm sure chief sleuth Cowgill is close to finding who, if anyone, was behind that accident.'

'There was nobody else. It was just a loose horse,' Dot said flatly. 'I think I saw the chance of pinning something on Battersby, but he did that for himself later. No, it's not that. D'you know what they found in Haydn's van?'

'No; Cowgill doesn't tell me anything more than he has to.'

'It was full of saddles and bridles and all that stuff. It were

Haydn who done the thieving, him and his gang of scum.
They used him, Mrs M. Threatened him, an' that.'

'But Cowgill didn't say a thing! Why didn't he tell me?
When did you find out? Did Haydn tell you what he was
doing?'

'No, o' course not, else I'd have said! No, the police told
me. I was so ashamed of him, and upset at losing him at the
same time, that for two pins I'd 'ave done meself in. But that
bloke Cowgill, who's got the hots for you – no, let me go on
– he took pity, and said they'd keep quiet if *I* did, seein' as
Haydn was dead anyway. Couldn't keep the accident out of
the press, o' course, but they wouldn't release the bit about
him bein' the saddle thief. Stay mum about it as long as
possible. O' course, they knew who the others were, and got
'em. Mind you, when I saw sense, I can't say I was surprised
about Haydn. Once a Nimmo, always a Nimmo.'

'I see,' said Lois, reluctant to believe Cowgill capable of
doing such a kind deed. She ignored the suggestion that she
and he had something going.

'So what about them twins? Joe Horsley's nephews?' Dot
continued. 'The Colonel and Horsley thought I eavesdropped
on their telephone conversation, didn't they? Well, I did hear
'em talking, and twins *was* mentioned. But I never made much
sense of it, so they needn't've bothered to 'ave me run down.'

'They're Joe's nephews,' Lois answered. 'They had a rotten
home, so Margaret said. Mother a tart, and no father around.
One of 'em had been in trouble before. Vicious, apparently.
They'll get what they deserve, I hope.'

'Don't bet on it,' said Dot. 'When you been teeterin' on the
edge of the law as long as I have, you can't bank on anything.'
She sighed again, and then her expression brightened. 'Drink
up, Mrs M, and we'll 'ave a second. Tomorrow's another day,
my Handy used to say. Only thing he was ever right about,'
she added, laughing wholeheartedly.

Postscript

It was the last point-to-point of the season at Beecham Cross. Warm sunshine lit up the still-fresh greens of the surrounding woods, and the crowds had blossomed forth in light colours and shirt sleeves. A perfect day, and this time Lois was not in a wheelchair. She and Derek walked up to the row of bookies, trying to decide which of them looked the most trustworthy. They decided on Trusty Clarkham, who smiled encouragingly at them.

Josie and Rob had come with them, but wandered off on their own. Lois wondered how long it would be before they decided to get married, and perhaps make her a granny. Derek said that dropping hints would only make them determined to put it off. But Lois had noticed a slight cooling off in her daughter's attitude to Rob, and wondered if, in Gran's words, they'd 'gorn past it'.

'Well, come on then,' she said. 'We must have a bet on this race, whatever else happens.'

The loudspeaker boomed, and a crackling voice said, 'Now we come to the Ladies' Race for the Darren Smith Memorial Trophy, which is kindly sponsored by Mrs Blanche Battersby.'

Lois and Derek watched the race holding hands, clutching tight. When the winner was led into the enclosure, Lois cheered loudly as Mrs Smith, accompanied by Blanche, walked with dignity into the ring. She greeted a beaming Floss Pickering and presented the trophy to her. Instead of shaking hands, Mrs Smith gave her a hug, and Lois reached into her pocket for a tissue.

'Very satisfactory,' said a friendly voice behind Lois and Derek. It was Hunter Cowgill, looking the part in his tweed jacket and tobacco-brown felt hat.

Derek nodded, but without smiling. Lois considered whether to suggest asking Mrs Smith just how satisfactory it was. But she didn't. It was not the time to spoil a proud moment, and she patted Cowgill lightly on the arm. 'A good result . . . for some,' she said, and added that they must be off to find Josie and Rob.

Cowgill watched them as they walked away, and then with a seraphic smile looked down at his arm. 'She touched me,' he said. 'See you soon, Lois.'